"Remember our first date?" Rob asked in a thoughtful voice.

"I remember how very afraid I was to be alone with you," she said, turning back to smile up at him.

"Afraid to be alone with me?" he probed further. The sparkle in his eyes let her know that the idea delighted him.

"Well, you were reputed to be quite a ladies' man and as you may recall I was rather inexperienced," she reminded him. Again Kara relaxed her head against his arm. "Your reputation terrified me so that I did everything I could not to be alone with you. I wasn't sure I could handle it."

"And are you still terrified to find yourself alone with me?"

"Should I be?" she asked, her dark eyes wide and expressive.

A smile played at his lips. Leaning forward, he took her wineglass and set it aside. "Yes, you should."

ABOUT THE AUTHOR

A Texas native who lists her hobbies as restoring old cars and making escape plans, Rosalyn Alsobrook claims to have been a storyteller for as long as she can remember. She has won numerous writing awards and at one time could claim as many as eighty-five pen pals from all over the U.S. and England.

A Tiny Flaw

ROSALYN ALSOBROOK

Harlequin Books

TORONTO • NEW YORK • LONDON
AMSTERDAM • PARIS • SYDNEY • HAMBURG
STOCKHOLM • ATHENS • TOKYO • MILAN

With love for the guys in my life:
my father, my sons,
and especially my husband.

Published July 1984

First printing May 1984

ISBN 0-373-16063-1

Chapter One

"Hold still," Kara Phillips ordered the overeager Irish setter as she tried to clip the leash to his wide leather collar. "Redwood, hold still."

The tall, amber-haired dog paced wildly about with his overabundance of energy while Kara worked to secure the leash. "Settle down, boy. There, I've got it; let's go."

Once they were outside the tall wooden gate, the long-limbed animal raced gaily ahead—as was his custom—practically pulling Kara along the walk in his haste to reach their destination.

It was a fifteen-minute struggle, the walk to Teague Park. It took quite an effort on Kara's part to keep the large rangy dog from breaking into a run and dragging her floppily behind.

When they finally reached the park, Kara led the now-reluctant dog past the pond to the shade of a huge pine tree. Tossing the paperback she had brought with her on the ground, she bent over Redwood, turning her head to avoid the dog's sloppy attempts at affection when he tried to lick her face. Unhooking the leash, she stepped back and watched him race back to the pond to chase a fat white duck that waited expectantly near the water's edge. As always, the duck was well out of reach by the time Redwood made it to the pond. Sometimes Redwood continued the chase right into the shallow water, but today he thought better of it. Instead, he chose to prance about chasing huge yellow butterflies flitting in the warm Texas sunshine. It was a beautiful Friday to be outdoors. The afternoon was warm, but a gentle spring breeze kept the temperature from becoming uncomfortable.

Sinking into the thick, cool saint augustine grass that carpeted the shaded ground beneath the tall pine, Kara watched Redwood at play. He was such a handsome animal, his long reddish-brown hair flowing freely as he ran. He had filled out nicely from the scrawny little pup he had been when Rob had brought him home to surprise her on her twenty-second birthday.

"He's adorable," she had exclaimed when she first saw the lanky little creature trying to wiggle free of Rob's firm grasp. Taking the puppy in her arms, she'd hugged him close, squealing with childish delight. He had rolled his tongue out happily when she'd scratched him gently behind his dangling ears. Smiling up at her husband, she'd told him, "He's precious, simply precious."

"You go for heavy panting, do you?" Rob had teased her. Leaning forward, he'd breathed several short, quick breaths in her ear and nipped lightly at her earlobe. He had been in one of his playful moods that day and soon the new puppy had been put in a large box with a ball to play with and temporarily forgotten. But that was five years ago, another lifetime ago, and she did not want to think about Rob now. The ache was still there; an emptiness throbbed somewhere deep inside of her whenever anything happened to remind her of him, which to her dismay still seemed to be almost every day.

Shaking her head as if to shake free all thoughts of her ex-husband, Kara picked up the worn paperback and opened it to where the bookmark divided its curled pages. She was nearly a third through the book and still could not fathom why her father had insisted she read it. It had a rambling plot that did not hold her interest, but she read on because her father was usually a good judge of books.

When she located where she had stopped reading the day before, she glanced around to see where Redwood was. She wanted to make certain he was not bothering anyone because he could be a pest at times. Sometimes Kara had to put him back on his leash just to keep peace. She was surprised to see him running across the grassy knoll on the far side of the pond with another Irish setter. His running mate was decidedly smaller but equally energetic as they romped happily together. It was the first she'd seen of the other dog.

Deciding Redwood was causing no trouble at present, Kara gazed back down at the book her father had loaned her and began to read, tuning out all the noise around her and only looking up occasionally to see what Redwood was up to.

She was deep in thought, rereading a passage she found particularly vague, when a deep voice sounded from behind her. "That's a fine looking dog you have there."

Something was oddly familiar about the voice. When she looked up to reply, her heart became paralyzed. It was he; it was Rob, standing only a few feet away. Kara was startled to find him so alarmingly close, even though she had known when she moved back to Longview she risked running into him again. She stared, too stunned to speak, at the strikingly handsome man that had once been her husband. His brownish-blond hair

was a bit blonder than it had been before and his mus-
cled arms a shade tanner, but he was definitely Rob
Phillips. There was no mistaking his powerful build or
those incredibly blue eyes surrounded by thick silky
lashes. Her gaze lighted briefly on the sensuous curve
of his mouth as he spoke again.

"Is that Redwood?" he asked, indicating the larger
of the two setters headed in their direction.

Kara nodded her reply before finding her voice and
squeaking out a trailing, "Yes."

"I thought so," he commented softly before looking
down at her. His eyes took in the lovely thick mane of
dark brown hair that framed the delicate features of her
face and fell in soft curls at her slender shoulders. His
gaze then roved over her body in easy familiarity, taking in every curve of her slim figure clad in a simple
pink cotton blouse and slightly tight cutoffs. His crystal
eyes lingered on the long tanned legs crossed casually
in front of her before lifting again to her face.

Indicating to the ground beside her, Rob politely
asked, "Is this seat taken?"

"N-no, feel free to..." Kara stammered, aware of
the inner exhilaration she felt at having him within
touching distance.

In one easy fluid movement he was seated on the
thick grass beside her, crossing his blue-jeaned legs Indian style before him. Her brown gaze met briefly with
a penetrating blue before she glanced nervously away.
A lengthy silence teetered awkwardly between them
before Kara finally spoke, "What are you doing here?"

"I come here every so often to unwind and let Princess play," he explained. "She loves it here."

Kara scanned the grounds looking for a little girl that
resembled Rob in some way. She had not heard anything about Rob's having a daughter but was not really

surprised such news had not reached her. Whenever anyone tried to broach any subject involving Rob, Kara quickly changed it. She was also not suprised Rob would have a daughter. He had spoken frequently of having children even before they had married. An odd little pain tugged at her midsection as she remembered how badly she had wanted to bear him a child. He used to tease her by telling her they would name their first-born Phillip if it was a boy. "Phillip Phillips. Doesn't that have a nice ring to it?" he would ask innocently, only to burst out laughing when she would wrinkle her nose in dismay and threaten absolute celibacy.

Unable to spot the likely child, she finally asked, "Which one is she?"

"The one playing with Redwood," he explained, then called out, "Princess, come." The smaller Irish setter turned immediately and came prancing over to where they sat. When Redwood realized he was being left, he came bounding right behind her. Princess came to a dainty stop in front of her master and waited patiently for what might come while Redwood skidded clumsily into Kara, knocking her over, and tried to force his wet affections on her.

"Nobody called you," she protested, trying to push the lanky dog off so she could sit up again. "Go away!"

"You used to love him to hop in your lap and nuzzle you," Rob commented, his face breaking into an amused smile.

"He used to be a small puppy, too. He's grown a bit, or haven't you noticed?" she asked, still trying to hold the dog at bay. "Now, Redwood, you goofball, get off of me!"

"Hey, boy," Rob offered a friendly hand as he spoke. "Come here, boy." Easily diverted, the gangling canine tromped over to Rob, wagging his tail ap-

preciatively as the lean muscular hand ran full length
down his shiny coat.

Sitting erect and readjusting her crumpled pink
blouse, Kara watched in fascination. The odd little pain
that had been plaguing her since Rob had let his presence be known twisted tighter as she watched his long
fingers gently stroking Redwood's neck. She knew
from experience what effect his gentle but command-
ing touch could have. It occurred to her that Juanita
now had the privileges his loving touch offered and she
grimaced. Shaking the thought, she forced a little conversation. "How long have you had Princess?"

"About four and a half years, I guess," he told her.
Rob had offered his other hand to his own dog who
seemed a bit edgy to have her master lavishing all his
attentions on Redwood. Now both dogs panted appreciatively as Rob ruffed up their coats and then smoothed
them again with a practiced hand. "I got her a few
months after...after you...left." His voice became
rigid as he spoke.

The harshness of his voice stung. She had never seen
him look so menacing. His eyes bore into her like cold
steel. His jaw became hardened and tiny lines deepened
at the corners of his firmly pressed lips. Suddenly Kara
was aware of how much the five years had aged him.
He had changed. He was not the same easy-going Rob
he used to be. But then she had noticed he was changing even then, during those last few months. He had
become so serious about his work, or so she had been
foolish enough to believe. Actually, the expressed concern and worry for his business had just been a cover-
up. She now supposed it was guilt that had shifted his
attitude so abruptly. Rob had grown quite somber those
final weeks. Whenever he was home, he was extremely
moody. His dangerously low moods had even begun to

rub off on her. The moodier he had gotten, the more depressed she'd become. But it wasn't long before she had discovered why he seemed so unhappy whenever he was home.

"Why did you come back?" His sharp voice broke into her thoughts, bringing them back to the present.

"I am managing a restaurant Dad just opened here in Longview."

"I know that. I read that much in the newspaper. But why this restaurant? Why Longview? Your father has restaurants all over North Texas. Why did you choose this one?" His eyes narrowed to cool slits, as if doing so would allow him to gauge her answer better.

Kara focused her attention on her hands, nervously twisting the paperback out of shape. "The man Dad had expected to run Pinewood had a massive stroke and is not able to do the job now. Dad needed someone to take his place. He was going to have to hire a complete stranger and you know how wary he is of strangers."

"Yes, I remember. He never did take a liking to me," Rob commented dryly.

"That's not true. He was just cautious at first, thinking every guy I dated was out to get his money. But he liked you a great deal and grew to respect you. He was very upset when our marriage fell apart."

"If he was so upset, why was he there bright and early the following morning wanting to pack your things?" he argued, his tone accusing.

"Rob, I don't want to rehash the past. There's no point in it," she replied, hoping to detour this conversation from its disaster course. She knew by the sharp pain twisting at some private part of her heart that old wounds were opening up, spilling sad memories into her bloodstream.

She realized Rob's tension was mounting as he continued to rub the red silky coats of the two dogs. His jaw flexed rigidly. The gentle stroking was turning into fierce movements, causing Princess to step back, but Redwood liked the rough treatment and lowered his head to allow Rob easier access to his neck and back. "Isn't that just like a female."

Kara wasn't sure if he meant her or the dog.

"The going gets a little rough and she backs away," he grumbled, then turned to face Kara. "Now, whom does that remind you of?" His eyes burned hot.

"Rob..."

"I know, I know. You don't want to rehash the past," he said curtly. "What's the matter? Can't handle the guilt?"

"What guilt?" she demanded, astonished. "Why should I feel guilt?"

"Well, you did run out on me."

This is ridiculous, she wanted to scream. Of course, she ran out. She had every right to. What could she possibly have gained by staying? Why hold on to a one-sided marriage? To stay would have been her final undoing. She would have destroyed herself completely by remaining. At least through her leaving she was able to keep a small thread of her badly shredded pride intact. Kara closed her eyes to the agony now gripping her. It was all rushing back to her, the memories she had tried so hard to block out. Her efforts had met with little success and now the tormenting images flowed freely. It was as if an inner dam had burst, a dam she had spent five years building and protecting.

Brenda had warned her what was going on, the real reason why Rob was working so late almost every night, but Kara had refused to listen. Even when Brenda had pointed out little telltale clues that kept popping up, Kara had refused to become suspicious. How naive she had been not to realize the merit in her neighbor's early accusations. Kara's love for her husband had blurred her senses. It all seemed so perfectly clear now, but that's the way with hindsight. It's always 20/20 vision. She was foolish to have ignored those many phone calls when the caller hung up just as soon as Kara had answered. And the necklace. Why didn't she speak up when she accidentally came across that woman's necklace in his car? Maybe deep inside she had been too afraid of learning the truth. After all, don't they say ignorance is bliss?

It was not until that tiny scrap of paper fell out of the pocket of the jacket she had picked up while cleaning that Kara's faith in her husband finally faltered. On it, scrawled in Rob's own handwriting, was written simply "J.B." followed by what was obviously a phone number.

With trembling hands, Kara had dialed the number. On the second ring a soft, sensuous voice had answered. This time it was Kara who'd hung up. The next few minutes were agonizing. Her initial reaction had been to pack up and leave, but a tiny part of her wanted to believe there was a simple explanation. She would confront him with the evidence and see what he had to say.

She waited for him to come home, pacing the floor of their small rented duplex like a caged animal and glancing at the clock every few minutes. Soon it became apparent this was going to be another one of his late nights. Unable to bear it another moment, Kara marched into the bathroom to touch up her makeup quickly. *War paint*, she mused sadly as she applied a bit of cheek blush and lip gloss. Why was it so important she look her best for this?

Knowing Rob ignored anyone banging on the doors

after closing, thus avoiding interruptions in order to get his work done, Kara thought to grab up the spare key from its special slot in Rob's wooden jewelry tray before heading out the door. Climbing into her Cougar, which had been a graduation gift from her father and the only thing they owned that was paid for, Kara sped across town to her husband's newly acquired auto parts store. By the time she reached her destination, her heart was pounding ferociously against her chest. She parked at the side of the building and quickly walked, almost ran, to the back door. She was not quite sure why a sense of urgency had taken over, but she frantically worked to get the key into the lock. Her hands shook so, it made the task almost impossible. When she managed to turn the key and open the door, she froze, suddenly reluctant to step inside. Her emotions were in a turmoil, first hot then cold. Was she losing her mind?

Cautiously, Kara stepped inside and eased the door shut. Standing in the darkened corridor that led to the offices, she thought she heard the shrill laughter only a woman could produce. As she neared her husband's office door, she was sure of the sound. A sliver of light fell across the hallway, guiding Kara directly to the noise, directly to Rob's partially opened office door. Through the narrow crack of the carelessly closed door, she had been able to get a clear view of her husband lying on his couch, bare from the waist up. He was asking someone across the room to hurry back as he tucked his arms behind his head, casually and comfortably. A satisfied smile spread easily across his face when the sultry voice assured him she would comply. The voice that had replied so sweetly to his command was definitely Juanita's, Rob's secretary. Although the door blocked her view, Kara could just imagine the voluptuous frosted-blonde in a similar stage of undress.

Stunned and humiliated, Kara had backed away from the door. In a strange state of shock, she had tiptoed quickly to the door, groping with tearstained vision for the knob. Quietly she stepped outside into the dusky evening and carefully relocked the door behind her.

From that point on, Kara's memory blurred. Somehow she had arrived back home and packed a suitcase without breaking down into an emotional heap. She remained in fair control, even when she'd carefully removed her wedding rings and laid them on the dresser. She had scribbled Brenda a good-bye note and taped it to the door of the adjoining duplex before loading the suitcase into the trunk and coaxing Redwood into the front seat. She was already headed west on I-20 before she actually broke into deep sobs. She wept off and on the rest of the trip.

Two hours later, when she had somehow arrived safely in Dallas at her father's front door, her face was puffy and her eyes so swollen that she could not have pretended she had not been crying. She had no idea how she would explain any of it to her father. She did not understand any of it herself. Luckily, he had not pressured her for an explanation and let her go straight up to her old room. Later he had brought up a tall glass of warm milk and offered it to her along with his strong shoulder.

Although she hated warm milk, Kara knew it was a loving gesture and had accepted the glass gratefully. Feeling she should offer him some sort of an explanation, she had told him she had left Rob. When he had asked why, she'd merely replied that she could not live with him anymore. Realizing his daughter's reluctance to talk about it, Edison Ewan made no further inquiries into his only daughter's problems. But wanting to help in some way, he'd offered to drive to Longview and speak with Rob. He would gladly try to patch things up between them.

Kara had accepted only part of the offer. She did want him to drive to Longview, but not to talk to Rob and try to set things straight. She'd wanted him to get her belongings for her. Her decision had already been made, she was never going back. All she wanted out of her marriage was her personal things, nothing more, but then there wasn't much more to take. The duplex had been rented and the furniture had not been paid for at the time. They had barely scraped up the down payment for the auto parts store. Since she did intend to keep her car, Rob could keep what was invested in the business. It had amounted to about the same.

"So now you're not speaking to me." Rob's harsh words interrupted her thoughts.

Answering anger with anger, Kara said sharply, "Not about the past." After a brief pause she managed to add in a more civil tone, "Now if you would care to discuss the weather, a book, or a movie..."

"Okay, okay, I get the idea," he grumbled, plucking at the taller blades of grass. Then suddenly smiling, he tossed the grass aside, stuck out his hand, and asked, "Truce?"

Reaching out to accept the unexpected gesture, Kara agreed, "Truce."

What started out as a light handshake did not end that way. Rob's fingers closed around her hand firmly, refusing to let go when the time came. She felt an old familiar fluttering in her heart as his thumb gently stroked the backside of her hand, sending tiny electrifying shivers up her arm. The awkward silence had returned as each gazed into the other's eyes, trying to think of something extremely clever to say, something that would not cause further conflict between them.

Rob was just about to speak when the snarling sounds of angry dogs caught their attention. On the far side of the park, Redwood was crouched low in a wary standoff with a huge, threatening German shepherd. The two dogs cautiously circled each other, emitting low, throaty growls. Princess was beside Redwood, yelping excitedly at the two as if ordering them to stop at once.

"Redwood!" Kara cried out impulsively, pulling her hand free of Rob's grasp and putting it to her throat. Upon hearing his mistress calling his name, Redwood was temporarily distracted and the other dog lunged forward. Redwood's painful bellows could be heard over the vicious barks of the larger dog.

Unable to free himself of his powerful attacker, Redwood was fighting back as best he could, but clearly he was losing. Kara froze in cold panic, watching helplessly as Redwood fell under the bigger dog's weight. Rob went into immediate action. He raced over to where the dogs were fighting, pulling the blue velour shirt he was wearing up over his head as he ran. When he reached the dogs, he successfully aimed the shirt at the angry dog's head, giving Redwood the chance he needed to escape. By the time the shepherd had shaken the shirt free, Redwood was a safe distance away, heading for Kara with Princess right behind him.

Turning his aggressions to the shirt, the German shepherd grabbed it with his teeth and shook it ferociously in the air before flinging it a few feet away from Rob. Kara watched in horror as the dog then began to move toward Rob, readying again for an attack.

Suddenly Rob began waving his arms erratically in the air, shouting at the dog while edging himself closer to where the blue shirt lay in a crumpled heap. Continuing to shout angrily, Rob reached down and yanked up the shirt, slinging it at the animal again. Although the shirt missed him this time, the large dog cowered and began to back away in confusion.

"Champ!" a rough voice shouted. "Champ, come here." The dog crouched low to the ground, slumping in defeat as a mountain of a man marched up and grabbed him by his collar. Jerking the animal to his feet, the man briskly apologized for his dog's behavior. He clipped a short leash to the collar and pulled the cowering animal away with such force the creature was gagging. Rob watched in disgust as the man opened the door to a yellow van and shoved the dog inside with his booted foot.

Gathering up his tattered shirt, Rob returned to where Kara knelt, carefully inspecting Redwood's wounds. "No wonder that dog is so violent," he commented, shaking his head. "What a repulsive way to treat an animal."

"I agree!" Kara stated, tenderly stroking Redwood's coat.

"How's Redwood?" Rob asked, kneeling down beside her and giving the dog a sympathetic pat on the head. "Hurt very bad?"

"Not too badly, thanks to you," Kara replied warmly. She was clearly appreciative of his help. Trying not to gape at his tanned muscular chest, covered only by the crisp blond hairs that grew in smooth patterns across his bronzed flesh, she told him, "He has a few cuts here and there, nothing too serious. I think the worst injury was to his pride."

"Poor fella," Rob said soothingly, rubbing Redwood's neck. "A wounded pride takes quite some time to heal."

There was a strange quality in his voice that Kara

could not quite fathom, making her oddly nervous. It was almost as if she could detect a trace of anguish in his words, but not quite. At any rate, she decided it would be better to steer the conversation in another direction.

"Thank you for coming to the rescue. I was too terrified to even move. Redwood could have been seriously hurt, maybe killed." She shuddered at the thought. "I'm so glad you were here."

Standing up and kicking at the ground in cowpoke fashion, Rob drawled in his worst Texas accent, "Aw shucks, twarn't much, ma'am."

Trying to be serious but unable to keep from laughing at his antics, she stood up and looked him in the eye. "Yes, it was. You very well may have saved Redwood's life. I just wish there was some way I could show you just how much I did appreciate it. Redwood didn't have a chance against that dog."

"There just might be," he said softly, suddenly seeming very serious.

"There might what?"

"There might be a way for you to display your gratitude."

"How?" she asked cautiously, highly suspicious of the glint in his eyes.

"Have dinner with me." Unbelievably, Rob stepped toward her and took her hand in his once again. "We could go dancing afterward. I remember how much you loved to dance. Do you remember how nice it was to be dancing in each other's arms?"

"You can't be serious," Kara remarked, awed at his gall. Here he was married to the other woman and flirting with his ex-wife. Well, she had no intention of reversing roles and becoming his present-day other woman. It was obvious that even his love for Juanita had not changed the ever-unfaithful Rob Phillips; he still wanted his outside playmates. The thought of it infuriated her. "You can't believe I would actually consider going out with you."

"Silly me," Rob stated through clenched teeth. "I thought you just might." He forced a throaty laugh. "I really did."

"Well, it's obvious we don't live by the same standards. There is nothing on this earth that could make me ever consider going out with a married man; it's just not my style," she spat bitterly. How could he? "I wonder what Juanita would have to say if she knew you had just asked your ex out?"

Rob winced at Kara's angry tirade. When he spoke, his voice was low and strained. "Juanita will never know."

"Don't be so sure," Kara returned.

"Juanita's dead," Rob stated in a flat tone. "She was killed."

Kara gasped as the impact of what he was saying struck her. Her voice fell to a whisper as she stumbled for the proper words to apologize. "I...I am so sorry, Rob. I had no idea. I thought you...when did it happen?"

"A little over two years ago. She had gone Christmas shopping downtown and was headed back to the car with her arms full of packages, which hampered her view. Witnesses said she waited for the light to change before crossing the intersection. The tall stack of presents prevented her from seeing the car barrelling down on her. The man's brakes failed. They say she never knew what hit her. She died instantly."

There was a strange hollow look in his eyes as he told Kara about the accident. She realized he still suffered, that time had not yet dulled the pain for him.

"I'm so sorry," Kara repeated, wishing there was something she could say to comfort him. "I had no idea."

"That's right, you've been pretty busy the past few years, haven't you? Too busy to keep up with your ex-husband," he said pointedly, his hands tightening around hers. "At that particular time it was rumored you would soon be marrying Wayne Gifford and be living wealthy ever after. Whatever became of that?"

"I don't know where you get such unreliable gossip, but Wayne and I were just good friends, nothing more," she replied. Why she felt the need to defend herself, she wasn't sure. "We enjoyed each other's company, so we went out together."

"Quite a lot, I understand."

"Often enough," she put in, noting that the conversation had certainly taken a nasty little turn. She wondered why Rob was suddenly so concerned with her social past. What difference did her dates with Wayne make anyway? She tried to pull herself free of his firm grasp; he was squeezing her class ring into her fingers and it was beginning to hurt. But when he felt her resistance, he did not release her. Instead he held on even tighter. "Rob, you're hurting me!"

He eased his grip a little, holding her hand lightly for a moment longer, then released her, letting the hand drop like so much dead weight. "I didn't mean to hurt you."

"That's okay. I understand," Kara lied, rubbing the flesh where the ring had left its imprint. She did not understand at all what had caused that quick show of anger. Maybe it was a reaction of some sort from having to discuss Juanita's death again.

"Here let me do that, after all I'm the one who did the damage," he explained and took her hand in his once again. He had regained his composure. With easy movements he gently massaged the sore finger, sending fiery tingles up her arm. It upset her to find she still reacted so acutely to his touch.

"How does that feel?" he wanted to know.

Before she could find the breath she needed to answer, Redwood wriggled his way in between them, demanding her attention.

"I think he's trying to get noticed," Rob chuckled, letting go of Kara's hand so that she could keep the dog from jumping up on her.

"Well, he's doing a good job of it all right. Get down, Redwood!" she ordered, pushing the gangling animal away. When the dog ignored her demands, she grabbed his front paws and firmly held them away from her. "Redwood, we're going home!"

"Need a ride?" Rob offered instantly. "My Blazer is just over there." He gestured to a nearby parking area.

"Not really. I don't live very far from here," she assured him as she waltzed Redwood over to where she had dropped the leash. Bending quickly, she snatched it up.

"Then I won't have to go very far out of my way, will I?" he grinned. Taking the leash from her, he quickly snapped it to Redwood's collar and led him toward the parking area. Princess was close at their heels.

Reaching down and scooping up her forgotten novel, Kara hurried to catch up with them. She was a little annoyed by his easy manipulation, always having his way, but decided not to make an issue of it. She was still feeling rather weak from Redwood's little encounter and would prefer a ride home. She refused to consider that part of her weakness had stemmed solely from Rob's presence.

After putting both dogs in the back of his dark gold

Blazer truck, Rob walked around to the passenger side where Kara waited to be let in. He slipped the key into the lock and turned it, but made no effort to open the door. He stared at her a long silent moment as if he were studying her features for the first time. She looked back at him, realizing how handsome he still was in spite of, or maybe because of, the tiny character lines that had formed at the outer corners of his crystal-blue eyes. She was aware Rob's nearness was stirring up old familiar feelings that existed only for him. She needed to put distance between them or chance giving into rapidly possessing emotions. As if he could read her thoughts, he reached out and caught her arm before she could move away.

His kiss was just as she remembered it, warm and masterful. Her initial resistance was melting as his lips worked their passionate wonders. Hands that had been laid on his chest in an effort to push him away relaxed then eased their way up to his neck, marveling at the feel of his firm, warm flesh. His kisses always had provoked her to the point of madness. She pressed her fingers against the back of his neck in an effort to draw him closer. Tears began to work their way into her dark eyes. How she loved the man she hated. He was her heaven and her hell. He still had easy control of her dearest emotions.

She felt his embrace weaken before he finally pushed her away. His face hardened as he reached for the door handle. "We'd better get going."

Chapter Two

Kara was a jumble of twisting emotions as she watched Rob's Blazer disappear around the next corner. Why had he invited her for Sunday brunch and a swim when it was obvious he found her and her kisses so repulsive? What astonished her even more was the fact that she had accepted.

"It's the least you could do after I risked life, limb, and one of my best shirts trying to rescue Redwood," he had pointed out to her, appealing to her sense of fair play. Maybe that was why she had finally agreed to go. He had made it seem as though it was her duty to do so. Whatever had prompted her to accept, she wished now she had not. After all, it certainly was not his undying love that had triggered the invitation. Something else had motivated him, but what? Her insides churned uneasily as she considered several possible motives.

It was Redwood's sharp tugging on his leash that brought Kara out of her reverie. Folding the piece of paper on which Rob had quickly scribbled his address and phone number, Kara tucked it into her hip pocket and allowed Redwood to lead her to the gate. At least she had possessed enough good sense to decline his offer to pick her up. That would have been too much like a date.

Once inside the yard of the small house she rented, she unclasped the leash knowing her dog would head straight for his food dish that sat empty beside the back door. Kara refilled the bowl before plopping herself down in the shallow depths of her canvas hammock. She stared blankly off into the distance, unaware of the awakening beauty that surrounded her. She completely ignored all evidence of spring's cheerful arrival. The huge stately trees were dappled in a bright array of green. Several of the mimosa trees had already begun to bloom, bursting out in a stilled explosion of airy pinks. The grass had already grown thick with its renewed color and tall stands of colorful irises and daylilies had pushed through to find places in the warm sunshine.

But Kara's attention was elsewhere. She was so confused. She still cared for Rob, darn it. Yet at the same time, she still hated him for what he had done. She had to admit she was somewhat delighted she would be seeing him again, but she also dreaded the outcome. What was wrong with her? Rob! That's what was wrong with her and she couldn't seem to cure herself of him.

By the time Sunday finally rolled around, Kara was so full of apprehension that she had picked up the phone several times fully intending to call Rob and beg off, but each time something had prevented her from dialing his number. She finally decided she really should go, having promised to do so, but would not make any more engagements with him. This would be it, no further entanglements whatsoever with her ex-husband.

Having made such a conviction, Kara felt easier about the day ahead as she drove slowly down Eden Drive watching both sides of the street for Rob's address. She had assumed it would be a fairly large apartment complex, after all it was in a nice neighborhood and it had a pool. She was impressed with many of the stately homes she passed as she made her way along Eden. Her own neighborhood was not nearly as elegant. The small brick house she rented was well kept and the yard roomy and neat, but paled in comparison to these two- and three-storied homes. She was stunned to find that the number scribbled on the scrap of paper corresponded with the number on a large open gate leading into a private residence.

When she drove her cinnamon-gold Corvette through the gateway, she was awed by the grandeur that greeted her. Perfectly manicured hedges lined the circular drive laid in dark brick and edged in black gravel. Tall stately pine trees shaded a newly mowed lawn. In among the many trees stood a lovely two-storied colonial-styled home fashioned from bricks of various earthtones and black mortar. The traditional colonial columns guarded a narrow walkway that stretched the width of the house. The home was beautiful to the point of being elegant.

Surely she had made a mistake. Rob could never afford this place. But, no, Rob's bronze Blazer was parked in the first compartment of the three-stall garage along with a royal blue Trans Am and a high powered ski boat. She must have the right address.

Her curiosity overcame her apprehension as she hurried to the front door. Although there was a doorbell to the side, she could not resist banging the heavy brass rings that adorned the tall double doors. Within minutes, one of the doors swung open and she was greeted by her ex-husband.

"Come on in," he said graciously, stepping back to allow her entry. He was dressed in a pair of faded cutoffs with a light-blue T-shirt that read "Made in Texas."

"Where's your swimsuit?" he wanted to know, closing the door behind her.

"I have it on underneath," she explained, feeling a

bit awkward at the close scrutiny she was receiving as his eyes wandered from her snug denim jeans to the low cut of her yellow-and-white terry top.

"Must not be much of a swimsuit," he commented, noticing that nothing was revealed under her blouse but the upper swell of her breasts.

"It'll do," she snapped, able to feel the color rush to her cheeks. Now she wished she had chosen to wear the one piece instead of her bikini. He had guessed right; there really wasn't much to it.

"Yes, I am sure it will," he stated with a glimmer of something devilishly evil in his eyes, then led her through the large, rambling house to the kitchen. He gestured for her to sit on a tall stool near a counter-bar while he checked on their food.

"How do you like my humble abode?" he asked while he peeked into the oven to check the bread.

"It's beautiful. What did you do, strike oil?" she asked, admiring the appointments of the room. The cabinets were made of a rich dark wood, as was all the woodwork. The cupboard doors were designed with thick panes of lead glass that matched that of the kitchen windows. The countertops were laid with oblong ceramic tiles in various shades of beiges and browns. Only a set of antique tin canisters and a coffee-maker had permanent places on top of his counter.

"No, I did not exactly strike oil, more like gasoline." He adjusted the thermostat.

"You struck gasoline?" she asked, more confused than ever.

"Have you noticed the new computerized gas stations going up around here?" he asked as he took the plates and glasses they would need from the cupboard. "Those automatic self-serves where you insert a credit card to get your gasoline?"

"Yes, those happen to be half mine," he stated simply. "Here, set the table and I'll explain how it came about."

Kara complied, carrying the stack of plates, silverware, napkins, and glasses to the small table that occupied the far corner of the kitchen. While she set the two places, Rob continued.

"Right after Juanita and I were married, her brother-in-law, Don Brunson, came up with a wild notion we should form a partnership. He had just read an article in one of his technical magazines about these computerized gas stations. With his knowledge of computers and my head for business, he figured the partnership was a natural. There was just one drawback; I didn't have the money to come up with my half of the capital needed to get into it and could not afford to take out another loan from the bank. I still owed on the one I'd taken out to open my auto parts store."

"So how'd you come up with it?" Kara asked, intrigued by this rags-to-riches story.

"Don had enough money for both of us since his parents own Brunson Construction and Realty. He said he would put up the entire amount, if I would manage the whole operation. My pride would not permit me to accept his generous offer, so we finally ended up compromising. I signed over half of the auto parts store to him to cover my end of it. He not only came up with the funds needed for the new gas station venture, he also spent thousands remodeling the auto parts store and almost doubling our inventory. He was a great guy."

"Was?"

"He was drowned in a boating accident on Lake o'the Pines about a year later," Rob explained solemnly. After a long pause, he added, "Don would be proud to see how far we've come with the business in the last three years. We just opened our sixth computer gas station and the auto parts store has also branched out. We now have three locations in Longview and one in Kilgore.''

"Who's we?" Kara asked.

Maria Brunson, Don's widow, and me, of course. That lady's just as shrewd as Don ever was when it comes to Phillips-Brunson, Inc.''

"Well, I must say, I am impressed," Kara stated quite honestly.

"You never thought I would amount to anything, did you?" he accused, a defiant tone in his voice.

Kara could see an argument coming on and chose her words very carefully, "I knew you would; but I must admit I never expected this much success this quickly."

The buzzing of the stove timer interrupted whatever Rob was about to say. Taking in a sharp breath, he hurried to get the hot pads and take the cheese bread out of the oven. The rich aroma quickly filled the room.

"When did you ever learn to cook?" she asked, breathing heavily of the delicious smells. When they were married, Rob could barely build his own sandwich.

"It was either learn or exist solely on TV dinners and restaurant food," he commented as he hurriedly put the steaming hot pan on top of the stove.

"What else are we having?" Kara asked, coming closer. Her appetite made her eager to discover more.

"I have a small ham in the smoker outside and in here," he told her, lifting the heavy lid off a small pot on top of the stove. "I have mushroom rice. Ah, perfect every time."

Replacing that lid, he reached over and picked up the

one on a slightly larger pot. "And we will also have glazed carrots. You still like glazed carrots?"

"When do we eat?" was her reply.

"Patience. I have to bring in the ham and slice it first."

Throughout the meal they talked about whatever they found they still had in common. Although they did reminisce parts of their marriage, they carefully avoided any mention of those last months or of the quickie divorce. They were getting along so well that Kara eventually quit worrying about whatever motives Rob had for inviting her over.

Kara reached her limit long before Rob finally pushed his plate away. After they cleared the table, Rob led her outside to a large tiled swimming pool.

"This is nice," Kara told him, staring at her surroundings in open admiration. The backyard was enormous, completely enclosed by a tall, wooden privacy fence. As with the front yard, the landscaping was absolutely flawless from the thick azalea bushes growing in unison along the fenceline to the potted exotics near the pool. The entire backyard was a garden paradise.

"I suggest we let our food settle awhile before going in." Rob pulled off his shirt and tossed it over the back of a redwood lounger before sinking into its thick floral cushions. He stretched out in order to get full benefit from the sun. Kara's eyes were drawn to the beautiful specimen of a man. Sleek muscles rippled with his every lithe movement. It was really a lethal combination, his strong masculine body and incredibly handsome face. She was extremely conscious of his nearness as she eased into the lounger beside his.

"Aren't you going to get some sun?" he asked. She still had on her jeans and yellow top. "You're going to be terribly uncomfortable if you don't shed some of those clothes."

"It is pretty hot out here," Kara admitted and pushed herself up out of the chair. She was aware of his keen attention as she reached for the zipper on the front of her jeans. How was she going to do this without feeling as if she were putting on a peep show? But then, in all honesty, she had chosen the bikini over the one-piece suit in hopes of arousing his attention. Why? She did not intend to see him again. It occurred to her she might be out to punish him for his past misdeeds by flaunting the body he would never again have the chance to possess. Kara felt it was a lucrative form of revenge, knowing well that although Rob had never truly loved her, he had indeed felt a strong physical attraction for her.

Ever so slowly, Kara eased the zipper down and left her jeans open to reveal her flat stomach while she smoothly slipped the yellow terry top over her head, unveiling a skimpy black bikini top that revealed the fullness of her breasts. She shook her head as her long dark tresses fell back in place around her shoulders and pretended to be unaware of her audience of one.

After draping the yellow blouse over the high back of the lounge chair she had previously occupied, Kara hooked her thumbs into her waistband and began to work her jeans downward. As she glided the garment over her smooth hips and down her slender legs, she leaned way over, purposely giving Rob a most provocative view. Picking up the jeans and placing them beside the blouse, she slithered back into her chair.

"You are right; this is much better," she said in a sultry voice while arching her back in an attempt to relax.

"Much," he breathed heavily, obviously aroused.

Kara was pleased with Rob's reaction but was dismayed to discover she was feeling similar effects. It was not supposed to work that way. It was to be his undoing, not hers.

Hoping the shock of cold water might do her some good in controlling her own heated desire for the man beside her, Kara got out of the chair and kicked off the sandals she still had on. She stepped over to the pool's edge and dove in head first. To her surprise, the water was quite warm, much warmer than it should be this early in May. It must be artificially heated. The warm water felt good to her skin as she swam the length of the pool underwater. She heard a muffled splash just before she surfaced in the shallow end and discovered Rob's sleek form headed straight for her like a deadly torpedo. His hands clasped around her narrow waist as his head broke through the rippling water. Wriggling free, Kara hurried to the side of the pool and pulled herself out. Perching on the edge with her feet dangling in the warm water, Kara eyed him warily. When he moved toward her, she splashed water at him with her feet.

"You realize you are going to have to pay for that," he half growled, half chuckled. Reaching out, he grabbed her by the ankles before she could get up to run.

Kara squealed in surprise, not having realized he was quite this close. A satisfied grin crossed his face when he pulled her in on top of him. As she fell, her arms automatically went around his neck to keep from going under.

"Ah, I have you right where I want you," he warned, his tone menacing.

"Not for long." She couldn't help but laugh, trying her best to break free. It was no use, he had her.

"Going somewhere?" he quizzed and glanced with a raised brow at her hands pushing against his chest.

"I guess not," she sighed, giving up the struggle. "What are you going to do to me, drown me?"

"There's a thought," Rob said playfully, his eyes widening as if he were demented and lusted to take her life. He tightened his hold and pulled her closer until their mouths were only inches apart. "Yes, I could drown you, or...worse."

"Worse?"

Narrowing his eyes, he warned, "Much worse."

"And make Redwood an orphan?" Kara asked, finding it difficult to swallow. She was not afraid for her life but was afraid of the emotions raging inside of her, emotions she could no longer fight. She wanted him to kiss her, make passionate love to her as she knew only Rob Phillips could.

When his lips moved to cover hers, Kara moaned with pleasure. The soft sound lost itself in the warm depths of his mouth, arousing him more. Wrapping her arms around his gleaming shoulders, she clung to him as though he were her lifeline, encouraging him by pressing herself against his firm wet body. Having denied her sexual needs for the past five years, Kara felt her body scream to be possessed. At the moment it did not seem to matter that he did not love her, that it was purely a physical act on his part. Kara stiffened at this last thought.

It *did* matter.

Sensing her sudden resistance, Rob withdrew his lips from hers and eyed her curiously, "What's wrong?"

"This," Kara sobbed. She hadn't wanted to cry but couldn't seem to help it. She was so confused and frustrated. "This is what's wrong."

"What's wrong with this?" he asked, anger beginning to show in his voice. "You've developed a thing against kissing?"

"It wasn't the kiss; it was where it was leading." She was just about to push herself away from him, when he let go and stepped back.

"So what you are saying is you don't want me to make love to you," he snapped, defiantly anchoring his hands on his lean hips. She could see his anger as he glowered down at her.

If only it were love, she thought miserably. But love had nothing to do with it, at least not on Rob's part. Tears had filled her eyes and now spilled over, blending with the water droplets glistening on her cheeks.

"Hell, Kara, I hadn't intended to kiss you. I thought you wanted to be kissed," he growled. Then his voice softened. "I guess I read the situation all wrong. I'm sorry." Although his tone was civil, he still sounded more argumentative than apologetic.

"Yes, I guess you did," she sniffed. Pushing herself through the water to the narrow steps at the corner of the pool, she added, "Maybe I should just go on home."

"Always the bird in flight, aren't you," Rob commented. "What are you running away from?"

"I'm not running away from anything," she lied in stubborn desperation that he not guess the truth.

"Then stay. I promise not to kiss you again," he offered, then sighed. "You make me feel like little Georgie Porgie...kissing the girls and making them cry."

Seeing the twisted pout perched on his protruding lips, Kara couldn't help but smile. She adored the little boy in Rob. "Okay, I'll stay awhile longer."

For the rest of the afternoon they got along just fine. After a tiring game of tag in which Kara did most of the chasing, they collapsed into the lounging chairs to rest. Once they had caught their breaths, Rob offered her a diet cola; he even remembered which brand was her favorite.

He returned shortly with their iced drinks, one in each hand. He also had two thick brown towels tucked under one arm and a bag of pretzels dangling from his teeth. Kara wondered if he had chosen the pretzels because he remembered they were one of her favorite snacks. Probably not.

"Care for a pretzel?" he asked once he had unloaded everything, setting it all on the small round table that sat on the far side of her chair. He pushed aside the watch and billfold he had left there before going into the water. "I couldn't find the kind you always used to buy, so I got these. I hope they'll do."

Rob had remembered. Helping herself to the contents of the opened bag, Kara was afraid to speculate as to why he had bothered to get pretzels, afraid she might put too much meaning behind the gesture. He was just trying to be a good host and provide something he knew his guest would like. Still, he had remembered.

When Rob sat back down, it was not in the other chair. Instead, he sat on the edge of the lounge chair she was stretched out on. Although he seemed to think little of it, she was totally unnerved to have him sharing her chair. Feeling it was a good time to keep a conversation going, she rolled over on her side, facing him at an angle, and asked, "Where's Princess?"

"Upstairs, I imagine," he replied. "She favors the rug in front of my bedroom fireplace. Even when there's no fire, she stakes out that rug."

A fireplace in his bedroom? Oh, that sounded romantic. Kara wondered how many women had been seduced in front of that fireplace. She supposed many had.

"Kara?" Rob spoke, as if asking permission to break into her thoughts.

"What?" she responded.

"There's something I've been wanting to ask but have not been able to find the right time. I suppose now is as good a time as any," he said with little-boy shyness. His crystal-blue eyes looked up but didn't quite meet hers as he considered the next words he planned to speak.

"Don't you two look cozy," a sharp voice sang out from behind them.

Rob was up instantly, sighing with relief as if he'd just been rescued from some terrible fate. "Maria, I didn't hear you come up."

Quickly he walked around the end of the chair to where a beautiful blond woman about the same age as Rob, early thirties, stood with her arms crossed defiantly across ample breasts. Emerald eyes bore down on Kara as Rob placed a brief kiss on a flushed cheek. "Maria, I'm glad you're here. I would like you to meet Kara."

"Your ex-wife?" she asked, stunned.

"The same."

"Pleased to meet you," she nodded politely, but her fiery green eyes revealed otherwise. She was hardly pleased. "I've heard so much about you."

Kara would have to have been a fool not to sense this woman's hostility toward her. Clearly Maria resented her presence.

"Kara, this is Maria Brunson, my partner," Rob continued with the introduction, oblivious of the silent slashing Kara was receiving. "You remember I told you about my sister-in-law, Don's widow."

It was more of a statement than a question, but Kara politely replied, "Yes, of course, I do, and I am just as pleased to meet you, Maria."

"Have a seat," Rob suggested to the newcomer. As the elegant beauty clad in a white flowing pantsuit took the seat offered, Rob asked, "Would you care for a drink?"

"Certainly. I'll have whatever it is you two are having," she said in a warm voice that was almost too feminine. When she heard they were having diet colas, she wrinkled up her pert little nose. "Do you have any of that lovely wine left over from our dinner last night?"

The woman cut her green eyes to Kara to see if the ex had caught the implication. They shared more than business interests.

"I'm afraid we drank it all," Rob shrugged.

"Oh well, I'll just wait to have something." Maria smiled sweetly. "Maybe you could run out and get a bottle before dinner. I'm rather fond of it."

Kara frowned, realizing she had stayed too long. She had only been invited for an afternoon swim. Maria was invited for the evening activities. Kara guessed that she was meant for an appetizer and Maria was to be the dessert. It was time to exit smiling.

Noticing Rob's watch on the table beside her, Kara picked it up and gasped, "It's four o'clock. I didn't realize it was so late. You two will have to excuse me, but I must be leaving."

"Oh, what a shame. Are you sure you can't stay?" Maria asked with little enthusiasm.

"Yes, please, Kara, stay for dinner," Rob put in. He sounded sincere in the invitation, but Kara knew better. Three was a crowd any way you counted it.

"I wish I could, but I have a prior engagement," she

lied as she gathered her clothes into a crumpled wad. "Sunday is my only night off, and I generally make plans for it way in advance."

"A date with Gifford?" Rob asked, speaking the name as if it depicted an infectious disease. Every muscle in him became taut as he waited for the answer.

"Why, yes. How did you know?" Now what had made her say that? She had not seen Wayne in ages. Maybe because it made her lie seem more plausible.

"Lucky guess," he spoke in a low, barely audible voice.

"Well, I really must be going. I certainly had a wonderful time; thanks for having me over," she rushed her words and began walking toward the nearest gate.

"I'll walk you to your car," Rob offered, trying to catch up with her.

"Don't bother. I can find my way," Kara said over her shoulder. As she hurried through the gate, she could feel a pair of emerald eyes encouraging her every step.

Chapter Three

Kara stared blindly at her reflection as one hand aimed the blowdryer in the general direction of the circular hairbrush held in the opposite hand. Her thoughts were submerged deep into the past. After having recalled the events of such a confusing day countless times, she allowed her overactive mind to wander back over the past five years...years she had spent trying to forget Rob and get on with her life.

When she had returned from the Caribbean with her divorce papers in hand, she was ready to become a recluse, ready to build a shell around herself and hide from all the pain the world had to offer. But her father had other plans for her. He quickly saw to it that her social calendar was filled.

At first she'd been reluctant to allow her father to manipulate her life so, but she soon gave in. It was easier than arguing with the stubborn man. Besides, going out with whatever men her father was constantly introducing her to was better than sitting around dwelling on the past, and attending the constant stream of parties he lined up sometimes kept her mind off her misery and loneliness for hours at a time.

During those first few years that followed the divorce, Kara went out with many different men, all types and ages. Several of the men were handsome enough and nice enough, but not one had ever been able to make her forget Rob. Everything she did seemed to refuel her memory, reminding her of something they'd shared in the three short years they had been married.

Within a year after their divorce, Kara had learned of Rob and Juanita's marriage, which served to confirm her belief that Rob had been in love with his secretary all along. Maybe he had married Kara for the money she would eventually inherit. She was amazed that she could have misjudged his character so completely.

After learning of Rob's remarriage, Kara continued to live the fast pace her father had set for her for almost another year. Finally she came to her senses. She needed a direction in her life. She decided to go back to college. She took courses that would prepare her for a career in her father's prosperous restaurant business. During this time Kara still dated occasionally, more for her father's sake than her own.

Because he was so much fun to be with and put absolutely no pressure on her to advance their relationship past that of friends, Kara had begun to see a lot of Wayne Gifford. Wayne was trying to get over his own shattered marriage. What they had sought in each other was strictly companionship. Kara wondered how a rumor of anything being between them quite as serious as marriage had ever gotten started. How absurd!

When Wayne had announced that he and his ex-wife were going to try to make another go of it, she had felt no remorse whatsoever. She knew she would miss their congenial nights out but was extremely happy for her friend. It was obvious Rob had not heard that Wayne and Gina had gotten married again, or did he think she was involved with a married man? After all, she thought ruefully, that's where she was supposed to be at this very moment, out with Wayne Gifford.

Switching off the dryer, Kara worked solely with the brush to shape her hair into thick curls that swept away from her face. She now was remembering how tired she had grown of the parties and going out with the men her father was constantly coming up with. It had gotten harder to pretend she was enjoying herself by keeping socially busy. She had finally begun to cope with the moments she spent alone and was beginning to resent her father's meddling in her life.

In order to prevent any further interference from her father and regain control over her own life, Kara had jumped at the opportunity to manage the new Longview restaurant. She knew the job included the risk of seeing Rob, but in a city of over 50,000 she felt the risk would be a slim one. She had not known of his wife's death and had felt Juanita would surely steer him clear of the restaurant. The move to Longview had seemed safe enough at the time she'd made her decision to move.

That seemed academic now. She had run into Rob again and the effects of the chance meeting were worse than she had imagined. Not only had she discovered she still cared for Rob deeply, but she discovered it hurt knowing he was getting along so well without her. And he certainly seemed to be getting along nicely with Maria, as well. The feelings Kara felt toward the shapely blonde could not be mistaken as anything but cold jealousy. It was obvious enough that the two of them were much more than business partners, much more. It was quite evident by the glimmer in Maria's emerald eyes that the two had to be lovers, and the thought of it caused an ache deep inside her. The old familiar emptiness plagued her, and although she went to bed early, it was hours before Kara managed to fall asleep.

The next day her thoughts seemed to be closing in around her. In an effort to keep from going stark raving mad, she decided to go to the restaurant early. Work would be the best cure for her. It would keep her mind occupied.

Clint Rutledge, the assistant manager whose duty it was to oversee the before-hours preparations, was surprised to see her so soon but glad just the same. He had just tried to call her to tell her that the day's shipment of fresh seafood had not arrived. The delivery usually came between 10:00 and 11:00 A.M. and it was now well past 1:00. Their supply was low and if the fresh food did not arrive soon, there would not be enough shrimp and crabmeat to start the seafood gumbo they were so famous for. It took three hours to simmer their gumbo to perfection, and time was running out.

Afraid the seafood would arrive too late if at all, Kara decided to commit the ultimate of sins and buy frozen. Quickly tearing a check out of the checkbook, she rushed to the nearest supermarket, almost missing the turn in her haste. Finding no parking places in front of the grocery, she had to park in front of a small drugstore that shared the same building. She hit her leg on the car door when she swung her legs around to get out, and as if things weren't bad enough already, the check slipped out of her fingers when she slammed the door shut. Just when she bent over to pick up the small slip of yellow paper, a breeze came along and carried it away. It was definitely Monday.

Kara followed the check halfway across the huge parking lot until it finally came to an abrupt halt under a small bright-red Gremlin. Cursing the tapered skirt she had chosen to wear, she knelt beside the car and tried to reach the check, but it was inches out of her grasp. She got up and went around to the other side. Kneeling down again, she tried to get the check. Still she could not reach it. In total frustration, she leaned her forehead against the side of the car as if its hard, cold surface would give her strength.

"What are you doing?" an all-too-familiar voice asked. "Paying homage to the great red-car god?"

Kára slowly turned her head and glared up into a pair of uncanny blue eyes that glittered with amusement. Rob stood only a few feet away dressed in a dark blue three-piece suit. A newspaper was tucked under one arm. The perfect image of a successful business man. Where had he come from?

"I'm trying to retrieve my check that the wind blew under this car," she stated as clearly as she could through her clenched teeth. How much more aggravation could she take? She tried again to get the check.

"Let me be of assistance," he said gallantly. Rolling the newspaper into a tight cylinder, he knelt down beside her. Using the wound newspaper, he carefully raked the check out from under the small car. As he picked it up and handed it to her, he wanted to know what wonderful thing he had earned by returning the check to her.

"How about a sincere thank you?" she stated simply as she straightened up, brushing her tan skirt smooth.

"You can do better than that," he commented, giving her legs the once over before bothering to stand. "Where's your gratitude?"

"What exactly do you have in mind?" she asked, regretting the question the instant it had left her tongue. It was obvious what was on his mind.

"I'll settle for a kiss," he grinned, leaning forward to make himself more available.

"Not here in a public parking lot!" she declared nervously, glancing around at the people headed to and from their cars. Quickly pushing him aside she added, "Besides, I'm in a hurry. The seafood for today did not arrive. I'll have to buy enough for tonight and rush it back to the restaurant."

"Here? I thought Pinewood prided itself on the best fresh seafood."

"I have no choice; this is an emergency," she explained, turning to leave. Her voice displayed the exasperation she felt.

"But you do have a choice," he offered as he ran to follow her. "There's a market on the north side of town that sells fresh fish and seafood."

"Where?" Kara stopped so suddenly Rob could not help but bump into her. The direct contact made her jump.

"Just off of Judson Road. Come on, I'll take you." He indicated she should now follow him. "My car's just over here."

"Why don't I follow you and save us having to come back here for my car? I really am in a hurry," she replied quickly, much of the frustration that had weighted her face lifting upon hearing there was a chance she might have fresh seafood after all, and her relief was evident when a bit of a smile began working its way across her face. "Just don't make a rally race out of it."

By the time they had reached the small shop that was situated in a side alley of a large shopping plaza, all of Kara's previous agitation was gone. She was almost singing aloud as she made her choices from the large selection of seafood. Having accepted Rob's offer to carry her purchases to her car, Kara played the gentleman and first opened the front door for him, then ran ahead to open her trunk. When he started to put the package into the trunk, he found very little space due to what Kara claimed were her necessities, things like her tennis rackets, assorted towels, a blanket, a large bottle of laundry detergent, and a deflated beach ball. Kara managed to scrape out just enough room for the large box. After Rob set the box down in the place Kara had cleared, he removed her keys from the lock and slammed the trunk lid down. He handed her the keys, then sniffed his hands, wrinkling his nose in disgust, and commented, "Of course, you realize that you are now twice indebted to me."

"Oh I am, am I?" Kara responded cautiously, remembering his earlier claim.

"As I see it, you now owe me two kisses. Two favors... two kisses seems fair to me," he told her, a satisfied grin settling on his face and his eyes twinkling with amusement, not unlike the cat that was just about to gobble up the canary. "And I do plan to collect what's rightfully mine."

"And you think you have two kisses coming?" Not as displeased with the idea as she had been earlier, Kara had to strain to keep a straight face.

"Definitely," he commented, stepping closer as if he were an animal stalking his prey. "And I will get them one way or another"

"Oh, you'll get what's coming to you all right," she warned playfully, "but not here."

"That sounds almost like a threat. I only wish I had time to follow you back to the restaurant and pursue this," he laughed, glancing at his watch. "But I have a two o'clock appointment scheduled and I'm going to be late as it is."

"Too bad." Kara grinned as she singled out the square-headed ignition key on her key ring.

"I'll just have to collect my kisses at a later time," he told her in a deep foreboding voice before returning to his car.

Kara shook her head slowly as if she were dismissing the idea while she pulled her car door open. It was all so silly, his expecting kisses for the two little favors he had done. Still, she couldn't help but hope Rob did indeed try to collect those kisses. She smiled openly as a flurry of provocative thoughts presented themselves, all dealing with how he might do just that.

The thoughts kept recurring throughout the rest of the day. By the time she finished work that evening and was headed home, Kara almost expected to discover either his Trans Am or Blazer parked in her driveway. She was somewhat disappointed when she found the driveway empty.

She chided herself for having even considered the possibility that Rob was again interested in her enough to actually be waiting for her so late at night. It was almost midnight. Why would he bother waiting for her when he has someone like Maria around? And that was probably where he was now, with beautiful, sexy Maria. Kara sighed as she reached into the mailbox and collected her mail. She should not allow herself to fantasize about Rob. She should try to be more realistic and remember the past. She should try to learn from past mistakes, and Rob Phillips was definitely one of her past mistakes.

Once inside, Kara locked the door behind her, then tossed the mail on the table beside her favorite chair as was her custom. She headed straight for the kitchen, opened the refrigerator, and extracted a diet cola. Absently, she walked over to the stereo, switched on Lionel Richie, and returned to her chair. She sank into its yellow-orange cushions, sipping her cold drink and listening quietly to several of her favorite ballads.

While sorting through the mail with her free hand, Kara came across a sealed envelope addressed to her that did not have any signs of postage or return address on it. Curiously, she ran her nail under the flap to open the strange envelope. Inside she discovered a most unusual billing. The statement declared she owed the amount of two kisses to Rob Phillips for services rendered. Kara smiled. This was one account she was looking forward to paying in full.

"What's gotten into that stupid dog?" Kara muttered as she pushed herself up on one elbow and eyed the alarm clock. It wasn't like Redwood to raise such a ruckus. Seven A.M.? It wasn't like Redwood to even be awake at this hour. He usually slept even later than she did.

Groggily she swung her legs over the edge of her bed where her dangling feet found the carpet. Flinging the covers to one side, she forced herself out of the bed. She'd have to do something to quiet him or the neighbors would complain and rightfully so. She considered strangling him, but that would mean getting dressed and straying farther from the warmth and comfort of her bed than she wanted to. What could have stirred him up so? If that dog knew how late she'd stayed up last night, he wouldn't dare risk barking this early in the morning, or would he? Knowing Redwood, he would.

Stumbling to the window, Kara pushed the curtain aside and yanked on the lever to unlock it. Stubborn thing was stuck. Pulling again, only harder, she managed not only to release it but smash her hand on the window frame in the process. Her hand throbbed with pain as she waved it frantically in the air. Strangling was too good for that dog.

Once she slid the glass up, she pressed her nose into the metal mesh screen and half-cried, half-whispered, "Redwood, hush!"

The huge red dog came bounding into her view with his usual eager silliness, still barking cheerfully.

"Redwood, if you don't shut up right this instant, I'm going to wrap that tongue of yours around your throat and hang you by it!" she shouted at the senseless canine who came to an abrupt halt in front of her window. He finally hushed when he jumped up on his hind legs and tried to lick her through the screen. To her surprise, a second Irish setter came prancing up right behind him and sat daintily at his side, silently watching them.

"Princess," Kara exclaimed breathlessly, rubbing her eyes to make certain she wasn't seeing double. Rob must be here, too.

Excited to the point of panic, Kara raced around the room hurrying to get dressed before the doorbell rang. She yanked on a pair of jeans, still draped over a desk chair from the day before, and pulled at a blouse hanging in her closet so hard that it sent the hanger flying.

As more and more time passed and she was able to get fully dressed, Kara began to wonder why the doorbell had not sounded or why there had not been a knock. Surely Princess could not have found her way over by herself. Rob lived in another part of town, at least three miles away.

Just in case Rob was out there on the verge of ringing the doorbell, Kara touched a bit of blush to her cheeks and quickly brushed out her thick mane of curls before opening her bedroom door. Having lived off and on at her father's over the past five years, Kara had been unable to break the habit of closing her bedroom door at night.

When she stepped out into the hall, she was greeted by a mixture of tantalizing smells. Coffee was one and either sausage or bacon was another. When she neared the kitchen, she could make out the sound of something frying.

"What the..." she mumbled, not at all sure she was awake. This just could be a dream. She used to sleepwalk as a child. She only hoped it didn't turn into a nightmare when she stepped through the kitchen door.

"Good morning," Rob greeted her cheerfully, waving a spatula in her direction. He seemed bright and chipper dressed in light blue jeans and a blue-and-white striped sport shirt. An unconcerned smile stretched lightly on his lips.

Kara stared numbly at him a moment, searching her logical mind for reasons why this man was in her kitchen cooking what was evidently breakfast. She retraced the events of the previous evening. No, she had been quite alone when she went to bed last night. So why was he here? Why was he making breakfast? How did he get into the house and where'd the sausage come from? She hadn't bought sausage in ages, rarely bothering to cook for herself these days. What was going on here?

"Have a seat. Breakfast will be ready in a few minutes," he commented as if nothing out of the ordinary was happening.

"What are you doing here?" she finally asked, still too confused to be angry.

"Cooking breakfast," he stated simply. "You still like your eggs scrambled?"

"It's pretty obvious that you are cooking breakfast, but why are you cooking breakfast in *my* kitchen? What's more, how did you get into my kitchen? The doors were locked," she demanded. Kara wanted to ask more, but she held some of the questions back because she also wanted to keep her groggy thoughts in order.

"Didn't you know? Redwood invited us to breakfast. Didn't he tell you?" Rob asked. Then acting shocked, he added, "Oh, that naughty dog forgot to tell you. It must have slipped his mind."

"Redwood invited you," Kara repeated flatly. "And I'm supposed to accept that."

"If you don't believe me, go ask him," he suggested, poking at the sausage like the whole matter was of little or no importance.

"You never explained how you got in here," she went on to ask, wondering if she was going to get any straight answers at all.

"Through the door, of course," he stated as if it were really a rather stupid question to be asking.

Sighing with total exasperation, she reminded Rob that the doors had all been locked and double-checked last night before she went to bed. Surely he didn't have a key. How would he have gotten it?

"Yes, the door was locked, and you really should have a talk with your landlord about that lock. A simple pocket knife can open it," he told her. Rob pulled his folded knife out and pitched it a few inches into the air to show her what a simple tool it was. When he reached up and caught it, he casually slipped it back into his pocket and returned his attention to the stove top.

"A lovely lady like yourself really should have better protection than that," he continued offhandedly. "You never know what sort of deviate might decide to break in and take advantage of you by cooking breakfast."

This was all so ridiculous. Kara knew she really

should be mad at him for this; but instead of anger, she found that she was actually pleased to see him and realized he had somehow complimented her. He'd indicated that she was a lovely lady. Hearing that from Rob delighted her. Still she wasn't sure she should let him know how pleased she really was. While she was busy trying to decide how she should react, he began removing the sausages from the hot skillet and placing them on a thick pad of paper towels. He set the skillet on one of the back burners and switched the stove off.

"I wasn't able to locate your regular plates, so I guess we'll have to use those paper ones I found," he said, nodding toward the small breakfast bar that was set entirely with paper and plastic—a far cry from the china and crystal Rob was used to these days.

"I haven't unpacked my dishes yet," Kara admitted sheepishly, knowing she had had nearly two months to have done so. "I don't eat many meals here. I have most of them at the restaurant. Generally I only have a doughnut or a Ding Dongs snack cake for breakfast."

"Tsk, tsk," Rob reprimanded her. "You really should take better care of yourself. Chocolate cakes for breakfast, shame. Don't you know breakfast is the most important meal of the day?"

"For some people," she defended herself. "I seem to get by just fine on a doughnut or a Ding Dongs cake."

Before they could pursue the pros and cons of a hearty breakfast any further, they were interrupted by another loud series of barks. Redwood was at it again.

"Before we eat you better feed that animal. I hunted for the dog food earlier, but I couldn't find that either. Don't tell me he eats doughnuts, too."

"I keep a sack of dog food in the hobby room," Kara explained, heading toward a closed door on the far side of the kitchen. She ignored the comment concerning the doughnuts.

"The hobby room?" he questioned, glancing at the door.

"Yes, I have more hobby stuff than one person could ever possibly use in a lifetime. Whenever I learn a new craft or skill, I go at it great guns until it finally bores me and I start something else. The thought that I might someday want to go back to a previous hobby keeps me from throwing anything away. I've tried everything from ceramics to needlepoint. Right now I'm deep into photography," she told him as she opened the door and stepped inside the darkened room.

"Same old Kara," she thought she heard him say, but wasn't quite sure.

"What was that?" She wanted it repeated.

"Oh, nothing," he mumbled in a low, spiteful voice. When she returned with a plastic bowl full of dry dog food, Rob was frowning noticeably at her. "I hope my breakfast doesn't bore you."

What did I say? Kara wondered silently. Something certainly ticked him off. Unable to figure it out, she shrugged her shoulders and went outside to feed Redwood and his guest.

When she returned to the kitchen after having put the dog food bowl back in the hobby room, Rob's harsh frown had vanished. His face lacked any expression at all while he carried the food to the little breakfast bar that divided the kitchen from the dining room. He set a plate of steaming sausage near the center of the small butcher-block counter and returned to get the biscuits and scrambled eggs out of the microwave oven where he was keeping them warm. Kara was impressed with how organized he seemed and had to admit he was far more adept in the kitchen than she was; but then whom did she have to cook for?

Rob probably had ample experience at preparing intimate little dinners for two, while she had absolutely no reason to cook. When she lived with her father, the cook prepared all of their meals. When she lived alone, she never felt it worth the effort, and in the past five years there hadn't been one single person she cared to cook for. It really was a shame because she used to enjoy it. But that was when she had a husband who was a more than willing guinea pig. She looked longingly at him, remembering some of the happy moments they had shared. In fact, except for the last months of their marriage, most of their moments had been happy ones, or at least they had been for her.

When Rob caught her staring so openly at him, he raised an eyebrow quizzically. Quickly she looked away.

"May I help you do something?" she thought to ask.

"No, all I lack is the orange juice and it's ready. I just have to get it from the refrigerator. All I want you to do is sit down and enjoy a good breakfast for a change," he said as he stepped over to the refrigerator and pulled out a small pitcher. "Just don't ask me to pass the doughnuts. They're not on today's menu." Thank goodness he was back in his playful mood.

"I wouldn't dare," Kara responded gaily, pulling her chair out and complying with his order. "Although I was wondering where the Ding Dongs snacks were."

"I'll ding-dong you," Rob threatened mischievously. Setting the pitcher down on the bar, he leaned over her. He stared menacingly into her sparkling brown eyes. Her heart quickened its erratic beating as his face grew closer to hers. She was certain he was going to collect those kisses and was as eager as she was afraid; but he only paused near her lips. When he ordered her to eat before it got cold, she could feel his warm breath fall delicately across her face. Then he pulled himself erect again and asked where she kept her salt and pepper shakers.

Knowing that it must make her seem awfully lazy, she had to admit they, too, were still in one of the many boxes overcrowding her garage. She had so much junk in that garage, she didn't dare park her car in there. It might never be seen again.

"When did you become so..." Rob paused, searching for the best word to use while he brought the large containers of salt and pepper from the stove and sat down in the chair across from hers.

"Messy?" Kara suggested, trying to help him find the word he was looking for.

"No, I was thinking more along the lines of disorganized. You never used to be like this. You used to think that everything should be kept in its proper place and that there was a proper place for everything. What you need is a housekeeper," he commented, piling his plate high.

"Oh, I plan to get organized around here one of these days," she put in, hoping he'd believe that. When he raised a suspicious eyebrow, she quickly added, "Besides, when you have a housekeeper, you can never find anything."

When Rob's other eyebrow came up, silently questioning what she was saying, Kara decided it was time to change the subject.

"These sausages certainly are delicious. I gather you brought them with you. No doubt Redwood warned you to bring your own food."

"No doubt," he grinned. Obviously he intended to stick to his ridiculous story. Popping a small piece of his own sausage into his mouth, he nodded in agreement, "You are right; these are good. My compliments to the chef."

As they ate their way through the huge breakfast, they discussed matters of little importance like the weather and the outrageous price of eggs. It wasn't until she caught him checking his watch that it occurred to her he should be on his way to work.

"I called and told Paula I wouldn't be in until sometime after noon," Rob explained when she had asked him about it. "I don't have any appointments this morning, and Paula can handle everything until I get there."

"Paula?" Kara questioned.

"Paula Jenkins, my secretary. The most efficient woman I've ever met. She knows nearly as much about the business as I do... no, make that more than I do. Without her I'd be lost in that office."

Kara wrinkled her nose. She did not have to meet this Paula Jenkins to know she probably wouldn't like her. Super efficient people made her nervous. Hearing all of the praise Rob had for the woman made her a bit jealous as well.

"Will it take you until after noon to recoup from your own cooking?"

"No, I had originally planned to talk you into taking the dogs over to Teague Park for a few hours this morning, but I've changed my mind," he said, pushing his chair back. Realizing he must be getting ready to leave, Kara's heart sank. It made her a bit angry that she even cared whether he stayed or left.

"I'm going to help you unpack some of that stuff in the garage instead, so the next time we can eat on regular dishes and I won't have to use the same skillet for the eggs and the sausage," he stated matter-of-factly. "We'll have to go to the park another time."

Kara blinked in astonishment. It seemed Rob was including her in his future plans and that both amazed and delighted her. She still cared for Rob, and although she wasn't certain where their relationship was going to lead, she realized now that she was willing to find out. Although she had photography class every Tuesday and Thursday morning at Kilgore College, she decided she could stand to miss today's. The keen interest she had developed for photography had dulled in comparison to the rekindled interest she had in Rob Phillips.

While Rob busied himself at the sink, washing the cups and pans he had used, Kara gathered up the plates and napkins and threw them away. She put the orange juice back in the refrigerator and threw the last three sausages to the dogs. Once the kitchen was back in order, Rob told her to lead him to the garage. He flipped the light switch as they entered but nothing happened. He mumbled something she could not make out and was afraid to have repeated. The only light came through the small windows in the huge garage door.

"Goodness, Karalyn, don't you ever throw anything away?" he wanted to know when he saw all the boxes and crates stacked up in the garage.

His mouth came open as he gaped at it all, trying to decide just where to begin. "Do you haul all of this around with you every single time you move?"

"No, I used to store it at Dad's, but he said something about getting rid of some of it and I decided I'd better rescue it. He might've thrown something really important out."

"It would be hard for the man to determine what was important and what wasn't in all this..." he paused, for lack of a word to describe it. He walked around where there was enough room, keeping his hands in his pockets as if he was afraid he might touch something.

"What on earth is that?" he gasped, staring down at

a large metal contraption peeping out from behind a tall stack of boxes. It seemed to be formed out of huge six-sided bands of shiny aluminum stacked one on top of the other and appeared to have a thick metal lid of sorts on top. It had dials and knobs on either side of a small metal box that was firmly planted on one of its sides.

"That is my kiln," Kara explained, laughing at his wide-eyed reaction to the oddly shaped oven. "Don't worry. It doesn't bite."

"But does it take prisoners?" he wanted to know, stepping back in mock fear.

"It hasn't yet," she chuckled. "I bought that when ceramics was my main hobby. You bake greenware and special clays in it to harden them into harder, more durable bisque. Then if you decide to paint it in glazes or underglazes, you bake it again. It's hard to explain . . . it's just a very high-intensity oven. It got to be too much of a hassle to run down to the nearest ceramic hobby shop every time I needed something fired."

"Fired?" he repeated.

"Baked," she substituted. "Anyway, I ended up buying my own kiln."

"Then, it is friendly by nature?"

"Quite," she laughed, following him as he moved on, pausing now and again to inspect anything that happened to catch his fancy.

"Well, where should we start?" Rob asked after he had made his way back around to where they had entered.

"You decide, after all it was your idea," she shrugged. One reason Kara had never done this herself was because she didn't know where to begin.

"Let's start with the dishes. Which boxes are they in?" he asked, pushing his sleeves up.

"I'm not sure. But I have a hunch they're in some of those boxes with the lids."

They made their way to the boxes she had indicated. There were eleven of them in all. Pulling the lid off one, Rob discovered assorted small appliances and decided they were on the right track.

Picking the heavy boxes up one by one, he carted them all inside the house and set them down on the kitchen floor. They started unpacking the box that had the appliances in it. First they washed the items, then decided together where everything should go.

The process reminded Kara of the weekend they moved their things into the duplex they were to call home for almost three years. They were getting married the following weekend and were blissfully happy discussing the merits of their different possessions and arguing over the placement of them all. A smile lifted her lips as she remembered the fight they'd had over whether the glasses were to go in the cabinet by the sink or the cabinet by the refrigerator. What had seemed like a major point to argue then seemed so silly now.

"You still got this old thing?" His question broke her reverie. She glanced over to see him examining an old toaster. "Whatever for? This hasn't worked right since your ring slipped off in it and I had to take the thing apart to get it out."

Sentimental value, she thought tenderly, but what she said aloud was, "Someday I'm going to get around to having it fixed."

"But why bother?" he asked, shaking his head. "You've already got another one. You really need to part with some of this stuff."

"Maybe you're right," is all Kara would say as she thought of a plan to sneak it into another room before he could toss it out.

Item by item, they worked their way to the bottom of the first big box. The last thing Rob pulled out of it was a handful of books that had nothing whatsoever to do with the kitchen. He glanced through them curiously before laying them aside. In the next box they opened, they found some of her dishes, several dish towels, and a few more books. When they came across more books at the bottom of the third box, which held sheets and pillowcases, he had to ask about them.

"If I had put them all in one box, I'd never have been able to lift them. By putting a few of them in each of the boxes, I was able to move them more easily," she tried to explain.

"I think I'm in trouble," Rob groaned, rubbing his chin thoughtfully. He was sitting on the floor staring up at her in wide-eyed amazement.

"Why?" Kara had been busy refolding crumpled dish towels at the counter but stopped at the mention of trouble.

"Because you are beginning to make sense to me," he grinned, managing to duck just before a wad of dish towels sailed by him.

Kara smiled sweetly at him when she went to pick up the towels she had thrown. She was contemplating throwing them again but from a closer range. She intended to bring his deep laughter to an abrupt halt. But, no, that was the reaction he probably wanted from her. She would not throw them.

"Missed," he taunted her, his long dimples deepening.

The towels she had just picked up seemed to have a will of their own as they went flying in his direction again.

"Missed again," he chuckled, dodging them once more.

"Well, I won't miss with this," she said, shaking her fist at him. When she got within punching range, Rob reached up and caught her by the arms, pulling her down on the floor with him. Instantly he was on top of her, straddling her waist with his knees and pinning her struggling arms to the tiled floor just above her head.

"You were saying?" He grinned, his eyes sparkling with amusement.

Kara did not answer him, she just stared up at him with a childish pout on her lips. Slowly Rob's grin faded and his eyes glittered with something more than amusement. His breathing was coming harder now, as was her own. His mouth came even closer and this time his lips lighted very gently on top of hers. As he released her arms, one hand went to caress her face softly. When he lifted his head to check her response, her childish pout was gone and open desire had taken its place. Having been given a tiny taste of his sexual prowess, she was clearly ready for more.

"I've missed you so much," he sighed before lowering his lips to hers again and easing the weight of his body on top of hers. This time his lips were more demanding, and while one hand remained at her cheek, the other slid down her side and came to rest at her waist. While his lips were working their magic on hers, she could sense that his hand was working its way up under her blouse. She wondered if she should stop him before things went too far; but the answer came back, no, let it go as far as it might. Her uncontrollable love for the man now outweighed her fears of being hurt again. Any reserve she had previously held had melted in the heat of her own passions. She still loved him and wanted him, if only for the moment. If she was headed for another fall, so be it.

Just before his hand reached her breast, her arms

slid up to encircle his neck. As the kiss progressed, she tried to draw him nearer. Her fingers wove into the soft thickness of his golden hair, and her hands pressed firmly against the back of his head. She wanted to crush him to her as if in doing so she could make him part of her. She felt on fire and wanted to pull him into the flames. With every stroke of his skillful hand and with each caress from his hungry lips, she wanted more.

The phone picked that particular moment to ring. Kara silently cursed Ma Bell and prayed Rob would ignore the ring. She planned to. But by the second ring, Rob lifted his head and gazed down at her. His hand had not left her breast. As if he had forgotten why he had paused in his lovemaking, he lowered his head once again. It was the third ring that finally brought a verbal response, "Answer that damn thing. It might be important."

Disappointment and anger mounted as she made it to the phone by the fifth ring. Who would dare call at such a moment?

"Hello?" she spat into the phone. If this was a lady trying to sell magazines, she planned to tell her off but good.

"Hello, this is Paula Jenkins, Rob Phillips's secretary. I need to speak with Mr. Phillips. Is he still there?" a soft, very feminine voice asked.

"It's for you," Kara said curiously as she held the receiver out for him.

Pushing himself up from the floor, Rob strolled over and took the phone. He seemed totally unperturbed by the interruption. He spoke in a mellow businesslike manner, "Rob Phillips here.... That's why I left you this number." He spoke clearly, responding to something Paula had said. "When?... She's certain?...

Okay, tell Maria I can be there within twenty minutes." He hung up the receiver.

Turning to Kara he explained, "I have to leave now. A problem has come up at the office. I will stop by later this afternoon before you have to go to work and help finish putting all this stuff away." Then in a foreboding voice, he added, "I always finish what I start."

Kara felt like screaming. She felt like crying. She felt like falling into his arms and begging him to stay, but instead she told him that she understood and smiled bravely as he kissed her cheek and went to the back door to call Princess.

Chapter Four

The bogus smile Kara had managed to keep until Rob and Princess were gone had slowly faded and now tears of frustration filled her dark eyes. Why did the phone have to ring? Why did that call have to do with Maria of all people? Beautiful Maria. He certainly wasted no time in leaving once he learned Maria needed him. It seemed like one minute he was on the phone and the very next she and Redwood were standing in the driveway telling them good-bye so he could rush off to be with Maria.

As Kara led Redwood through the gate to the backyard, he began to whimper softly. "I know how you feel, old boy," she told him, kneeling down to give his head a sympathetic pat. "I feel the same way. But we can't let it get us down like this," she sniffed. "After all, I already had guessed that Maria was very important to Rob. I could never really expect to compete against the likes of her. If I wasn't able to compete with Juanita, then I certainly could not hope to compete against Maria. There is just no comparison. You should see her, Red. She's got beautiful frosted blond hair that falls in perfect curls to her slender shoulders and large, sultry, green eyes. She wears designer clothes on a body you wouldn't believe. Look what I have to compare with that. Mud-brown hair and eyes the color of day-old coffee. Even my nicest clothes can't do very much to help this plain-Jane figure," she sighed hopelessly, dabbing at one of the tears that had been welling up in her dark eyes and had finally plunged down her cheek. Redwood nuzzled her lovingly, which encouraged a half-smile from her. Sometimes she felt like Redwood was the only one who really understood. It's what made up for all of his clumsy behavior.

"But you, Red, a handsome animal like you has nothing to worry about. With that princely face and shiny red coat, Princess would be a fool to even glance at another dog," she said, fondly stroking his silky red fur.

"Come on," she spoke with an enthusiasm she did not really feel. "We've got a few hours before I have to shower and get ready for work. Let's run down to the park for a while."

Taking the trip to the park and a longer route home did little to lift Kara's downtrodden spirits. Then when Rob did not return that afternoon as he had told her he would, her dark mood worsened. He had lied to her just to make leaving a little easier for himself.

In spite of an extremely busy evening at the restaurant, Kara found herself constantly thinking of Rob. She considered all the reasons she should try to forget about him, the main one being that she never had and never would totally possess Rob's heart. He would never truly belong to her no matter how much she wanted him. He had too many gorgeous women and she was not the type of woman who could share her man. That's why she'd left him in the first place. His love for other women should still be reason enough to want to give it up and have nothing further to do with the man, yet it seemed all he had to do was look sideways at her with those sexy blues of his and she was ready to offer him anything. Why was that? What power did he have over her? What had become of her common sense?

Kara was still wondering what she should do where Rob was concerned when she pulled into her driveway just before midnight. She killed the engine and turned out the headlights. She sat in the dark trying to get up the energy to get out. She was drained. Her weary muscles ached more from the tension that had plagued her than the actual work she had done at the restaurant. She could hardly wait to slip into a tub of hot water and soak until the stiffness melted away. After the usual ritual of procuring her mail, unlocking the front door, and relocking it beind her, Kara discarded the mail on the chairside table and proceeded to the kitchen for her diet cola. Only tonight the mail could wait. She would head straight to the bathroom for that badly needed hot bath just as soon as she got her cold drink.

Automatically she flipped the light switch just inside the door. When she walked into the kitchen, she went directly to the refrigerator. It was not until she had her drink in her hand that she realized the boxes were gone. She hadn't bothered about them since Rob had left that morning. When he didn't show up that afternoon as he suggested he might, she assumed the task would be hers to finish, but she'd intended to do it tomorrow.

Her first thought had been that Rob might still be in the house, but she cancelled that idea when she realized his Trans Am had not been outside and all the lights except the usual one in the entryway had been out when she arrived. But he had been here. He had to have been.

Her eyes searched the room for further evidence of

Rob's having been there. It was when she glanced at
the door he could so easily open with his little pocket
knife that she saw the note. It was taped to the small
window centered high in the upper half of the door.
Kara rushed to yank the note free from the glass and
anxiously read:

Karalyn,
　　Hated having to leave when I did, but it was an
emergency. It took me longer than I had expected
to take care of the problem so I wasn't able to get
back over here before you left for work. I felt
guilty leaving you with all that work so I decided to
finish unpacking all those boxes while you were
working. Most of it is in the kitchen cabinets, but I
put some of it in the bedroom. A few of the things
I saw no need for I put back into a box and returned it to the garage. The rest of the boxes are
folded and ready for the trash.
　　I will stop by tomorrow at lunchtime so that you
can thank me properly.

Kisses,
Rob

P.S. You really should ask your landlord for a better lock.

A knowing smile crossed Kara's lips when she considered what Rob probably was considering his proper
thanks. And if she was right and he wanted another
kiss, she really would not mind obliging him. That is if
she could actually believe it had been an emergency
that caused him to leave so readily that afternoon as
promised. She truly wanted to give him the benefit of
the doubt, but history warned her to be careful in that

respect. She had been way too eager to give him the benefit of the doubt when they had been married and look what happened. Kara felt uneasy about it, but still she decided to chance believing that there indeed had been an emergency at work. After all, Rob had returned to put the stuff away and now hinted at a pleasurable reward.

Kara did not feel as tired as she had when she had first come home, but she still wanted to soak awhile in a hot tub. It would give her a chance to better consider how she felt. Ever since Rob had re-entered her life, her emotions had been subject to constant change.

Taking the note and her drink with her, she turned out the kitchen light and walked down the hall to her bedroom. As she switched on the overhead light, she noticed the pile of books and linens Rob had heaped on her unmade bed. He must have unpacked more than the boxes they'd brought inside.

Kara decided to go ahead and put everything away so she wouldn't have to worry about it after her relaxing bath. Gathering up the linens first, she wondered where she should store them. Remembering that the closet in the spare room was not yet full, she put them away in no time but was left with no room for the books. This house did not have built-in shelves like the last place she had rented. Not really eager to lug the books very far, Kara stacked them in the nearest corner. She was surprised when she ended up with two stacks as high as she was tall, equal to her own five and a half feet. She had not realized she had that many books; but then she rarely visited her dad's library when she didn't latch on to at least one book that caught her interest.

Having finished clearing the bed, Kara turned to go into the adjoining bathroom for that long-awaited bath.

She glanced down at the dresser when she passed by and noticed something new had been added. There sat an old picture she had not seen in five years. It was still in the same gold frame she herself had bought for it.

Gingerly she picked it up and stared at the happy bride and groom pictured before her. Deep sorrow engulfed her as she took in their young, blissful, smiling faces. A knot began to form in her stomach. It was as if she were viewing the dead. In a way she was, for what she saw was the ghost of something she once held very dear—the ghost of her marriage.

The sudden appearance of the photograph puzzled Kara. She had purposely left the picture behind, along with her wedding rings and anything else that she felt represented their farce of a marriage. She'd wanted nothing around that would remind her what a complete fool she had been. She had given her father strict orders not to return with that sort of thing the next day when he had gone back for her things. And although he only brought back what he considered to be practical things, each and every item held memories for her; yet once she had them, she could not bear to part with them, like the broken toaster. It hurt more to part with them than to keep them around as reminders.

Rob must have brought the picture and placed it on her dresser where she would be certain to see it, but why? Did he think she had left it behind through an oversight or was this his way of letting her know how unimportant the memories of their marriage were to him. Maybe he would rather do without it. She wished she knew exactly what his motive had been.

And now that she had the picture, what should she do with it? Part of her wanted to leave it right where it sat, but another part of her knew her memories would grow and haunt her unmercifully if she did. Kara considered simply returning it to Rob but was afraid he would refuse to take it. He might not care what became of it. That would hurt too much. And what if it had not been a cruelly perverse act on his part? What if he'd brought it because he honestly thought she might want it? Then to return it would be an insult. But if she chose not to keep it and simply threw it away, he might become angry that she did not offer him the chance to take it back. What should she do with it?

Right now she did not have the energy to sort through it all. Until she did and could clearly think it through, she would allow the picture to stay where it was.

The first thing Kara did the following morning was call Mr. Clifton, her landlord, about the lock. She really did not mind Rob's being able to get in and out whenever he wanted. It was sort of thrilling that he could and did. But the fact that anyone else wanting to enter her house for whatever reason could do so made her more than a little nervous. When she made the call, she was told Pete Clifton was not home at the time but his wife Shirley promised to have him stop by later that morning.

After a quick breakfast of orange juice and a doughnut, Kara took extra care in getting dressed. Instead of her favorite morning wear of faded jeans and a baggy shirt, Kara chose a pink-and-blue floral sundress with narrow string ties for straps. She selected pastel pink sandals to wear with the dress. She worked with her thick brown hair until every curl was in place, sweeping away from her face. Then Kara brushed her cheeks with frosted peach blusher and blended violet and blue on her eyelids before applying a thin layer of pink lipgloss. Wanting everything to be perfect right down to her jewelry, she chose a gold necklace with a simple diamond pendant that hung close to her throat. The ring she selected was a grouping of small opals and diamonds that resembled a tiny blue-and-white flower. Simple but very pretty.

Before leaving her bedroom, Kara straightened up and carefully made the bed. She was not quite sure why she did it when there was no reason for Rob to see it, but she felt she should . . . maybe because she had left it in such a mess yesterday and Rob had seen it when he brought the books and linens in. She did not want that to happen again. He already had such a low opinion of her—claiming she needed a housekeeper.

The note had left Kara unsure of whether or not Rob expected lunch. Just to be on the safe side, she decided to have something ready; but what? There was very little to choose from. About all she had was canned tuna or frozen chicken. She never had been much of a red-meat eater. Deciding on Italian baked chicken and knowing there was not time to allow the chicken to thaw simply by setting it out at room temperature, Kara tossed the frozen package into the microwave oven and set it on defrost.

While the chicken was defrosting, she began to search for her apron. She certainly did not want to splatter tomato sauce or anything equally offensive on her dress. During the hunt she located several items she would need, but not the elusive apron. With no more time to search, she went to her room and put her robe on over the dress.

Italian baked chicken used to be one of Rob's favorites, and Kara had made it often enough that she did not have to refer to a recipe. It was a good thing, because her cookbooks were somewhere in those tall stacks of books in the bedroom.

Finding everything she needed to make the chicken except mozzarella cheese, for which she substituted the one cheese she did have, cheddar, Kara quickly had the chicken ready to go into the oven.

Next she made the only salad she could from the little produce she had on hand. She grated the carrots and celery she'd purchased to snack on and mixed in salad dressing and raisins. It made just enough for two.

Having used all of the carrots, Kara was left with little choice for the vegetables. She had canned corn and, what luck, Italian green beans. If the Italian bread she had bought last week to make hogie sandwiches and never got around to using had not gone bad, she could round the meal out with garlic bread.

While Kara was crushing the garlic cloves, there came a light knock at the back door. She had not expected Rob for at least thirty more minutes. Hurriedly she yanked off her robe and threw it into a cabinet. She checked her reflection in the chromed toaster just before answering the knock.

To her disappointment yet relief, it was Pete Clifton, her landlord. She had forgotten all about his wife promising to have him stop by. When she explained the problem with the lock in as few words as possible, Pete slowly scratched his head, nodding.

"And these days you need a good lock on the door," he agreed, putting a finger to his lips while he studied the door. "Tell you what, I should have a security chain out in the truck I can put up for today, and I'll try to get you a deadbolt by the end of the week. Is that all right with you?"

"Yes, fine," Kara spoke hurriedly. She wanted to get back to her cooking. She still had to get the bread ready and wanted to clean up the mess and recheck her hair before Rob showed up. And there was still the table to set. Glancing at the wall clock, she knew she would not have much more than half an hour to finish.

"I'll just go on out to the truck right now and get that chain for you," he explained and turned to leave. "I'll be back in a minute."

Kara closed the door behind him. She doubted Pete Clifton did anything within a minute. Although he did not look much older than she did and was actually rather virile-looking, he moved around like an old man with nothing to do. Slow and easygoing, that was Pete Clifton.

Grabbing the robe from the cabinet and wrapping it around her once again, Kara mixed the garlic juice with melted butter and began brushing the bread generously. She had to hurry. Time seemed to be working against her as usual. Tearing off a large piece of aluminum foil, Kara wrapped the loaf of bread and placed it in the oven with the chicken. She had just begun to tackle the mess around her, when the knock sounded at the door again.

Not wanting to take the time to answer the door, she shouted, "Come on in, Pete."

"And who is Pete?" Rob wanted to know just as soon as he had opened the door.

"What are you doing here?" Kara gasped, dropping the bowl she had melted the butter in. Luckily it was plastic.

"Didn't you see my message?" he asked, peering around the door to see if the note had been removed.

"But you said you'd be by at lunchtime," she complained, wanting to stamp her foot in protest but managing to control herself. "It's only eleven thirty."

"I lunch early," he shrugged, coming in and closing the door. He was wearing a pair of dark blue dress slacks and a matching vest over a light blue shirt. Kara guessed that he had shed his jacket before coming in. On a day like today she could easily understand why he had discarded his jacket. He was absolutely handsome dressed in different shades of blue.

"I still want to know who Pete is," he restated.

"That man outside," she told him over her shoulder while she rushed to put things in the dishwasher.

"What man outside?" Rob wanted to know, searching through the door window for signs of a man.

"The one with the truck," she went onto say, never pausing in her work.

"What truck? I saw no truck when I drove up."

"You didn't? I wonder what happened. He was supposed to go back to his truck and get a chain to go on the door."

"Who was?"

"Pete Clifton, my landlord!" she sighed in exasperation. "When I heard the knock, I thought you would be Pete returning with the chain."

"And do you usually ask your landlord in while you are dressed like that?" he asked suspiciously, indicating the robe she still had on.

"Not usually," she admitted sheepishly and explained how she had been unable to find her apron. She immediately removed the garment to prove that she was indeed properly dressed.

"Nice," he commented, allowing his gaze to sweep downward. "Did you wear that for my benefit?"

"No," Kara lied, not wanting to admit the truth. His ego certainly did not need any more boosting. "It's just that it's such a beautiful day, I simply felt like wearing a summery dress."

"Too bad, I was hoping I had something to do with it," he stated, right to the point. "Whatever the reason, you look gorgeous."

"Thank you," she remarked uneasily. For some reason, Rob's compliments were making her want to blush.

"Mmmm, something smells good. What is it?" Rob asked, breathing deeply the rich aroma that filled the room.

"Italian baked chicken," she replied proudly, knowing Rob would be pleased.

"Am I invited?" He took in several more deep breaths when he opened the oven door to peek inside.

"Only if you'll set the table," she informed him cheerfully, putting the last items into the lower rack of the dishwasher.

"Seems fair enough," he agreed. Knowing more about where everything was than Kara herself did, he had the table set in no time and was offering to help with the food. She made him sit down and stay out of her way while she got everything ready.

To Kara's delight and relief, the chicken was delicious, as was the rest of the meal. Rob had seconds of everything. How he could eat so much and not get fat was beyond Kara.

After they had finished eating, they sat at the table chatting. Rob explained his problem at work the day before. It had involved an irate customer who was threatening to sue because a faulty gas nozzle had leaked gasoline all over her. The gasoline had not only ruined her new outfit but had blistered her leg before she could get it washed off. Rob had spent the afternoon trying to calm the woman enough to reason with her. In the end she was willing to accept his offer to pay the medical bills and a check for five hundred dollars to buy a new outfit, which was far more than the original one had been worth. Kara decided it sounded plausible and did not feel as bad about his having left when he did. Although the problem had been fairly serious, she was perversely delighted to hear it. Her spirits lifted considerably.

Finally the topic of his having returned to put away the rest of the things while she was at work came up.

"That's why I came over, you know," he reminded her. His eyes danced with anticipation. "I wanted you to have an opportunity to thank me properly."

"Yes, of course, I do want to thank you. It was very considerate of you."

"And?" he prompted her eagerly. He leaned forward with his elbows on the table and his chin resting lightly in his hands, ready for his reward.

"Oh, you want a reward?" Kara hedged, pretending she did not know what could be on his mind. "Let me get my purse."

"No need. Your money is not good enough."

"It's not?" she asked innocently. "Then what?"

Narrowing his eyes until they were two threatening slits of silver ice, he claimed, "I think you know very well what."

Kara's heart fluttered with expectation when he pushed his chair back and slowly yet determinedly stood up. A mischievous grin possessed his handsome face, causing narrow indentations to form in his lean cheeks. By curling his index finger toward himself, Rob motioned for her to come to him. He did not have to say what was on his mind. She could easily read it in his eyes.

The knock on the door came before Kara could respond to his silent command. When she got out of her seat, it was not to go to Rob, but to the door instead.

"Sorry it took me so long," Pete apologized when he stepped inside. "The chain wasn't in my truck after all. I had to go back home to get it, and since it was nearly noon, I went ahead and ate lunch. Hope it didn't inconvenience you any." Spotting Rob still standing beside the table, he nodded a hello and went about the business of installing the security chain. If he thought it strange that Kara had a man in her kitchen, he did not show it.

Kara began to clear the table as Pete talked to Rob over his shoulder. "That sure is a beautiful Trans Am out there in the driveway. That must be yours."

Rob admitted it was and thanked him for the compliment, waiting impatiently for the man to finish his work.

"I almost bought a Trans Am myself last year, but my wife wanted a car more suitable for the family. We got three boys, you know."

The fact that Rob did not have anything to reply did not stifle Pete's gift for gab. "Just a few more minutes here and I'll be finished. Now this won't keep an intruder out if he really wants to get in, but it'll have to do until I can get up to the hardware store and get you that deadbolt I promised. A deadbolt ought to keep 'em out. Leastwise they won't be opening your door with a credit card or screwdriver."

"Or pocket knife," Kara muttered only loud enough for Rob to hear. She cut her eyes over to Rob to see his reaction. His eyes narrowed cautiously as he returned her gaze. He had his arms crossed and was impatiently drumming his fingers on his arms.

"Of course, they can still bust in a window in order to get in, but more than likely a burglar won't bother. He'll just go on to a house that is a little easier to get into," Pete continued while he tested the chain.

"Another thing, most prowlers won't pick a place that's got a dog in the yard. Too risky. So I wouldn't worry too much."

Scratching the back of his head with the worn yellow handle of his screwdriver, Pete stood back looking at the chain. "Looks a mite crooked, don't you think? I better raise that right side a mite."

"Looks straight enough to me," Rob offered as he quickly stepped over to escort the man out of the door. "It was nice of you to come over and see to the problem as quickly as you did."

"That's part of owning rent houses," Pete grinned, allowing Rob to maneuver him outside. Kara wanted to follow them and watch Rob practice the art of giving Pete the old heave-ho, but she decided to stay behind and finish cleaning up the kitchen. She put what she could into the already half-filled dishwasher and left the rest of the dirty dishes in the sink to soak. She was nervously keeping an eye on the door while she gave the table a quick wipe with a sponge. Would the interruption deter Rob's earlier plans or would he return still wanting to be rewarded?

The question was answered only moments later when Rob came back inside wondering aloud, "Now where were we?"

"At the table." Kara sounded extremely casual, considering the state of utter turmoil her insides were in. Her heart pounded fiercely when he stepped closer to where she stood with her sponge still in hand.

With clever foresight Rob removed the wet sponge from her hand and tossed it in the general direction of the sink. No words were spoken. His gaze held hers as his arms slid around her. Kara's lips automatically parted and her arms went up to encase his neck as his mouth came ever closer and finally claimed hers. The feel of his lips against hers were maddening. A burning passion scampered through her veins, quickly warming every inch of her, releasing a fever only Rob could relieve.

What Kara had expected to be a long fervent kiss turned out to be extremely sensual but short, for all too soon his lips had released hers and he lifted his head in order to peer down at her.

"I'd better leave," he spoke in what was barely above a whisper. His breathing came in short erratic fragments. "I...we...I just...better go."

Kara tried not to let the disappointment show. She eased her arms down and allowed him to back away. Why did he suddenly decide he should leave? Did he feel guilty? Was he concerned with Maria's feelings should she find out? Or was he just as afraid of what was happening between them as she was?

Her head was spinning with so many questions that it was hard to concentrate on what he was saying. It was something about a one o'clock appointment he wished he didn't have.

Kara's insides were a painful whirlwind of confused emotions as she walked with him to his car. It was obvious she was still very much in love with Rob by how badly she ached whenever he left her. Some wounds had never quite healed.

After opening his car door and before climbing in, Rob paused a moment. It was as if he had something he wanted to say yet he was hesitant to speak. He stared at her a moment, seeming uneasy about whatever was on his mind. Finally he leaned forward, kissed her on the cheek, and told her that he would see her soon. Then he was gone.

Chapter Five

For the rest of the afternoon, Kara occupied herself by shopping for a bookcase. She seemed to have a renewed interest in decorating. Until now she had been satisfied with adequate, but for some reason she now felt like sprucing the place up with something really nice. She went to six furniture stores before deciding she liked best the bookcases she'd seen at the first place she had visited. Although she knew she could make do with less, she ended up purchasing a complete four-piece wall unit with recessed lighting, which would certainly put a strain on her pocketbook. Most of the manager's fee she earned went for clothes, rent, or her car. But this was something she really wanted; besides, the unit was a very practical choice in furniture. The maple coloring would go well with her Early American furniture and the small compartments at the base of two of the pieces would give her a place to store things other than her books.

Having spent so much time looking around before finally making her decision, she did not bother going home to freshen up. She did not really have time. Kara left straight for the restaurant after giving the salesman her address for delivery the next Saturday.

Shortly after she had settled in behind her desk and

was looking over the previous day's report, which Clint always left in her top basket, she spotted a memo beside the phone that simply said, "Rob phoned—will call back."

Setting the report aside, Kara picked up the slip of paper with both hands and stared at it curiously. While wondering if she should try to call him or wait for his return call, the phone buzzed, startling her so that she tore the paper in half.

"Pinewood, Kara Phillips speaking," she managed to say calmly.

"Where have you been all afternoon?"

Kara closed her eyes in reaction. It was Rob. "Shopping."

"Well, I've been trying to get a hold of you for hours," he explained. "What were you shopping for?" he wanted to know, as if he had called for no other reason than to chat.

"Furniture," she stated simply, then added, "I bought a wall unit for the living room. I needed someplace to keep all those books you unpacked and heaped on my bed."

There was a long, awkward pause before Kara decided to come right out and ask, "Why did you call?"

"I wanted to see if you would like to have a late supper with me on Saturday night, or should I say Sunday morning, since it's well after midnight when you leave."

"Where?"

"Wherever you say," Rob replied quickly, letting her know he was eager for her to say yes.

"How about here, at Pinewood. I could have the chef prepare two lovely dinners right at closing time," she suggested, not really interested in any of the all-night restaurants. Besides, Pinewood was the best.

"No, that won't do. After seven or eight hours' work, you would be tired of the place, ready to leave. I know I would be. How about that new place on the Loop? No, better yet, I know a place that serves exquisite food, has wonderful atmosphere, and is open at all hours. Its specialty is catering to private parties of two."

"And where might that be?" Kara asked suspiciously.

"Over on Eden Drive. You remember, you've eaten there once before. How about it?" The invitation sounded earnest.

"I don't know," Kara began. Again her common sense was doing battle with her heart, warning her what could happen if she were to find herself alone with him at his house so late at night. Look what happened when she was over there in the daylight hours. Her common sense warned her that she just might find herself caught in a very compromising situation, which happened to be her heart's main argument for her to go.

"I'll plan a special surprise for dessert," he tempted her, his tone melodious.

"What's that?"

"Something sweet, rich, and chocolatey..." he replied, hoping to lure a yes from her.

"Sounds fattening," she said cautiously. An alarm was sounding in her head, telling her to come up with an excuse not to accept. At the same time her heart was continually beating out the message for her to go...go...go.

"So, you'll diet the next day. It'll be worth it," he assured her, then in a coaxing little-boy voice, he added, "Please?"

Rob sounded so sincere in his invitation that Kara pushed her common sense aside and decided in favor of her heart. She promised to try to be at his house a little after midnight and wanted to know if she should bring anything.

"Just yourself," he said sweetly. "See you then."

He hung up.

Kara stared at the now-silent receiver in wonder and amazement as she slowly returned it to its cradle. It seemed too good to be true. Nervous excitement surged through her, making it impossible to continue concentrating on her work. Finally she returned the daily report to the top basket and leaned lazily back in her large over-stuffed desk chair. She stared up at the white acoustical ceiling, contemplating the plans she had just made. After the way Rob had abruptly broken off that kiss earlier, she had not expected to hear from him for quite some time, if ever. She'd tried but hadn't really been able to convince herself that it was for the best, not completely. Now she had hope again, however slight.

Kara could have spent the rest of the evening fantasizing about what might happen Saturday, but moments later, Clint stuck his head in the office and told her he was leaving. Time for her to go out front and greet the patrons as they arrived. It was a good thing Wednesdays were slow; she'd have a hard time concentrating on her duties this evening.

For the rest of the week Kara did not see Rob, although he called her at work each evening to remind her of their date. She also found a note on her door Saturday morning when she came home from a quick trip to a nearby convenience store to get the extension cord she needed in order to place the wall units where she wanted them. She was disappointed to have missed him.

The note had been tucked into the crevice between

the door and the doorframe. Kara supposed he'd noticed the deadbolt had already been installed. Rob had merely explained in his note that he'd stopped by and would see her after she got off from work. Part of her was worried about the evening ahead, yet another part could hardly wait. The rest of the day seemed to pass at a snail's pace. It was almost unbearable.

The furniture store had promised delivery before noon, but it was after two before the wall units arrived. It took the delivery boys over an hour to install them properly, leaving Kara with about forty-five minutes to shower, dress, and drive to work. Any other day but Saturday, she could just have called and told Clint she would be a little late, but Saturdays were their busiest days. On Saturdays Kara came in half an hour earlier and Clint stayed two hours later than on weekdays. Sundays would probably be just about as busy, but her father was opposed to business on Sundays. Actually it had been her mother who had been opposed to opening on Sundays and her father had willingly respected her wishes and never allowed any of his restaurants to open on a Sunday, even after her mother's death many years ago. It seemed odd he would remain so adamant about it when he was not an extremely religious man. The only times Kara knew of that he had ever stepped inside a church had been to get married to her mother and again for her funeral. Kara supposed his reasons for remaining closed on Sundays were more personal than religious.

The fact that they were closed on Sundays might account for the huge crowd they always had on Saturday. Tonight would be no exception.

Kara took special care in selecting her outfit for the evening. She always wore something extra-dressy on Saturday nights, but she had reason to be especially choosy tonight. Not having the chance to change after

work and still be at Rob's on time, whatever she chose
to wear for work would also be what she would wear
later at Rob's. She flipped through her many hostess
gowns until she found the one she was looking for. It
was long and clinging and black. The narrow slit up the
right side of the skirt was almost as daring as the deeply
plunging neckline.

For footwear she selected a pair of shiny black heels
fashioned from a network of tiny interwoven straps.
She brushed her hair out to its fullest and after adding
several long gold chains around her neck and applying
an extra touch of color to her cheeks and lips, Kara felt
very much the temptress. She could not help but try
out a few sultry flirtations in the mirror.

Look out, Rob Phillips, she thought with a wicked
smile.

Kara was thirty minutes late when she finally rushed
through the back door of the restaurant. She'd expected Clint to be more than a little annoyed with her,
having to take care of her duties as well as his own, but
he seemed to have everything well in hand.

"That ought to whet their appetites." He grinned as
his gaze deliberately swept over her gown. "Is there
someting special happening tonight that I don't know
about? You haven't worn that since opening night."

"I have a date." Kara shrugged, as if it was not as
special as he had made it sound. "I just wanted to wear
something nice for him."

"Lucky guy," Clint commented with a sly raise of
his brow. He let out a low whistle when he had to come
closer in order to hand her the restaurant's register into
which he had logged all the evening reservations as
they occurred. His eyes continued to scan her slinky
attire. "If I weren't already engaged, I think I'd propose
marriage to you right here and now."

"Wouldn't work. I enjoy being boss too much," Kara chuckled, placing the reservation register over the lowest part of the neckline and folding her arms around it self-consciously.

"Who's the guy?"

"My ex," Kara answered briefly. Clint knew about her past. He was the type you could easily confide in.

"Husband?"

"That's the one."

"Why are you bothering with that guy? He already had his chance and blew it."

Kara shrugged. She hated to admit that she still loved the man in spite of everything. It didn't seem the rational way to feel, but she just could not help it.

"You must have a screw loose."

"Probably do," Kara had to admit. It was the only plausible explanation. If she had half a brain, she would not allow Rob this second chance to hurt her.

"A beautiful woman like you could have almost any man she wanted... especially wearing a dress like that. Ouch!" He brought his hand to his mouth and playfully bit his knuckle as if looking at such beauty was sheer torture. Kara knew he was prone to exaggerations but loved it all the same.

Every time Clint's path crossed hers until it was time for him to leave, he let out a low wolf whistle and gave her the once over. It did wonders for Kara's ego. She only hoped Rob would react with the same enthusiasm.

Kara locked the front doors promptly at eleven thirty and waited anxiously for the last diners to finish. When midnight neared, she hinted to the small number of dawdlers remaining by asking them repeatedly if there was anything else they needed. Had any of them requested dessert, she was sure she would have suggested they get it packaged to carry home.

Finally she had let the last customer out and was free to go. Although it seemed an eternity had passed, it was not yet midnight. She would not be late.

Apprehension mixed with eager excitement as Kara retouched her makeup and ran a quick brush through her hair. A few minutes later she was in her car headed north on Fourth Street and watching for a street sign that read Eden Drive. The closer Kara got to Rob's house, the harder her pulse raced. That common sense of hers was again warning her she might be headed for trouble, that her decision to go had been a foolhardy one; but her heart refused to listen.

When she drove up the lighted drive that circled in front of the house, she was immediately aware that the curtains in one of the lower floor windows moved. Her heart fluttered at the thought that Rob must have been watching for her. Parking off to the side of the house, she had to pass the window to get to the front door. She was a little disappointed to discover Princess was the one peering out from the narrow part in the curtains.

Kara tapped lightly on the window as she passed by, which caused Princess to bark excitedly, announcing her arrival. Placing a finger to her lips, she tried to quiet the overly zealous animal. When Princess only seemed to bark louder, Kara gave up and hurried to the front door. Just as she reached for one of the large brass door knockers, she heard the knob rattle and the door swung open.

"Hell-ooo," Rob chimed. His eyes widened as they slowly roved over her, lingering momentarily on certain curves that were revealed by such a daring neckline.

"I didn't take time to change after work. I was afraid I would be late if I did," she started to explain, worried he would realize she'd planned to wear the gown anyway. Now though, she felt suddenly overdressed. Rob had on a pair of brushed-denim fashion jeans and a casual V-neck cotton shirt, white with light blue trim.

"That's perfectly all right," he stated adamantly. "In fact that dress is about as perfectly all right as it can get. It might make breathing a little difficult for me, but I don't mind... believe me, I don't mind at all." He continued to stare at her in amazement.

Kara smiled inwardly. This was just the sort of reaction she'd hoped for. She could feel his gaze still on her as she passed through the doorway and greeted Princess who pranced around the room barking jubilantly, causing quite a commotion. Kara knelt down to pet the excited animal, knowing the slit in her skirt would offer Rob quite a provocative view.

Princess stopped barking and wagged her tail appreciatively when Kara stroked the dog's head.

"Craving a little attention, huh, girl?"

"She's not the only one," Rob commented, letting out a few little playful barks of his own. When Kara's only response was a curious raise of her brow, he began to whimper pitifully. Kara stood as he began to come closer, still whimpering softly.

Unable to resist, Kara reached out and patted him gently on the head, "There, there now."

Instantly Rob's tongue came out and he began to pant heavily. "I don't know if I should be doing this," Kara commented dryly. "Have you had your shots?"

Rob stopped in mid-pant and began to laugh. He assured her he had been properly vaccinated but warned her that he had flunked out of obedience school. Kara laughed, too.

The two of them continued to poke lighthearted fun at one another as they enjoyed the Dijon pork chops that Rob had prepared for their late-night supper.

Rob had set a magnificent table, using fine china and sterling silver. Included in the fresh floral centerpiece was a pair of tall white tapers. Rob certainly had developed exquisite taste over the past five years.

The meal was delicious and Rob's continuous joking was delightfully entertaining. It was like old times. Kara was enjoying herself immensely, unaware of just how much she had eaten until Rob announced it was time for his extra-special, super-duper, ultra-deluxe dessert.

"I'm sorry, but I can't possibly eat another bite," she apologized, patting her tummy tenderly. "I'm just too full."

"Me, too," he admitted. "Why don't we forget the dessert for now and finish our wine in the den. We can relax while we let our food settle. Maybe we will feel more like having that dessert later on."

The den was lighted by only three very dim amber lights in narrow cylindrical casks that protruded from the wood-slat ceiling above a small wet bar. A small conversational grouping of sofa and chairs faced a huge ceiling-to-floor window in a close-fitting semicircle. A large schefflera, every bit of nine feet, thrived near the window.

Through the wall of glass, the view included most of the gardens and part of the pool. Several tiki lamps flickered intermittently throughout the back yard, forming islands of soft light in the darkness.

As Kara eased into the thick softness of the over-sized blue-and-beige sofa, Rob leaned over his stereo unit just long enough to flip a switch and then joined her on the sofa. A soft instrumental recording full of violins and clarinets gently surrounded the two of them.

Kara sipped nervously on her wine, more in an attempt to occupy herself than to satisfy a thirst. It seemed almost crucial that her hands have something to do.

If Rob was equally apprehensive, he did not show it. Casually he placed an arm behind her, resting it lightly on the back of the sofa. He stared silently at her a moment before finally commenting, "You are so incredibly beautiful."

"And you have obviously had too much wine to drink," Kara teased, trying to keep the mood light. She just did not know how to handle such an open compliment, had never been confident of the validity of such statements. She had been handed a line by too many men who were just out to score points.

"The wine has nothing to do with it. I have always been amazed at your beauty. Especially those eyes. I'll have you know those dark, mystical eyes of yours have haunted me constantly over the past five years. I never was able to get them out of my mind," Rob said softly. Moving his hand forward, his fingers began to play with a lock of her hair. "And I often wondered if you'd cut your hair. I'd so hoped you hadn't. I love your long hair. It's so thick and sexy."

"I thought about a shorter hairstyle. I felt like I was getting too old for long hair, but I could never quite bring myself to get much of it cut," Kara admitted. She was unable to resist leaning her head back against his strong arm. She could smell the gentle fragrance of his cologne. The soft tug at her hair along with a bit more wine than she was used to was having a calming effect on her.

Rob stared into her eyes a moment and she felt as if she were floating in a sea of blue. "Did you ever think about me over the years, Kara? Did you ever wonder what I was doing or how I was?"

"Of course, I did," Kara replied tenderly. "I could

never put you, the man I was once married to, entirely out of my mind.''

"And did you try?"

"At first, I did," she admitted. "But soon I realized it was useless. You were burned permanently into my memory."

"Was it really so bad?" His voice was deep with feeling.

"Was what really so bad?"

"Being married to me." Rob's jaw flexed with troubled emotion while he waited for the answer.

"There were good times." For no apparent reason tears clouded her eyes, and her throat constricted so that her voice wavered when she emphasized, "Rob, there were so many good times."

She felt his gentle touch when he brushed aside a tear that had settled on her cheek. The tenderness in his action triggered more tears. She turned her head so that he could not see the raw emotion flooding her eyes. Where did all of these silly tears come from?

"Remember our first date?" Rob asked in a thoughtful voice.

"I remember how very afraid I was to be alone with you," she said, turning back to smile up at him. Her eyes were still damp, but she felt she had the tear-flow under control.

"Afraid to be alone with me?" he probed further. The sparkle in his eyes let her know that the idea delighted him.

"Well, you were reputed to be quite a ladies' man and as you might recall, I was rather inexperienced. You were several years older and in a league all your own," she reminded him. Again Kara relaxed her head against his arm, only closer to his shoulder this time. It felt so right to be in his arms again. It was as if the past five years had not existed. She could easily forget that there had ever been a divorce and the reason behind it. She was that affected by his nearness. "Your reputation terrified me so that I did everything I could not to be alone with you. I wasn't sure I could handle it."

"And are you still terrified to find yourself alone with me?"

"Should I be?" she asked, her dark eyes wide and expressive.

A smile played at his lips as he thought it over. Leaning forward, he took her wine glass and set it aside. "Yes, you should."

His lips closed over hers, gently at first. They were warm, tender, and extremely persuasive as they worked their magic on her. Passion quickly mounted and the kiss became more demanding. His arms tightened around her, drawing her ever closer to him. Kara responded by sliding her own arms up around his neck and returning his embrace. In a natural response, she slid her tongue into his mouth and sampled the familiar taste that was uniquely Rob.

"Kara," he murmured softly past her lips. She felt his hands move her hair out of the way of her zipper, while his lips were continuing to cast their sensuous spell over her. When his fingers worked the zipper down, Kara felt the fabric slacken around her. His fingers left tantalizing trails of warmth as they moved along her sensitive skin. Sliding beneath the fabric, his hand slipped the gown from her shoulders and it fell down around her waist. The hand quickly moved to cup one of her breasts, gently caressing the tip with his thumb until it burned with intense desire.

Kara quivered with anticipation as his lips made their way down her throat. She arched her back eagerly when his lips neared her breasts. Gently he laid her back on the couch and slipped the gown over her hips and to the floor. The tiny scrap of lace that was her only undergarment quickly followed.

Continuing to caress her breast with one hand, Rob managed to pull his own shirt off then lowered himself on top of her. Her breasts flattened against his chest. It seemed so natural, so right, to have him there. She ran her palms across his naked back, marveling at the feel of his muscles.

When his lips returned to reclaim her breast, she ached with arousal. Reaching for his buckle, Kara knew she wanted him. Her need was too intense. Five years had been a long time. She had to have him now.

She tugged at his belt and he brought a hand down to stop her. Raising up on one elbow, he stared down at her. His thumb continued to play idly at her breast as he spoke, "Kara, tell me why you left me."

"What?" she asked, trying desperately to catch her breath.

"Why did you leave me?" His voice was low and determined. "Before we make love, I want you to tell me exactly why you left. I think we need to discuss it."

Kara's passion instantly turned into anger when she realized the game Rob was playing. "I think you know exactly why I left," she spat at him. Pushing him off her, she sat up and made a grab for her clothes.

"I think I do, too, but I just wanted to hear you say it," he told her, his nostrils flared with the emotion that consumed him.

"Well, I'm certainly not giving you that pleasure," she cried. Humiliation flooded her as she struggled to get back into her clothes. How could he be this cruel? Here she was ready to give herself to him and all he wanted was to hear how terribly hurt she'd been to find out about Juanita. Tears stung her eyes at the realization that this had all been a big ego trip for him, nothing more.

"I don't want you to leave here until you've admitted to me why you left me."

"I don't care what you want, Rob Phillips. I'm leaving." Grabbing her shoes, she stomped out of the room in her bare feet.

"Karalyn, come back here!" he shouted after her.

"Forget it!" she shouted over her shoulder. She was practically running in her haste to get out of Rob's house. When she banged the front door behind her, she could tell it did not close, but she was not about to take the time to go back and close it. She rushed down the sidewalk to her car. Tossing her shoes to the passenger side of the car, she jumped in. She had turned the key and had the car moving in reverse in less time than it took to close the car door. When she threw it into drive, she spun gravel everywhere.

Anger consumed her while she sped along Eden Drive. She was just as mad at herself as she was at Rob for having allowed herself to get in such a vulnerable situation. She should have had better sense than that. Where had her brains been? Out to lunch? Had she really believed he might have changed?

"Never again!" she swore aloud, hitting the side of her fist on the steering column. Rob had used her for his own amusement for the last time. No more hoping for miracles.

When she reached Judson Road, Kara turned right instead of left and headed out of town. She did not want to go home for fear Rob was not through playing his perverse little games. She needed time to pull herself together. Having nearly a full tank of gas, Kara put her foot down on the accelerator and headed north. It was not until she'd driven through the small town of

Diana and was nearly to Ore City that she decided on a destination. Turning east on Highway 155, she drove on to Lake o' the Pines.

Pulling off at the first lakeside picnic area she came to, Kara got out and started walking along the moonlit shoreline. Whenever she felt like she was about to burst into a flood of angry tears, she would bend over, pick up a rock, and hurl it as far as she could across the water. She was determined not to cry. She'd wasted enough tears on that man.

When a dense thicket prevented her from going any further along the narrow embankment, Kara sat down on the side of a tree that had fallen but somehow still lived. Sadly she stared out across the dark water that so well matched her mood. Her attention was drawn to the long silvery path the moon left rippling over the lake's ebony surface. That and the tranquil sound of the water softly lapping against the rocky shoreline had a soothing effect on Kara's frayed emotions. Soon she had them back under control. She was no longer possessed by anger, nor did she still feel like crying or screaming. Instead she seemed almost numb, as if the whole ordeal had drained her dry of any feelings. She felt only a strange emptiness.

She sat for hours, hypnotized by the flickering trail of moonlight. Occasionally it occurred to her that she should be getting home, but she failed to follow through on the thought. Even after the moon had disappeared and the sky began to lighten in the east, Kara continued to sit and stare out across the huge lake. It was not until an early-morning fisherman buzzed past her in a small yellow boat that her reverie was finally broken.

Standing to leave, she became aware of how sore her feet were. She had not bothered to put her shoes on before heading out across the rocky terrain and had been so wrapped up in her anger and humiliation that she had not paid any attention to the sharp rocks. But now as she limped back toward the car, the rocks had her full attention.

The sun came up to her left as Kara drove back to Longview. Slanted sunrays flickered through the thick branches of the tall trees, most of which were pines, that graced the East Texas roadside. The long drive made her sleepy. When she got home, she quickly showered and crawled into bed. She was too tired to worry about Rob anymore. She was too tired to worry about anything. She fell asleep almost instantly.

Chapter Six

A week had past and Kara had managed to avoid Rob entirely. Whenever the phone rang, she refused to answer it. To be on the safe side, if it rang in the afternoon while she was still home, Kara would always call the restaurant and make certain the caller had not been Clint with a problem that needed her attention. The only other person who ever called her that she cared to speak to was her father, but he usually called her at work after the early evening rush was over. He rarely phoned her at home.

Rob had tried calling her at the restaurant several times, but Kara was inevitably too busy to come to the phone. He always left messages for her to return his calls, but she ignored them as best she could. Whenever she felt herself weakening and actually wondering what he could possibly have to say to her, all she had to do was think back to that Sunday morning's escapades and the heartless games Rob was capable of playing.

Kara had just enough pride, wounded as it was, to keep from returning a call. She was not about to give him another opportunity to exploit her emotions further for his own personal gratification. He knew only too well the effect he had on her and it was all just a big joke to him. The man must actually thrive on his ego to be going to such lengths to feed it.

Kara decided Rob was probably very angry that she did not play the game out and give him all the delicious details of how hurt and utterly destroyed she had been to find out about Juanita. Why else would he want to talk to her? She felt an odd satisfaction in the fact that he must really be upset with her. Kara's own anger had slowly returned. She was especially angry with herself for even having admitted to him that she had thought of him since the divorce. She wished now she'd kept her big mouth shut, instead of feeding his ego. What else had she been foolish enough to say? She could not recall the conversation word for word, but the parts she could remember made her stomach ache.

The events of Sunday morning were all Kara seemed to think about, even though she tried not to dwell on them while she endlessly pulled assorted weeds out of her flower beds. Having neglected them so far this year, the horrid little green invaders were in all her beds, surrounding and taking her flowers and bushes hostage. She was hoping to work out some of the hostility that had been slowly building up inside her over the past week by doing a little constructive yard work. But the longer she worked at yanking the cantankerous weeds out, the more she seemed to think about Rob's obvious intentions... about his little game. Instead of easing some of her tension, she seemed to become more incensed with each passing moment.

The sun slowly burned off the cloud cover that had kept temperatures rather mild all morning. Kara could feel the increasing heat bearing down on her back and the backs of her legs as she continued to jerk the stubborn weeds out of her beds.

The higher the temperature climbed, the more irritated she became. Redwood had long since decided it was best just to leave her alone. He watched her work from the cool shade of a nearby mimosa tree. By the time she had cleared out all the beds in the backyard and had bagged up the many huge piles of weeds and garbage, she was hot, tired, and in the worst of moods.

Before going inside to shower and change, Kara turned on the garden hose and began rinsing the dirt off her legs. The water cooled her skin but not her temperament. When she turned the faucet off, she could hear the faint sound of the phone ringing inside. Hurrying to the back door, Kara decided she would answer it this time. If it turned out to be Rob, she knew just what she was going to say to him. The time had come to tell the joker off.

Kara rushed to the phone, leaving a trail of wet footprints on the kitchen floor behind her. She grabbed the receiver and put it to her ear just in time to hear the click of someone hanging up. Angrily she slammed the receiver down and stalked off to the bathroom to take a shower, grumbling all the way. How she wished she had gotten to the phone in time. She would have given Rob an earful, that is if it had indeed been Rob.

Even after she had bathed away the grime and finished shampooing her hair, Kara remained under the steady flow of the showerhead, letting the lukewarm water run over her sunbaked skin until the water began to turn cold. Stepping out, she gently blotted herself dry with a thick, soft bath towel. She was feeling much better by the time she sat down to blow dry her hair.

After finishing with the last curl, Kara switched the dryer off and laid it down. She applied a light layer of spray to help her hair keep its shape because it was always so flyaway right after she washed it. Slipping into a pair of terry shorts with a matching tank top, Kara went back outside to check her handiwork.

Upon examination, Kara realized she had neglected to water the plants. The freshly turned earth was slowly drying out to a dusty white. Turning on the garden hose again, she pressed her thumb across part of the nozzle, creating a wide spray of water. She lightly showered all of the flower beds and the two hanging plants on the patio.

Spotting Redwood lazing comfortably under the shade tree, Kara was unable to resist slipping her finger further in across the nozzle, making a much more powerful spray that could just reach the spot where he lay in peaceful bliss. Giggling to herself with menacing delight, she let the animal have a solid blast of the cold water.

Redwood opened his eyes wide, then instantly took off running. Once he was out of range of the mysterious shower and no longer was getting wet, he stared up into the now-cloudless sky, then scanned the area around him. When he saw Kara holding the water hose and laughing devilishly, he perched his head at an angle and began to bark his protests loudly.

"I'm sorry, Red. I just couldn't help myself," she chuckled, leaning over to turn off the water. It certainly felt good to laugh about something for a change.

Still sharply barking his opinion of what she'd done, Redwood pranced over to her side and gave his dripping amber coat a hard shake, scattering water everywhere.

"Why you..."

Kara was just about to turn the water back on and let him have it once more, when she realized the phone was ringing again. Her smile dropped and her angry mood returned as she ran to answer it. Redwood trotted ahead of her to the back door and stood directly in her way. By the time she'd pushed the defiant animal aside and reached the phone, it had stopped ringing again. Her heart was pounding fiercely when she picked up the receiver to make absolutely certain the caller was no longer on the line. She heard the annoying buzz of the dial tone before slamming the receiver down. It was extremely infuriating to have missed another call and possibly an opportunity to tell Rob Phillips off. Well, what was preventing her from calling him and telling him off anyway?

Yanking up the receiver again, she began to dial the number. When she got to the last digit, her hand froze. What she wanted to say would be much more effective if said in person. She should drive over and say it right to his face. That was exactly what she would do.

She decided her shorts were not the appropriate thing to wear for telling off an overbearing ex-husband. She went to her closet and pulled out a pair of light blue slacks and a white gauze blouse with blue embroidery stitched across the yoke. Shaking her head she put back the blue and pulled out a pair of pale pink slacks and a pink floral blouse that billowed out light and airy, but she was wearing a belted yellow-print sundress when she finally made it out of the door.

The drive over seemed endless. Kara managed to hit each and every red traffic signal. Her nerves were drawn tight and her stomach ached by the time she pulled up in front of his house. She was glad to see both cars parked in the garage. It meant she had not made the drive over for nothing. He was home and was going to hear what she had to say.

Impatiently she knocked on the door and paced about while she waited for Rob to appear. What was taking him so long? She tried the doorbell.

"Kara," he exclaimed curiously when he opened the door to find her standing there with her fists clenched at her sides.

Kara avoided looking directly into his devastatingly blue eyes, knowing the disastrous effect they might have on her determination. Instead she focused on a tiny white thread peeping out from behind the top button of his open safari shirt.

"Have you been trying to call me?" she began, according to plan.

"Yes, I have," he answered. He opened his mouth to say more but her words cut him short.

"Well, I want you to stop," she told him firmly. So far she had managed to keep her temper in check. "No more phone calls."

"But..." he started to speak again.

"But, nothing. Don't call me anymore, Rob. I don't want to be bothered by you ever again. Not after last weekend. That's it. I've had enough. I don't care for your little games and I refuse to play them." Her voice was rapidly growing louder.

"What games?" he asked in exasperation.

"You very well know what games."

"If anyone is playing games, my dear, it's you."

"Me?" she replied, breathing heavily under the strain of her anger.

"That's right. Now you've got it," he stated firmly. "You!"

"Rob Phillips..." She paused, her anger and confusion had the best of her. How had he turned this around on her?

"Rob Phillips," she began again. "You...you...just go to blazes!" She was screaming now. Blast it. What she'd wanted to tell him was to "go to hell" but it just hadn't come out. Angrily she turned and stomped off. She was clenching her fists so tightly that her nails were digging tiny trenches into her palms, but she was only vaguely aware of it.

Rob must have been left speechless, because he did not have a reply to make. He just stood in the open doorway and watched her leave.

Kara rolled up her car window and turned on the air conditioner while waiting for the long line of cars ahead of her in the commercial window lane to finish their banking business. She needed to make the deposit and get the proper change to start the day. Unfortunately the lines always seemed much longer the first few days of each month and June was proving no exception.

Clint usually took care of the banking chore but had chosen this week following Memorial Day for part of his vacation. It was just as well because Kara could not seem to find enough to do these days. With Clint gone, she went to work around nine and did not get home until nearly midnight or after. There was little time to dwell on her personal problems, which suited her just fine.

A week and a half had passed since she had promenaded over to Rob's and ordered him to leave her alone, to stop calling her. Apparently her words had managed to sink into his thick skull because the calls had stopped. She had neither heard from nor had seen him since.

Her heart still seemed to stop whenever she spied a dark blue Trans Am approaching, but it was never Rob. She would scold herself for letting such a thing upset her even occasionally. But she was keeping busy enough that she no longer dwelled constantly on her misery. She had managed to get along before without having Rob Phillips in her life, she could do it again. She had to. It would only feel like the end of the world for a little while.

A slow, twangy tearjerker came across the radio airwaves. Impatiently Kara switched to other frequencies until she found something a little more upbeat. The last thing she wanted to hear was depressing music.

When the bright yellow Chevette in front of her finally pulled away from the window, Kara eased forward. She was delighted to see Patricia Ray, Clint's beautiful fiancée, smiling down at her through the spotless glass.

"Hi, Pat. What are you doing working the drive-through?" Kara asked as she waited for the huge metal drawer to slide open. When it did, she laid the zipper bag inside it.

"Covering for Jean while she's gone to lunch. Marian Pole usually takes Jean's lunch shift, but she's gone to Shreveport for a few days. Being shorthanded, I was elected," Patricia explained, leaning forward to be certain she was within range of her microphone.

"Think you can handle my deposit and get me the right change?" Kara teased good-naturedly.

"I think I can manage," Patricia chuckled, shaking her short blond curls.

"How are you getting along without Clint?" Kara asked loudly, never certain how well the outdoor intercom picked up her voice.

"I miss him, but I'm bearing up pretty well. I really wanted to go with him and meet his parents, but I'm only allowed two weeks and I'll need all of that in August for the wedding," she grinned, searching the inside of the zipper bag. "Where's the change? The slip says there should be forty cents."

"Drat," Kara breathed aloud. "Just a minute." She hurriedly rummaged through her console for the money.

"How about taking in a movie Sunday? It'll help me keep from missing Clint so much," Patricia suggested while she watched Kara scramble for the coins. Kara had pulled out gas receipts, gum wrappers, bottle caps saved for a now-outdated contest, pens, a deceased candy bar, wadded paper, a comb, and two hair brushes. Finally she singled out the forty cents she needed and tossed them into the waiting drawer.

"A movie sounds great. What? When? Where?"

Having removed the change, Patricia replaced the bulging zipper bag in the drawer and tossed in a few pieces of candy usually reserved for children before sliding it out to Kara.

"I'll call you later and we can make our plans. Maybe we could go out somewhere for a pizza first."

Patricia had just said the magic word—pizza. It had been ages since Kara had gone out for pizza. The TV commercial showing thick, steaming slices of pizza with everything on it, being picked up from a tray and leaving behind long strands of cheese as a smiling face awaited the first delicious bite came to Kara's mind.

"Yes, call me this afternoon. I'll be at the restaurant," Kara told her as the car started to move. She hoped Patricia had not made the suggestion in passing. She really would enjoy going out to eat pizza and see a movie. It would be a welcome break in her monotonous routine and would keep her mind off "things."

Shortly after five that same afternoon, Patricia did call, still enthusiastic over the idea of pizza and a movie. Being a realist about the fact that they were not as young as they once were and that Patricia would have to be at the bank for work by eight thirty Monday morning "bright-eyed and bushy-tailed" as she put it, they decided on an early movie. By the time Kara hung up, the plans were for Patricia to pick her up around six and they would eat first, the pizza having been given priority over the movie. They could decide on which movie while they stuffed themselves.

Minutes later the phone rang again. Patricia had come up with another idea and wanted to know if Kara would like to take in the flea market. When Kara admitted she had never been to the Longview flea market, Patricia insisted they go. The change meant Patricia would be by around three o'clock. She claimed that it took a couple of hours to really stop and look at everything and Kara agreed that she did not want to miss anything.

Having pushed herself unmercifully all week, it was nearly 1:00 P.M. Sunday afternoon before Kara woke up. She had intended to get up early and catch up on her laundry, having neglected it for over a week.

"Best laid plans," she mumbled to herself when she'd examined the clock and discovered the late hour.

Stumbling into the kitchen, still rubbing sleep-weary eyes, Kara headed straight for the refrigerator. She always had been slow to wake up, even when she'd had more than enough sleep. She never could understand how Rob always would wake up so cheery, almost breaking out into song with his enthusiasm over a new day. Now how had that thought slipped in? The reason must be that she was still too sleepy to control her disorganized thoughts. What she needed was a diet cola and a doughnut—in that order.

She had set the doughnut aside and was pouring the soda from her can into a large ice-filled glass, absently mumbling the jingle that did not even advertise this particular diet drink, when the phone rang. The sudden noise startled her, causing her to jump. The soda splashed across the countertop and spilled onto the floor.

"Drat!" she muttered as she reached for the phone. "Hello?"

There was no reply.

"Hello?" she repeated as she watched the cola form a puddle on her floor.

Still no reply.

"Pat, is that you?"

Then there was the sharp click of someone hanging up.

"Get your number right next time," Kara grumbled into the receiver, having assumed the call had been a wrong number. Clumsily she replaced the receiver and stared at the mess she'd made. The puddle on the counter had reached and saturated her last doughnut. If she didn't know better, she would swear it was Monday.

Being the extremely punctual person she was, Patricia arrived promptly at three. Kara had found something still clean to wear and managed to get a load of laundry done with no further incidents or complications. She was in a better mood, being fully awake now and eager to go.

The day was hot, but the indoor flea market was air-conditioned. So much so, Kara was glad she had decided on a short-sleeved blouse and jeans instead of shorts.

Keeping up with Patricia in the crowded market wasn't easy. Patricia flitted from booth to booth, examining all sorts of odd-shaped items, searching for anything she could make an unusual planter out of. Plants were Patricia's passion, second to Clint, of course. And in spite of some of Patricia's expert maneuvers, Kara pretty well was able to stay with her. It wasn't until she happened to notice a stack of very old books that Kara paused to browse momentarily. Some of the books dated back to the late 1800's and Kara couldn't resist stopping. When she was through, she glanced around the crowded area and realized Patricia was nowhere in sight, but was probably on the other side of the huge building by now.

Slowly she scanned the crowd again, more closely this time, hoping to catch sight of Patricia's blond curls, but what caught her eye wasn't Patricia's blond, curly hair, it was Rob's. He was standing only a few booths away, busily examining an old brass clock. When he finished looking the piece over, he handed it to a woman standing very close to him. Kara could not see her face, but she knew the woman was Maria. They both were dressed in crisp, white tennis outfits and looked all the world like a pair of models picked right from the pages of a summer fashion magazine.

Kara's insides burned as if acid had spilled into her veins when Rob bent very close to Maria's ear and spoke, shaking his head slightly. As he turned to walk away, Maria lightly placed the clock back on the table and quickly followed him. Two tables down they stopped to examine another antique clock. As Rob studied the craftmanship of the wood, Maria wrapped her arms around one of his and studied his expression. After a moment she laid her cheek against his arm and gave it a tiny hug. The intimate little gesture made Kara ill; her stomach tightened. How absurd that she should be so very close to tears over a man that she absolutely could not tolerate! Why should it hurt so to see him with Maria? She shouldn't care whom he was with, yet seeing them together hurt deeply.

Kara wanted desperately to run away, but the over-crowded aisles prevented it. Slowly she began to take tiny steps backward, allowing more and more people to come between them. When she could no longer see the two of them, she turned and began to push blindly through the crowd. Her eyes stung for want of tears, but she was determined not to cry.

Making her way back the way she'd come, Kara began to wonder how she was ever going to locate Patricia again without running into Rob. Since Patricia was moving at twice the rate that Rob and Maria were, Kara decided not to go searching for Patricia at all. She would wait at the same entrance they had come in and watch for her there. No longer interested in the many treasures to be found at the flea market, she just hoped Patricia continued to hurry.

It was almost an hour that seemed like an eternity before Kara spotted Patricia in the crowd. Her friend was loaded down with various packages and was wearing a large western straw hat that she hadn't come in with. The price tag was still dangling from the back of the brim.

A modern-day Minnie Pearl, Kara thought to herself, managing a smile that made her feel a lot better.

"Where'd you go?" Patricia asked, when she noticed Kara coming toward her. "One minute you're right behind me and... poof... the next minute, you're gone."

"I stopped to look at books," she explained, holding out her small package as evidence.

"Books?" Patricia wondered aloud. "All this neat stuff and all you buy is books?"

Kara's only explanation was to shrug her shoulders.

"Come back to the car with me to unload all of this. Then I want to head back to that booth in the corner with all those beautiful, unfinished wooden pieces."

Horrified at the thought of running into Rob, Kara volunteered to carry everything to the car while Patricia went back to make whatever purchases she still had to make. Kara would wait for her at the car. She felt very clever at having thought of this.

"You sure? I've got quite a load here," Patricia pointed out.

"That's obvious enough," Kara chuckled, for Patricia rather reminded her of a prospector's donkey with so many bundles and packs.

Carefully Patricia began to hand over the many packages that overburdened her. Once her arms were completely free, she ended the transfer by plopping her hat down on Kara's head. Kara realized she must have the hat on backward when she noticed the price tag dangling just above her right eye, but she could do little about it with her hands full. When she opened her mouth to ask her friend to turn the hat around, Patricia quickly inserted the green plastic disc that was attached to her key ring.

"You'll need the keys," Patricia explained briefly. "The doors and trunk are locked."

As Kara clamped her teeth down on the little disc that advertised the bank where Patricia worked, Patricia asked, "Now are you sure you can manage?"

Unable to answer anyway, Kara just nodded and turned to leave. She took four steps toward the entryway and froze. There, just inside the door she intended to use, was Rob with Maria still clinging to his arm. They were talking to an older woman Kara recognized as his aunt. Giving one pleading glance heavenward, Kara hoped to ease by unnoticed.

No such luck. Just as she was about to pass quietly by, Maria glanced around and spotted her. Kara nodded politely in her direction and continued walking. An amused smile played at Maria's lips when she tugged at Rob's sleeve. Kara's teeth bit deeper into the hard plastic when Maria pointed a perfectly shaped nail in her direction.

Rob's eyebrows arched in odd speculation as he took in the sight of Kara with such a ridiculous load.

Kara smiled weakly around the keys still clamped between her teeth, aware again of the price tag dangling at her right eye and the fact she still had that stupid hat on backward.

Not exactly the sophisticate, she thought grimly. She wanted to spout a stream of explanations concerning her predicament but could only continue to smile as she took several more rapid steps toward the door, which happened to be slowly closing in front of her. Having to turn her back to the door and push it back open, she was able to see Rob headed in her direction with Maria close at his heels.

"You need help," he stated, his voice simple and flat, while reaching over her head to push the door open for her.

She couldn't very well argue with him with a mouthful of keys so she meekly turned and preceded them on through the door. Once they were outside and out of the way, Rob began to take some of the packages away from her.

"Where's your car?" he asked, glancing around the crowded parking lot.

She nodded toward Patricia's car, which was parked at the far end.

"Where? I don't see it."

Shifting the packages she still carried to one arm, she was able to remove the keys and explain that she was here with a friend and pointed in the direction of her friend's car. She felt a little awkward, if not totally surprised, at having Rob offer to help, and judging by her grim expression, Maria was more than a little surprised herself.

"I'll be right back," Rob told Maria before turning to follow Kara to the car.

"But..." Maria started to protest, then changed her mind. Instead she turned and walked briskly back inside the building.

Rob followed Kara silently for a while; then in an attempt to make polite conversation, he asked what was inside the cloth-bound package.

"I really don't know," Kara explained. "Most of this is Patricia's."

"Patricia's?"

"Yes, Patricia Ray. I don't think you've ever met Pat. She's a more recent friend."

Rob paused a moment as if trying to sort something out before going on with the conversation. "Where is your friend?"

"She went back for more," Kara explained. "I have no idea where she plans to put anything else."

"I see the problem," Rob commented lightly when Kara stopped to slip a key into the trunk of a small, green MG. After several different arrangements, Rob managed to get everything they were carrying, except one small sack, into the tiny trunk.

After tossing the leftover sack onto the canvas roof of the car, he carefully eased the trunk lid down and gently pressed it shut. When he stood back up, he stared curiously at her. Neither spoke for a long time and when one of them finally did break the awkward silence, it was Rob wanting to know if that was her hat or her friend's.

Having forgotten all about the thing, Kara quickly reached up and jerked it off, wondering how badly it had messed her hair. "That is another of Patricia's purchases."

Hurriedly she turned her back to him and pulled the keys from the trunk lock where they had been temporarily abandoned. She hoped Rob didn't notice how her hands were trembling when she unlocked the passenger door. They weren't trembling out of fear exactly, more from the uncertainty of the situation. It seemed absurd that she should tremble at all.

She quickly tossed the hat and the small sack Rob had left on the roof through the open door. Without bothering to look up, she could sense that Rob had followed her around to the side of the car.

"So much for that silly hat," she mumbled and slammed the door closed a little harder than she had intended, causing the keys to pop out of the lock with the impact and fall to the pavement. Before she could kneel down to retrieve them, Rob had bent over and picked them up. Silently he held them out for her.

"Thank you," she said graciously as she accepted the handful of keys. She felt she should smile, but her face was frozen—almost as if she were in a state of shock.

"You're welcome," he said matter-of-factly. This time he asked for no reward for his good deed. He simply was being very polite, maybe overly so.

Neither one of them had noticed Patricia's presence until she asked Kara to pitch her the keys, and neither of them spoke again until they realized she planned to unlock the trunk and put in her final purchase, a small wooden planter.

"I don't think you're going to be able to put that in there," Rob commented, watching Kara's friend work to get the key to turn. Just then the trunk lid popped up and Patricia caught sight of the crowded contents. She had to agree. The trunk was definitely full.

"Did I really buy that much?" she exclaimed. Rubbing her chin, she looked down at her new plant stand. "Sort of creates a problem, doesn't it?"

"If it would help, I could give Kara a lift home. Then you could just put that thing on the seat beside you," Rob offered politely.

"Thing?" Patricia repeated defensively, reaching down to pick up the planter and hold it close.

"I think we can manage if I hold it on my lap," Kara quickly put in. The thought of being a third party to Rob and Maria did not sit very well with her. "Besides, I'm not headed home right now; we've got plans for this evening and we are running late as it is," she added, glancing at her watch.

"Plans? I see. Well, I'll leave you two to solve this dilemma. I've got Maria waiting."

Kara watched sadly as Rob walked away. He did indeed have Maria waiting. Rob would always have some beautiful woman waiting for him and rightfully so. He was too handsome, too charming, not to. It was just a miserable fact of life, handsome begot beauty.

"That's some hunk!" Patricia exclaimed as she unlocked her side of the car. "Where'd you ever meet him?"

"That's Rob."

"Nice looking."

"My ex."

Patricia froze with one leg in the car and the other on the ground. She first looked at Kara to see if she was serious, then again at Rob's retreating back. "*That's* your ex?"

"That's him," Kara replied quietly. Oddly she took pride in Patricia's reaction to Rob, despite the fact that he was no longer hers.

"You must have some set of standards for your men if that's one of your throwbacks," Patricia continued while she settled in behind the steering wheel. Her eyes were wide with astonishment.

Rather than explain that if anyone had been the throwback, she had been it, Kara changed the subject. And although he never became the topic of their conversation again, Rob and Maria continued to plague her thoughts, ruining the entire evening for her.

Chapter Seven

For the third time Kara shuffled through the stack of assorted invoices and packing slips that now over-flowed her top basket. Here it was June tenth, and because she had managed to get behind while Clint was away, she had two dozen or more checks to get out today. And she could't locate all the invoices she needed to verify all of the accounts due. She was two daily reports behind. The bank ledger was long overdue a reconciliation. And her head hurt. Worst of all, it was Monday again.

"Clint!" she shouted at the top of her voice. Her hand went to her temple at the violent reaction her throbbing head had to the sudden strain. There should be a law against Mondays.

She was picking her way through the mass of multi-colored papers in her top basket for the fourth time when the door finally opened and Clint stepped inside.

"You called?" he asked in an old-movie butler style. He clicked his heels and nodded his head, causing his thick black hair to bounce forward and back into place. Kara was amazed at how his hair seemed to be in constant animation yet never mussed.

"Do me a favor," she began, barely looking up from her task, "Go ask Kathy if she's seen an invoice for one hundred and twelve dollars from Langford Paper Company lying around the cashier's booth anywhere. I need it."

"Will do," he answered, turning to leave.

"And Clint," she asked, almost pitifully, "would you see if you can round me up a couple of aspirin?"

"Will do," he replied again before disappearing through the door and closing it securely behind him.

Pushing aside the statement from Langford's until she could find the missing invoice, Kara picked up the water bill. She did not need invoices to pay this one. Moving the already-opened checkbook closer to her, she quickly made out the check and was addressing the envelope when her pen began to skip. It was out of ink.

"Drat!"she squealed with frustration. Childishly she threw the pen as hard as she could. It hit the door with a loud crack just as Clint was opening it.

"I surrender," Clint said from behind the partially opened door. Only his hand could be seen, waving frantically with his first two fingers extended in what was now an outdated symbol for peace.

"Come on in," Kara sighed, too tired to laugh at Clint's ridiculous overreaction.

"If you are not satisfied with my work, you should fire me, but don't fire *at* me," Clint said cheerfully when he peered inside as if he weren't quite certain it was safe to come in.

"Oh, get in here," she told him. "Did you find the invoice?"

"No, Kathy hasn't seen it. I looked around for it myself but didn't see it either. Are you absolutely sure it isn't in your basket or on your desk?" he eyed the clutter suspiciously.

"Yes, I've looked everywhere for the blasted thing."

"You want me to help you look for it?" he asked,

reaching for the scramble of paper in her top basket.

"No, thank you. I've got enough problems," she assured him good naturedly. "Did you find any aspirin?"

"Sure did. You need any water to take them with?" he wanted to know as he pulled a small bottle out of his shirt pocket and set it in the only clear spot he could find on her desk.

"No, I still have soda here," she told him, indicating the can standing bravely in a sea of scattered papers. Quickly she grabbed the bottle and began to wrestle with the childproof cap. Once she had it opened, she tried to shake out two tablets onto her palm. The bottle emptied itself in her hand. She picked out two and laid them aside before putting the rest of the pills back into the reluctant bottle.

Tossing the two aspirin to the back of her mouth, she reached immediately for her drink. A big swig of lukewarm diet cola and a horrible twist of her face later, she had the tablets down. She paused a minute with her drink still in her hand as if waiting for a miracle to occur.

"This just proves you need me around here," Clint informed her matter-of-factly. "I left for only one week and look how far behind you got."

"You're needed all right." She threatened him with a raised brow. "Right now I need you to get out of here so I can get my work done."

"Tell you what. Since I'm such a good guy, I'll answer the phone and fend off all pushy salesmen for you. I'll even stay a few hours late if you aren't caught up by the time for me to leave," Clint offered. "And that happens to be the extreme sacrifice for me. After all, I do have a hot date with a certain blond fiancée that hasn't seen me for a whole week."

"Oh, and you think Patricia actually missed you?" Kara teased.

"Yes, that woman's crazy about my body," Clint threw back at her before turning to leave.

"Clint?" she called after him, setting her empty drink can down. "I appreciate the sacrifice," she slowly smiled. "Thank you."

"I'm here to help," Clint told her. Then lifting the corners of his mouth into a devious grin, he added, "And by the looks of you, you need all the help you can get."

He darted out of the doorway just as her cola can hit the doorframe. He quickly reached back inside and grabbed the knob, slamming the door shut before she could throw anything else.

Kara rubbed her tired face. She couldn't blame Clint for such a remark, even though it had been made in fun. She looked terrible and was well aware of it. She had dark semicircles below her eyes, which makeup hadn't been able to hide. It wasn't even noon yet and she was already tired. Her whole face felt like it was sagging from her lack of sleep. She'd had trouble falling asleep last night because her mind had been so determined to work overtime. She could not seem to keep her thoughts off Rob. Something about their chance meeting earlier in the day had bothered her. It was more than the fact that he had been with Maria. She had long since realized she was jealous of that relationship and had been from the very beginning. What really was eating away at her had to do with the way he had acted, being so overly polite, as if he was forcing himself to be civil toward her. Why had he bothered to speak to her at all? If he was angry at her, as well he should be, why didn't he just ignore her or better yet show his anger by some rude action? It was the way he forced himself to be nice that plagued Kara's thoughts until the early hours of the morning. When she had finally managed to drop off to sleep, she had dreamed about him. It had been a most disturbing dream.

In the dream they had come running toward each other, arms outstretched, in a rolling meadow thick wtih bright-yellow wildflowers. She was dressed in a white billowing dress. He was in a white satin shirt and white slacks. When they'd met halfway, he'd lifted her up and swung her around before allowing her to slide down the length of him into his wild, passionate embrace. It had been the classic love scene, right through to the end when she and Rob lay naked in the field, making love in the warm sunshine, given their privacy by the tall fragrant flowers.

The emotions her dream had aroused within her had grown until she felt as if she would explode. The intensity was so strong that it caused her to wake up gasping for air. When she'd realized it had only been a dream, the frustration was great enough that she had been unble to keep from breaking into tears. The dream may have been part of her imagination, but the emotions it evoked were very real, too real. She'd been unable to go back to sleep afterward. Her mind had kept replaying the dream over and over again despite her efforts to concentrate on something else, anything else.

She was still having trouble pushing the dream to the back of her mind, even this afternoon. Her work should have had top priority, but flashes of that dream kept intruding on her thoughts, another from a long list of annoyances the day had brought.

Having failed to locate another pen on her desk, Kara began to search the drawers. When she pulled open the small drawer she kept her envelopes in, she found the missing invoice from Langford's. She couldn't imagine how it had gotten in the drawer but didn't take time to worry about it. After all, she hadn't been functioning at her top efficiency lately. Before she could lose the invoice again, she pulled it out of the drawer to staple it to the proper statement. When she did, she discovered a pen right under the invoice. Things were looking up at last. If she could keep her mind on her work and off Rob, there might be hope of getting caught up after all.

Working through the afternoon, Kara had somehow managed to keep any further stray thoughts of Rob off limits and finally began making headway at last. She had hunted down all of the invoices and packing slips she needed, still amazed that things were finally going well. She was actually smiling to herself as she filled out the last check she needed to get out by the tenth, when Clint tapped lightly on the door. It was the first interruption from him since he had made his mad dash for safety almost three hours before.

"There's a phone call for you. Claims it is important," he stated softly, hoping it would be less of an interruption if he were to be quiet about it.

"Right when I was making a little progress here,"she frowned. "Who is it? Did they say?"

"Rob Phillips. Do you want to take the call?"

An emotional alarm sounded, warning her that this phone call definitely meant trouble.

"No!" she stated emphatically. "Tell him I can't come to the phone. Tell him I don't have time to talk right now because I'm...oh, tell him anything...that I've recently died and am too busy getting embalmed to come to the phone."

"Hey, I like that one," Clint grinned. "But I'll just tell him you're unavailable at the moment."

"Thanks," she offered, breathing a sigh of relief after he had closed the door behind himself.

"Where was I?" she said aloud, trying to regain the concentration she had going for her before the interruption. But now Rob was back in her forethoughts. She couldn't help but wonder why he had phoned. Until now he had met her demands not ever to call again. What could have prompted him to call today and why had she been so afraid to accept the call? What could he do to her over the phone anyway? She knew the answer to that one. He could easily destroy her emotional self, turn her insides into permanent gelatin. She shuddered at the power Rob had over her. He didn't have to lay a hand on her; he could literally destroy her with just his words or even a look.

Kara's mind was so preoccupied with the phone call and what implications there might be that she sat several minutes staring numbly at nothing in particular with her pen poised over the checkbook in position to write. She was so deep in her reverie that her whole body shuddered when she came out of it. She was brooding again. Here she had finally been able to push aside all thoughts of him and fully concentrate on her badly neglected paperwork, and with one little phone call he'd managed to destroy all of her momentum. She was exasperated over the fact that she couldn't control her own thoughts anymore and dearly wished she could reach inside her brain, rip his image out of her memory, and remove him from her past.

Trying once more to refocus her attention on her work, Kara finished filling out the final check. When she started tearing it out of the checkbook in order to place it in a waiting envelope, she was horrified at what she saw. She had signed the thing Mrs. Rob Phillips.

Furiously, she tore the check into many jagged little pieces instead of simply voiding it as she should. Kara then threw it at the trash can, grimacing when the confetti-sized paper scattered over a wide area, landing everywhere but in her target. Rather than bother picking all the pieces up, Kara began filling out another check, careful to get the signature right the second time. She did not even want to think about why she had reverted back to her use of his name.

Having stuffed the check and the top portion of the statement into the envelope, she lifted it to her tongue in order to moisten it. As she ran her tongue beneath the flap, the edge caught the corner of her mouth, leaving a razor-sharp cut. She sighed. The way everything was going, she should have anticipated that.

Tending to the painful nick with the tip of her tongue, Kara sealed the envelope and tossed it onto the stack with the rest of the outgoing mail. Needing postage stamps, she pulled open the top drawer and was almost amazed to discover the roll of stamps right where they were supposed to be. But she was not really surprised to find that there were only twenty-one stamps when she needed thirty.

Glancing at her watch, she noted that she still had fifteen minutes before the post office closed. If she hurried, she could get there in time to get more stamps over the counter and not have to wrestle with one of those confounded machines that were supposed to dispense stamps but never did. When the machine claimed to take quarters, it usually meant for keeps.

Tossing the stamps she already had back into the drawer, Kara reached into the petty-cash box for money and gathered up the envelopes that needed to be in the mail that day. Hurriedly she pushed away from the desk and glanced around the room to see where she'd flung her purse when she'd entered early that morning. That seemed like ages ago.

Just as she spotted her purse in one of the chairs that faced her desk, Clint opened the door and looked in expectantly. She paused in order to hear what he had to say.

"There's another urgent phone call for you. This time it's a guy with OakMinter Linen," he said sheepishly. He really didn't want to deliver this message.

"Did he say what he wanted?" she sighed, setting the envelopes back down.

"Something about Pinewood being late in payment," he told her, looking as confused as she was. He had never known Kara to neglect payment.

Throwing the money down on her desk in a wad, Kara let out an expletive that was totally out of character for her.

"He said he needed to talk with you about it," Clint continued, shrugging his shoulders helplessly.

"Late?" she cried out through clenched teeth. "Where do they get off telling me I'm late with my payment? The blasted thing wasn't even due until today!"

Flipping through the stapled packets of invoices that were now stacked neatly in her bottom basket ready to be filed, she yanked out a small group of blue invoices stapled behind the lower portion of OakMinter's latest statement.

"See there? Due June tenth. It can't be overdue. Today is June tenth and I've got the check right here ready to be mailed. It won't be overdue until tomorrow."

Clint shrugged his shoulders again. "He's on the phone. Explain it to him, not me."

Tossing her hair back, she jerked the receiver off the hook and placed it to her ear. She took a deep silent breath and in her best businesslike voice spoke. "Kara Phillips. May I help you?"

Absently she picked up her pen and began to fiddle with it as she waited for a reply. She rolled it continuously back and forth between her fingertips and thumb.

"Phillips? Any relation to that wonderful and talented Rob Phillips, who is not only exceedingly handsome and debonair, but a financial wizard as well?" she heard Rob's familiar singsong voice reply.

All her frustrations gave way to outrage. Her anger became so great she felt as if she was strangling on it. Unable to speak or yell or shout or cry, she stared furiously at the phone, then slammed the receiver down, causing the phone to jump slightly from the force.

Closing her eyes tightly, she wanted desperately to scream, but it didn't come. Exasperated, she hurled her pen across the room as hard as she could. It bounced off the far wall with a smack, barely missing the open aquarium as Kara let out a bloodcurdling cry that would easily put a swarm of rampaging Indians to shame.

By the time Clint had bounded into the room, wide-eyed and out of breath, Kara was leaning face down on her desk sobbing uncontrollably. He rushed over and tried to comfort her, but his efforts only seemed to make her worse. He could not imagine what the laundryman could have said to cause her to react so.

"Look, Kara, there are other linen services," he offered, patting her gently on the back. "Heck, I'll wash the damn stuff myself if you'll just quit crying."

Suddenly her sobs turned into hysterical laughter. He didn't know if this wicked cackling was much better than the crying. She was still out of control.

"Hey, it's not that funny," he complained, acting totally insulted. "I know how to work a washing machine. You women don't have the market cornered on laundry know-how."

Kara grabbed her sides, letting her laughter slowly subside as she listened to Clint.

"In fact, down at the local washeteria, I'm clearly

known as Clean-Clothes Clint. I'm actually a wiz with the Biz.''

Kara's laughter finally stopped as Clint continued to explain his laundry prowess. She was no longer listening. She now stared sadly into space. He realized he was being ignored, and since she was no longer crying, he decided to leave her to her thoughts, whatever they might be. At this point he only wanted to leave well enough alone.

Although at the time it had seemed the ultimate disaster, the next day, Kara could not explain, even to herself, why she had reacted so severely to Rob's little prank. She should've expected him to do something like that after having refused his call. His incredible ego would not accept her refusal easily. She had to worry what he might do now that she had hung up on him and she was afraid that his overgrown pride was not about to let it end there.

Every time the phone rang that following day, Kara held her breath in anticipation, waiting for Clint to come in with some disastrous word from Rob. It never came. By the end of the evening she had decided he was either going to take his sweet time about calling back, maybe hoping to catch her off guard, or worse. He might be planning to do his evil deed in person. But when several days went by and she had neither heard from him nor had seen him, she decided she had come to the wrong conclusion and that he must not be considering getting back at her at all. He might not consider her worth the effort. Realizing this, Kara quit worrying about every phone call and every interruption from Clint. Oddly she felt a little sad once she had realized he wasn't going to bother with her at all. She probably never crossed his mind again, yet she seemed to be constantly reminded of him day and night. It wasn't fair. Rob had continued to plague her dreams, but he was no longer cast in those sinister, villainous roles as he had been shortly after their divorce. Instead he was now certain to appear as her lover and hero. It was quite upsetting.

Kara was unable to find a way to prevent him from invading her dreams. She had come to terms with the fact she must learn to accept them for what they were—simple traces of silly fantasy. Although she found she couldn't completely ignore the dreams, she avoided analyzing them in any way. There wasn't any point in it.

Her anger had slowly dissolved and all she was left with was heartache where Rob was concerned. It was not a sharp pain that afflicted her; it was more of an all-consuming sadness. Kara almost preferred the anger. Her misery had begun to affect her sleep and especially her appetite. The only food she now ate was what little it took to sample the daily dishes at Pinewood.

Few things made her smile these days. Her only pleasant moments were in her dreams, which quickly turned to gloom when she'd awaken to discover that she was deceiving herself again. The real Rob was not the same as the Rob in her dreams, and the relationship they shared in her sleep was far from reality. Things were not to be changed simply by dreaming.

Clint tried to cheer Kara up several times but failed, as did Redwood. Kara had entered what Clint referred to as "a deep-purple funk."

Patricia thought she'd come up with the perfect solution to Kara's depression when her brother phoned from Houston to tell her he planned to come visit for a week. Andy Ray was an almost-six-foot-tall, muscular, blue-eyed blond, who Patricia decided was just the right cure for Kara. And if Andy couldn't manage to pull Kara out of her depression, she'd invite Tony, her other brother from Shreveport, for a little visit. Tony was a charmer. One way or another, Patricia was determined to get Kara to forget whatever it was that had given her the blues.

As Patricia had predicted, Kara wasn't too enthused over the prospect of a blind date with her brother.

"Please, Kara. I want to show Andy a good time while he's here without having him feel as if he's intruding on Clint's and my privacy. He hates being a third party," Patricia pleaded when she sensed Kara was about to decline the invitation she'd just presented so eloquently. She followed Kara from the kitchen to the restaurant's main dining area, still determined to see her plan through.

"I don't know. Dad's supposed to call Sunday evening. He always calls me on Sunday to get a report on Pinewood and see how I'm doing," Kara hedged, knowing it was a weak excuse, but it was the only one she could come up with on such short notice. She continued to make her rounds, checking to see that everything was in order before they opened.

"You could call your father earlier that afternoon and go ahead and tell him what he needs to know," Patricia pointed out, not about to give up. She followed Kara around the salad bar, while Kara gathered a sample of everything onto a small plate.

"To tell you the truth," Kara said as she tasted each thing on her plate, "I've sworn off blind dates. Dad burned me out on them years ago."

The two of them had to step away from the salad bar while Jan, one of her waitresses, placed a tall stack of clean plates and salad forks in the compartment below.

"I rarely have anything in common with guys I've been set up to go out with," Kara continued while she watched Jan carefully restock the bin.

"Please? As a favor to me? Andy's a real nice guy, even for a brother. He's good looking and has a great sense of humor, just like his sister. He makes good money working for Drake Petroleum and I know you'll have at least one thing in common. You both drive Vettes. Besides, if you find out you don't like him, you'll still have me to talk to and Clint."

"Sounds good to me," Jan butted in as she closed the doors on the side of the salad bar. Then while she smoothed out her uniform, she said with a wink, "If you don't grab this guy, I certainly will." She gave a prissy wiggle of her well-rounded hips before heading back to the kitchen.

"Now I'm begging you," Patricia said, watching Jan flounce through the double doors and out of sight. "Andy's had experience with all kinds of women, but he just isn't ready for a woman like Jan."

Kara had to chuckle at Patricia's remark. Jan was well-noted for being rather outspoken as well as completely liberated, and the pretty little redhead was not opposed to having a good time.

"Oh, all right. I'll go, but don't expect anything to come of it," Kara conceded cautiously. "I'm only doing this as a favor to you."

"Wonderful," Patricia sighed with relief. "We'll pick you up somewhere around seven thirty unless I call and tell you differently."

When Patricia left to find Clint and tell him the good news, Kara couldn't believe she'd agreed to go. In her recent mood she would only ruin Patricia's chances of entertaining her brother. She hoped she wouldn't end up spoiling the evening for everyone. Sunday was three days away. Maybe she could think of a way out of it by then for Andy's sake as much as her own.

By Saturday afternoon when Patricia called to confirm the time, Kara had been unable to come up with a plausible excuse that would get her out of the blind date. Reluctantly she agreed to be ready for the big night on the town by seven thirty. Having resigned herself to the fact that she was stuck, Kara began to wonder what Patricia's brother was like. He just might be all the things Patricia claimed him to be. Who knows, she might even enjoy herself.

With that thought in mind, Kara's mood lifted slightly. She even managed to smile that evening as she greeted the many patrons Saturday always brought to their door and escorted them to their tables. She was just beginning to feel that there might be hope for her yet, when Rob and Maria entered the restaurant arm in arm.

Chapter Eight

"A table for two?" Kara inquired, being cordial yet trying to seem indifferent as she greeted the pair. She silently wished she could wipe that cagey smile from Maria's cranberry lips.

"Please," Rob replied smoothly. "I believe we have eight-thirty reservations for two."

"Reservations?" Kara asked, obviously confused. She hadn't noticed a Phillips on the reservation log. Had she, she certainly would've prepared herself for this moment.

Leaning over the podium and quickly running her finger down the smooth page to read the eight-thirty listings, she discovered why. There in Clint's familiar print was the name Brunson and beside it was plainly written two. The reservation had been made in Maria's name. She wondered whose idea it had been for them to dine at Pinewood and whose idea it was to use Maria's name. They certainly had some nerve!

Maria's smile widened victoriously. It was a spiteful smile that let Kara know just who the culprit was. There was a silent message here that Kara couldn't possibly miss. This was Maria's way of telling her, "This is my man. You may have had him once, but now I've got him. Hands off."

The sudden anger Kara felt made her wish she could snatch Rob away from her and have him declare his undying love right here in front of her, but she knew it was much more than revenge making her want such a thing.

"You do have our reservations down, don't you?" Rob asked with a little concern. Looking over her shoulder, he had already spotted the name Brunson.

"Yes, Brunson, party of two," Kara observed aloud as she checked off the name. "It will be just a moment before we have your table ready. Please have a seat."

With a quick gesture to several lounge chairs near the entrance, Kara turned her attention to an elderly man who had just walked in escorting two younger couples. As it happened, a table for five had just been prepared, allowing her to escape Rob's intimidating presence in order to seat the new arrivals. She didn't hurry back, although it was inevitable she would have to return.

When she did return to the podium, her phone line was flashing. She avoided looking at Rob and Maria and turned to face another direction when she picked up the receiver. While she explained to the person on the phone that they were pretty well booked for the evening, she could feel two pairs of eyes watching her intently, as if they were gauging her every move. She felt strangely like a mouse at the mercy of two hungry cats.

All too soon the phone conversation was over, but Kara continued to hold the receiver and picked up her pencil, pretending to be making notations of some sort in her reservation log. To her relief Jan walked up and whispered that there were now two tables ready in her area, a table for two and a table for six. Although a group of six had been waiting longer than Rob and Maria had, Kara decided to go ahead and seat her ex.

She wanted Rob and Maria in another room, although she would prefer to seat them in another restaurant.

Taking a deep breath, she gathered two menus and walked casually over to where they were sitting, Maria in her beautiful, flowing, white silk gown and Rob in a pale-blue three-piece suit. As she neared the pair, Kara saw Maria glance away, pretending that she hadn't been keeping a keen eye on her. But Rob was staring openly at her.

"Your table is ready. Please follow me." She waited until they were both standing before slowly walking toward the room in which she planned to seat them. She felt very self-conscious about having them following her, wondering if her hair looked all right from the back and whether or not her long, blue skirt was hanging evenly. She hoped her white satin blouse was tucked in properly and prayed she wouldn't trip on the ruffled hem that almost reached the floor.

Pulling a chair out, Kara quickly laid the menus on either side of the small table covered with a deep royal-blue cloth. Running her hand across the smooth back of the chair, she recited with a slight smile, "Your waitress for the evening will be Jan. She'll be with you in a moment. Enjoy your meal."

Kara hated that this tiny table was tucked away in an intimate little corner where the already-dim light was even softer and there were few distractions. But there was little she could do about it now.

"Thank you. I'm sure we will," Rob said briefly as he laid a hand on the back of Maria's chair and waited for his beautiful companion to be seated.

When Kara reached the hostess's podium again, she let out a sigh of relief. She wondered if she had been holding her breath the whole time. It certainly seemed that way.

Now that the two were seated in another room, she would only have to be bothered by their presence when she escorted someone into that area to be seated, and whenever there was a choice, she would place patrons elsewhere. She'd had it with having to pretend all was right with her world when, in actuality, her world was crumbling into tiny pieces. She just wasn't very good at those types of games. Rob would surely guess her true feelings and chalk it up to a technical victory. She hated the thought.

Plastering another congenial smile on her face, Kara went to tell the Johnsons their table was ready. She told herself just to ignore Rob; after all, she had work to do. Although she'd decided to just think of him as another customer, her heart did somersaults while she led the Johnsons to the table next to Rob's.

She tried her best to avoid looking in Rob's direction at all while she laid a menu at each place around the large table. She stood back and watched as three of the five young men who so closely resembled each other reached for the older woman's chair. Kara had already decided that this must be a group of sons taking their mother out for a night on the town, when the oldest of the group, a young man close to her own age, stepped over and whispered in her ear, his breath tickling her cheek and causing her to smile.

"It's Mom's birthday. We want the evening to be special."

Kara's smile widened. She knew he was hinting at one of the little cakes Pinewood served for special occasions. Quickly she leaned over and whispered back to him, "I'll take care of it."

He returned her smile and nodded his appreciation before sitting in the vacant chair and joining the group in their conversation. When he was certain his mother wasn't looking, he glanced over at Kara and gave her a knowing wink. His mother had been kept so preoccupied by her other sons that she hadn't been aware her oldest had been whispering in Kara's ear, but Rob hadn't missed any of it.

Still trying not to notice Rob, Kara explained to the little group that their waitress for the evening would be Jan and that she hoped they would enjoy their meal. But as she turned to leave, her eyes betrayed her. They seemed to have a will of their own when they sought out a glimpse of Rob.

As she had halfway expected, Rob was watching her closely. When he was certain she was looking his way, he narrowed his eyes as if trying to deliver a very unfriendly warning. Judging by the flex of his jaw, Kara was certain she did not want to know exactly what was going through his mind. She didn't even care to guess. It angered her that he continued to silently harass her. Clenching her fist, she listened as her heart beat wildly, pounding out a coded message. This message was quite clear to her. It was time for her to stage a prompt retreat before she let her anger get the best of her. She had her other customers to consider. Stopping only long enough to tell Jan about the cake for table four, Kara made a rapid exit.

As was usual for Saturday night, Pinewood was very busy. Not only were there the patrons with reservations, there were the usual drop-ins. Kara always had someone waiting to be seated. Each time she escorted someone to a table in the room Rob was in, she could feel an angry pair of eyes following her. She was glad Maria's back was to her or she'd surely have a second pair of unfriendly eyes upon her.

Kara was engaged in a constant struggle to keep her anger under control. Rob continued to stare at her. His very presence seemed to crush her and was beginning to affect her work. She started to fumble things in her attempt not to let the other customers see her anger. Knowing she needed a moment to cool her emotions, she hurriedly went in search of Clint. She could not let the customers suffer because she could not contain her anger. They deserved a more congenial host.

Clint usually left around nine on Saturdays, and since it was a few moments past that, she hoped he was still around. To her relief and Clint's dismay, Kara caught him just as he was leaving through the back door and asked him to please stay late. She convinced him that she had a terrible pain in her head and needed to take two aspirin and lie down a few minutes. It wasn't a total lie. She did have a bad pain, only it was more in the vicinity of her heart than her head. How could anyone be so cruel?

Reluctantly Clint agreed to greet the guests and seat them for a little while. He made a quick call to tell Patricia he would be late before relieving Kara up front.

"Thanks, Clint," she sighed weakly. Knowing Rob and Maria had just been served their main course, she promised, "It'll only be for about twenty minutes. I just need time enough to let the aspirins start to work."

Clint gave her shoulder a comforting squeeze and ordered her to her office. He then turned to greet a couple that had just entered, giving them one of his most charming smiles.

Kara went by the cashier's cubicle to get the office key. She usually kept the office locked when she wasn't in it. Once she had located the key, she went straight there and let herself in, closing the door securely behind her.

Out of habit she reached for the light switch but stopped herself before she actually touched it. She decided there was enough light for her present needs. It wasn't so dark that she couldn't see. The light in the aquarium was still on and the faint light from the street filtered through the wooden blinds left open at her window. At the moment she preferred the darkness.

Her first thought was to sit at her desk, but she realized she was too restless for that. Instead she paced about the room, trying to work off some of her anger. She wondered if Rob or Maria would consider it a form of victory that she had deserted her duties because of them. She was sure that's how they would see it and felt they would have an enjoyable laugh at her expense. She didn't particularly like that idea; in fact it hurt that Rob could be this vengeful toward her.

She certainly resented the fact that they had chosen to dine at Pinewood, invading her territory and tampering with her private feelings. They were playing a cruel game of seek-and-destroy and had made her emotions their target. They were out to hurt her and regrettably had scored a direct hit.

Taking in short, hard breaths, Kara fought back the tears burning the outer edges of her eyes and the tightness squeezing her chest. She wouldn't allow herself to cry. She just wouldn't. He wasn't worth a single tear, not a single one.

Afraid she was losing the battle with herself and feeling the turmoil inside of her continuing to build, Kara slammed her fist into her hand. She couldn't believe that her emotions were this vulnerable when she had spent five years trying to toughen them.

Despite her valiant effort to prevent it, the tears still came. They clung to her lashes when she finally opened her eyes and soon were rolling wet trails down her cheeks. Rob had won; he'd gotten his revenge.

Sadly she walked over to the window and leaned against the opened wooden blinds. She folded her arms across her chest as if to brace her aching heart while she watched the heavy traffic flowing along Marshall Avenue. Her vision was blurred, but her eyes continued to follow the steady movements of the many cars and trucks making their way to their various destinations. There were so many people out there. She wondered if any of them were as unhappy as she was right now.

Kara felt so forlorn, so deeply hurt, as she continued her unseeing vigil by the window. The steady movement was beginning to have a calming effect, almost hypnotizing her, but the tears continued their trek along her cheek, down her neck, and into her blouse. She didn't bother to search for a tissue to wipe them.

When the knock at the door resounded through the room, it startled her. She glanced at the clock on her desk then at her watch, but she could not make out the time in the darkness. Her twenty minutes were over, she assumed, and she went to let Clint in, hoping he would give her a few more minutes to regain her composure. She was confident he would. Clint was the most understanding person she knew. She wished Rob had even a trace of the true compassion Clint had been blessed with. She shook her head sadly at the thought while she stepped over to open the door. It was so useless to wish such a thing.

Not taking the time to wipe away her tears, deciding Clint would be more agreeable to stay a while longer if he was to see them, Kara started to make her pleas as soon as she had her hand on the knob.

"Clint, would you please—" She stopped midsentence, having opened the door enough to see who was standing on the other side. It was not Clint in the lighted hallway as she had expected. Instead she found herself staring up into Rob Phillips's icy-blue eyes.

Not waiting for an invitation to come in, for fear it

would give her a chance to slam the door in his face, Rob pushed the door open wider and marched inside the dark room.

"Shut the door," he said in a cool, even voice. Staring down at her, his eyes narrowed as if daring her to disobey what he had told her to do.

Her common sense told her to close the door and not make matters worse. Rob was in a very unfriendly mood, but it was her stubborn pride talking when she spouted, "Only if you are on the other side."

"Karalyn, close the door. I want to talk to you in private," he explained, running a hand through his blond hair. His voice was low and determined.

"We have nothing to talk about, in private or otherwise. If it is conversation you seek, why not try your charming little dinner companion?" Kara asked, meeting his angry gaze directly as she stepped aside to let him leave. She kept her hand on the knob, ready to close the door as soon as he was in the hall.

"Kara, close the door," he repeated, pronouncing each word clearly with meaning. His lean, muscular jaw grew rigid when she continued to ignore his request. Reaching out and taking her hand off the knob, he held her wrist firmly with one hand while slamming the door shut with his other.

"Thank you," he muttered, letting go of her wrist.

"You're not exactly welcome," she informed him, rubbing her wrist where he had just held it. It was a subconscious reaction to his touch. He hadn't held it tightly enough to actually have hurt it.

After a long awkward moment of staring at each other in the dim light that the aquarium against the far wall provided, Rob gave a weighted sigh. "Kara, we need to talk about this."

"About what? About your dating Maria and bringing

her here to my restaurant? You don't need your ex-wife's blessing in order to date other women, you know. And this being a public restaurant, you can pretty well bring whoever you please here—as long as you mind your manners." Kara continued to be sarcastic. Then pretending to have become suddenly bored with this conversation, she stepped over to the aquarium and sprinkled a pinch of food across the top of the bright blue-green water. The only sound for a long while was the slight hum of the air pump and the bubbling sound made by the air stream as it continuously surfaced.

"I want to know why you insist on ignoring me. First on the phone, awhile ago out there, and now in this room," he said, moving to stand beside her. He would not easily be deterred.

"I wasn't aware I was ignoring you," she responded, her voice overly sweet and not quite sincere. She never even bothered to look up.

"Ah, come on, Kara. You refuse to talk to me on the phone, you avoided looking my way out there most of the time, and now you turn your back on me," he pointed out, knotting his hands into fists. It was evident Rob was angry, but he managed to keep the anger out of his voice.

Kara continued to stare down at the many colorful fish darting through the water and capturing the tiny tidbits as they floated slowly down. She was remembering a time when Rob had turned his back on her and their marriage. Her eyes followed the movements in the water, but her thoughts were on the rapid movements that seemed to be skitting about inside her. Anger still thrived as did the hurt and humiliation of having actually cried. Yet right along with that was the electrical feeling that charged her system whenever

Rob was close to her. Her insides were churning with so many different emotions, she couldn't possibly sort them all out and was afraid to even try.

"Well, Kara?"

"Rob, I'd rather just ignore you than fight with you," she finally said.

"Why do we have to fight?" he wanted to know. "Why do we always have to fight?"

"I guess because we both have such different values and beliefs. And we both feel so strongly about them," Kara replied logically. Looking up at him, she added, "And our needs are so different."

In the gentle glow of the aquarium, Rob could see that Kara had been crying. He reached out to take her in his arms, hoping to comfort her, but she moved to avoid his touch.

"Rob, I think you should go," she said firmly, trying not to notice his cologne as the light scent drifted past her, assaulting her senses. It was a familiar scent that triggered still more emotions and memories.

Rob sighed and stepped away from her, but instead of heading for the door as she hoped he would, Rob turned and walked over to her desk. Moving a stack of papers aside, he sat down on the edge and crossed his arms across his chest. He was reaching the end of his patience. "Not until I find out just what your problem is."

"My problem?" she asked, noticeably confused. "You are the one with the problem, buddy."

"Hell, Kara, at the moment my only problem seems to be you!" he said angrily, dropping his arms and placing his fists on his narrow hips. He had reached his breaking point.

"That's one problem you can rid yourself of easily enough," Kara spouted back. "Just leave."

"Simple as that, huh?"

"Problem solved," she said with a defiant nod.

When Rob made no move to leave, she pointed at the door and glared at him. When he still made no move to leave, she prompted him further, "Maria is probably wondering where you are."

"Let her wonder. I'm not leaving here until we talk this out."

"Even if we did have something to talk out, which we don't, this is not the time nor the place. I have to get back to work." Having said that, Kara stepped over to the door and placed her hand on the knob. Frowning at the way her hand trembled as she turned the knob and opened the door, she added, "Now if you will step out, please, I can lock the door and relieve Clint up front."

Rob walked toward the door, but before stepping through to the hall, he leaned close to her ear and quietly warned her, "Kara, I'm not giving up."

"Might as well," she told him before turning her back on him in order to lock the door. She wondered what her makeup must look like as she fumbled with the key. She could feel the dried trails from her recent tears on her cheek and knew her makeup must've streaked horribly. She hoped it wasn't bad enough to frighten away the customers. Turning quickly, she marched bravely past Rob, who had obviously waited with the intention of walking with her down the hall.

"Kara," he called out behind her after she had breezed past him. When she did not respond, he called out, "I'll talk to you later."

Kara didn't reply, but her mind cried out for him not to waste his breath. And although she went back to her duties as hostess and allowed Clint to leave, she refused to acknowledge Rob's presence again even once.

When only moments later, Rob walked by her escorting a somewhat-annoyed Maria, she failed to issue them her usual invitation to dine again at Pinewood.

Later she realized how proud of herself she was for not having let Rob manipulate her, yet her curiosity began to get the better of her as the evening wore on. She wondered what it was he was so determined to talk about. Did it have to do with Maria? Was he going to warn her of a possible marriage between the two? If that was the case, more power to them. They deserved each other. Then it occurred to her that he might have intended to settle their differences so he could continue playing his little cat-and-mouse game with her. He probably got a perverse pleasure out of tormenting her and watching her suffer. Maybe manipulating her the way he did made him feel all-powerful.

Kara decided that was probably it. Rob's ego had an insatiable appetite and Kara was tired of being the one it fed on. She had suffered enough and refused to be humiliated any further. Let him find some other patsy. It was time to take a stand. She made herself a solemn vow to be more careful of him in the future and avoid him whenever possible. She decided her life was easier to tolerate without him.

The first chance to prove to herself that she could follow through with these new convictions to simply avoid him came later that same evening when she went home. It was just minutes after midnight when she turned down the small street that ran in front of her house. As she neared her driveway, she spotted the large, dark object sitting in the shadows there. She knew instantly that it was his Trans Am, and as she pressed her foot down on the accelerator, she caught a glimpse of Rob sitting on the front fender of his car and staring down at his dangling feet. He looked up just before she had passed by and hopped down, waving his arms above his head. She could hear his shouts even over the loud rock music playing on the radio.

Pressing her lips in determination, Kara turned left at the next street corner and kept going. When she reached the first traffic signal, she stared angrily at the light glowing such a bright red, impatient to keep moving. Even though she had promised herself she would avoid the man, she had a compelling urge to go back. Taking out a piece of gum and chewing thoughtfully, she began to realize that simply avoiding him was not the best solution. It was actually the coward's way out. She knew she should go back and have it out with him once and for all.

Taking a deep determined breath, Kara turned at the next intersection and headed back home. Chewing her gum as rapidly as her jaw would work, Kara began to consider just what she would say, but to her disappointment she found the driveway was empty when she pulled in. She debated on whether or not she should drive over to his house but decided to wait until morning. That would give them both a chance to cool off.

Turning her headlights off but leaving the car running, Kara got out of the car and went to pull up the garage door. Ever since Rob had cleaned it out, she had actually been able to use it for her car.

Glancing around at the shadows, she slowly heaved the door up. When she looked back to make sure the door was high enough, she was so stunned at what she saw in the dim glow of the street light that she sucked in a silent scream and swallowed her gum. There sat that Trans Am and standing only inches away from her was Rob Phillips.

As the gum slowly slid down her throat, her heart

jumped to meet it. Kara's mouth fell open, but she made no effort to speak. She just stared in amazement.

"Surprise," he muttered with little feeling and reached out to grab her arm. Before she could think to move, he had her firmly in his grasp.

"You're hurting me," she complained when he stalked over to her car, pulling her along behind him.

"That's nothing like the pain you've been putting me through lately," he said, almost growling. Yanking the door open with his free hand, he reached in and turned the ignition off. He immediately extracted her keys and put them in his own pocket. "You're not going anywhere until we have had our little talk."

"Now wait just a minute," Kara began to protest, wincing as his grip tightened.

"I've already waited here for several hours," he muttered, dragging her back toward the front door. "Hell, Kara, I've waited five years to have this conversation and we are damn well going to have it."

Kara bit back her reply. She had seen him angry many times before, but never anything like this. She wisely decided not to antagonize him further, at least not while he still had such a strong hold on her arm. This was not at all a good time to protest.

Rob reached into his pocket and pulled out her keys once they had reached the door. Selecting a likely key, he tried to ease it into the lock. It wouldn't fit. The next key he tried slid easily in but wouldn't turn. Holding the keys up high so that the dim light from the nearest street light fell across them, Rob singled out the only other key that wasn't an automobile key. He had to jiggle it a little, but it eventually turned and unlocked the door. Impatiently he swung the door open wide, letting it bang against the door stop.

Rather than wait to be dragged in, Kara willingly

stepped inside. When he felt she was going to cooperate at last, he let his grip loosen but didn't let go completely as he followed her in. It wasn't until the door was closed and Kara had reached inside a nearby doorway to flip on the living room lights that Rob finally released her.

"So what is it you want to talk about," Kara asked as nonchalantly as possible before turning to go into the living room. Choosing her favorite chair rather than the couch where Rob would be able to sit beside her, she made herself comfortable.

"About us," Rob stated bluntly.

"What about us?"

"About the other night."

"What about the other night?"

"About our problems."

"Rob, will you please get to the point?" Kara demanded, ready to get on with it.

"Why did you leave me?"

"The other night?"

"No! Five years ago," he replied, anger sparking in his eyes.

Kara sighed; she was afraid he was back to that. He still wanted to hear all about how hurt she had been to find out about Juanita. He was determined to have all the details of the agony and humiliation she'd suffered. Well, she just wasn't going to give him the answer he wanted. His ego would have to do without bolstering this time.

"I believe you already know the answer to that," she stated firmly, looking directly into his silvery-blue eyes. She wished he would sit down; it made her feel uneasy to have to look up at him.

"I think I do, too, but I want to hear it from you," he claimed. Slipping his hands down to pull back his coat, he jammed them into his pants pockets.

"There's no reason to rehash the past. Look, we both know what the problem was, so why discuss it? Why open up old and painful wounds? Why not just let it be? What's past is past."

Rob stared down at her in cold silence for a long moment, then he glanced away. When his eyes returned to meet hers, there was a definite change. Some of the anger had left them, and he finally conceded, "Maybe you're right."

Kara was temporarily stunned. She had expected him to argue with her until she finally gave him all the delicious little details of having found out about his big affair. She wondered if she might not have misjudged him on that point, and if so, had she misjudged him in other areas as well? He might not be nearly as terrible and insensitive as she had assumed, not that she felt he was by any means near sainthood.

"It isn't really that important anyway. That particular problem doesn't even exist anymore, does it?" Rob spoke quietly, adding, "I should let such memories go. Forget them and put them behind me."

Kara thought he was referring to his memories of Juanita when she told him, "You can never completely forget the past. Don't expect yourself to. But don't dwell on it either. It's too frustrating. You can't allow those memories to hurt you for the rest of your life. You'd be miserable. You can't undo it, just accept it and go on. Give your tomorrows a chance."

Rob stepped toward her and knelt down in front of the chair. His eyes peered into hers as if searching for something in their brown depths. "Tomorrows can be meaningless if you face them alone."

There was so much truth in the profound statement Rob had just made. She reached out to him, taking his hand in hers in an effort to comfort him. She could see the agony in his eyes. Rob was a tortured man. Suddenly all the hostility of the past was gone. Caressing his hand gently, she sighed, "I know."

"Share my tomorrows," he said softly, almost pleading with her. Standing abruptly, he pulled her up to stand before him. "Please, Kara, marry me again. I need you so much."

The proposal seemed to come out of the blue. Kara stared blankly at him, wondering if he even knew what he was saying. He must be reacting to the grief this conversation had to have stirred up. Even as his arms went around her and pulled her to him, she felt he couldn't realize what he had just said.

"Give my tomorrows meaning again," he continued as his lips sought hers for a brief kiss. "Kara, please. We can make it work this time. I know we can. The reason you left me before no longer exists. You'll have no more worries in that department. I promise you."

She was stunned by his enthusiasm. Shaking her head, she reasoned, "Rob, a marriage has to be based on love, not need."

"You will learn to love me. I can make you love me." His brows went together to emphasize what he was saying to her.

"That's not what I meant," she explained, wondering how he ever decided she needed to be made to love him. Looking away from him, she openly admitted, "I do love you. I never stopped loving you. But love has to flow both ways, Rob. Who's to say that you will ever grow to love me?"

His hands slid to her face to touch the warmth and softness there. Placing one on either cheek, he forced her to look up at him so that she could see the sincerity evident in his eyes. "Kara, I do love you. I thought you knew that. I've loved you since the day I met you. I never stopped loving you."

"Now you've gone a little too far," Kara said, her voice tinged once again with anger, knowing that that was a lie. "You can't honestly say you have *always* loved me. Rob, a man in love with one person doesn't have an affair with another."

"An affair?" he asked, truly bewildered. "Me?"

"And Juanita," she added, pulling abruptly away from his arms.

"Me and Juanita?"

"Rob, I saw you two with my own eyes," she explained, becoming flustered.

"What?" he shouted, his eyes widening to their limit. "What are you talking about? I never laid a hand on Juanita.

"Never?" she scoffed. She shook her head with disbelief as she plopped back down in the chair.

"Well, not until we were married," Rob expounded.

Throwing herself back into the softness of the chair, she looked at him warily like a canary would a suspicious-looking cat. "Think back. On the same night I left, did you or did you not tell me you were working late, when you actually had no intention of working at all?"

"I *was* working," he said with indignation, crossing his arms over his chest.

"Rob, I came by that night. The door was open a crack and I saw you lying on the couch half-naked, and I could hear Juanita giggling in the background, probably with very little on herself."

"And that's why you left?" He quickly knelt in front of her so that he faced her directly. "You thought I was getting it on with Juanita? No. Kara, you jumped to the wrong conclusion—and so did I."

"You did?" she questioned. Reaching down, Kara

absently played with the band on her wristwatch, but she continued to look Rob in the eye.

"Yes. I was working late, trying to get ahead. I was afraid I would lose you if you had to go too long without all the luxuries you were used to having. That's why I had become so obsessed with the business that I was working late almost every evening. On that particular evening I had been sitting at my desk so long that my neck got a little stiff. Juanita and Mike had not gone home yet, and when she noticed how I kept twitching my shoulders trying to relieve some of the strain, she demanded I take a break and let her give me a neck massage. She had me remove my shirt so she could knead the muscles in my neck and shoulders. When she was finished, I lay down on the couch, since Mike had suggested we all take a break. We asked Juanita to make us something to drink."

Shaking his head, he said sadly, "If you had come on in, you would have found Juanita, still fully dressed, standing at the desk preparing the drinks, and you would have seen Mike was there, too, leaning back in his chair with his feet propped up in another chair. Absolutely nothing happened."

"B-but," Kara began to stammer. "What about the phone number?"

"What phone number?"

"The one I found in your pocket with Juanita's initials on it."

"You found a number in my pocket with J.P. on it?" Rob asked curiously, trying to think back.

"No, J.B. Remember, she was a Buchanan at the time."

"J.B.? that wasn't a phone number. That was a part number. J.B. is a line of import auto parts. That was probably just a part number I needed to find and had written it down before I could forget it. I'm always having to do that."

"But I dialed the number and it rang. A woman answered," she defended the conclusion she had come to. "And there was women's jewelry in your car," she went on to explain. She had not left simply because of one incident but because of several.

"Right. That was my cousin's. Don't you remember? Karen had borrowed my car for two days earlier in the week. She came by several weeks after you'd left, looking for her necklace and hoping she might have lost it in my car."

"I threw it away," Kara admitted shamefully.

"Then we owe Karen a necklace."

And those phone calls in which the caller would hang up were just wrong numbers, Kara thought, deciding not to even mention those.

Rob looked at her in amazement. "And I thought you had run out on me because you were bored. I thought you just wanted to return to the rich life. In fact, I kept tabs on you for a while and was convinced that you had left because I could not provide well enough for you. I heard about all those wild parties and rich boyfriends, about your life in the fast lane." There was a twinge of jealousy in his voice. "That's why I worked so hard to finally become a success, to prove to you that you had made a mistake about me."

"But I only went to those parties and dated those guys for Dad's benefit. He was the one who kept finding me dates. I only let him because it helped keep my mind off you and Juanita, especially after I heard you two had gotten married," she put in accusingly.

"Hey, I only married her to help get over losing you," he explained, finding this all so incredible. "I was lonely and miserable after you left. Juanita began to take care of me. She provided me with the companionship I needed at the time. She was the one who suggested we get married. I knew from the start I could never love anyone the way I love you, but I did not want to be alone forever. I was also grateful to her for all she had done for me, so I decided to go ahead and marry her. I thought that ever marrying for love again was out of the question, so I settled for gratitude."

"But you grew to love her. I saw the sorrow in your eyes when you talked of her death."

"I don't think it could have been sorrow you saw. It was more likely guilt because I did not feel the sorrow and grief I should have after her death. She was good to me. She knew I still loved you, but she was convinced she could change that. She tried her best to earn my love right to her dying day, and I could not even feel sorrow at her death, only loss." The pain Kara had detected earlier in his eyes had returned, but he was right, it wasn't sorrow. She could see that now.

"Oh, Rob, I can't believe we were such fools!" she cried out. Having a sudden need to touch him, she reached out and placed her hands on his lean, muscular face. "Such stupid, awful fools."

Rob smiled, filling her hands with his dimpled cheeks. "You realize that if jumping to conclusions was an Olympic event that we'd both be gold-medal winners."

Kara laughed, tears forming in her dark eyes. "That's for sure."

Rob's laughter sparkled in his eyes. "Kara, I love you. Will you please marry me again? We can't get back the years we lost, but we can still have all the years ahead."

Quickly frowning, as if the subject was bothersome, Kara retorted, "Marry you? Can't we just be good friends?"

"Kara," he said slowly, warning her to be careful.

Unable to conceal her joy any longer, she leaned forward and placed her nose against his, grinning broadly, "Of course, I'll marry you, you big dummy."

"Such endearment," he chuckled as his lips protruded to take a brief kiss. Reaching into one of the pockets of his jacket, he pulled out a small cloth-covered box. Kara recognized the little blue box with the tattered gray edges. Her eyes filled with sentimental tears when he eased the hinged top of the little worn box open. There, protruding from a narrow slot, was her wedding ring. The same ring she had left on the dresser as her last defiant act before walking out the door of the duplex forever.

Easing the ring from its long-time resting place, Rob commented lovingly, "I always hoped that someday this golden ring, symbol of our love, would reclaim your finger."

That sounded so poetic to Kara. Her heart soared with the love and ultimate joy she had forgotten she possessed. She had suppressed such emotions for so many years, they seemed to explode inside her when he reached for her left hand. Lifting it gingerly, he slid the ring onto her finger.

Kara smiled timidly, feeling suddenly shy, sort of like a blushing bride. In fact, she felt just as she had the first time he'd proposed, except something deep down inside her was nagging her. At first she had no idea what it could be. Then she remembered Maria. The glowing smile faded; her stomach knotted.

Rob was immediately alarmed. "What's wrong?"

"What about Maria?"

"What about her?" He clearly didn't understand the question.

"Aren't you and Maria... aren't you two..." Kara

couldn't find the words, but her eyes revealed her thoughts. Impatiently she pushed him back, almost causing him to topple over, and stood. She walked around him to the window and lifted the curtain back so that she could stare out at the blackness of the night. She hardly breathed while she waited for his reply.

"Maria is a friend and a business associate, nothing more. True, she is a dear friend and I love her, but as I would a sister," Rob told her while he came to stand beside her at the window. She turned to look at him, wondering whether or not to believe him. A guilty smile played at his lips that made Kara a little nervous. Then he explained further, "I may have led you to believe there was something more, but there never has been anything but a close friendship between us. We were a comfort to each other after Juanita's death and a friendship grew from that."

Kara eyed him suspiciously. After all, she'd seen the "hands-off-he's-mine" look Maria had flashed her. Warily she asked, "Are you sure there isn't something a little stronger than friendship between you two?"

"Quite sure. It is strictly a platonic relationship."

"You've never made love to her?" Kara wasn't sure she had a right to ask that but needed to know.

"That almost sounds absurd! About all I've offered her are a few brotherly kisses. As I said before, she's like a sister to me," he told her with a slow shake of his head. The sparkle in his eyes showed he was slightly amused by her jealous suspicions.

"Brotherly kisses?" she probed further.

"Yes, like this," Rob said and promptly leaned forward and pecked her cheek lightly, stifling a grin. "Nothing like the kisses I have planned for you."

Having said that, he lowered his mouth to hers and, upon finding no protest, slipped his arms around her and pulled her body against his in a passionate embrace. Kara was so relieved to know Maria was nothing more than a friend, she was totally overwhelmed with joy and excitement, still finding it all so hard to believe. She'd never dreamed that there was a happy ending in store for her where Rob was concerned. Easing her arms up, she encircled his strong neck and returned his caresses, meeting each kiss with a passion she knew she could only feel for Rob.

"You are mine again," he breathed softly against her cheek while he continued to hold her close. His hands slowly slid up her back and became entwined in the dark depths of her hair. Holding her head tilted slightly upward, he pulled away a few inches and gently allowed his other hand to explore the face he loved so dearly. It was as if he wanted to make certain she was real. Bringing his face close to her again, his lips traced the delicate contours of her cheeks where his hands had just been teasing her skin with a tantalizing, fiery sensation. When his lips once again demanded hers, it was with such ardent, molten kisses that sparks of searing heat shot along her nerves, warming every inch of her.

Kara's eyelids grew heavy with desire as Rob's kisses trailed fire down her neck and his lithe fingers worked with the many buttons of her blouse. Soon he had the blouse undone and slipped it readily from her shoulders. He tossed the garment carelessly across the chair and her long skirt and undergarments soon followed. At last she stood completely naked before him, and for a brief moment he simply viewed her lovely body, knowing he would once again claim it as his own.

"Rob," she sighed and her breath fell sweet across his cheek. He knew he could never love or need a woman the way he loved and needed Kara. He wanted to crush her to him, but chose instead a gentle caress when he again pulled her near.

Kara trembled as he gently lifted her naked body into his powerful arms and began to carry her down the hallway to her bedroom. Her trembling was not from fear, nor was it from the cold, but from the desperate need she felt for this man, her man. Rob was going to make love to her and finally soothe the consuming ache she'd suffered from having wanted him for so long. And she knew only Rob could assuage the fire vividly burning inside her.

Rob buried his face in her thick hair and breathed deeply the familiar scent that was Kara as he gently laid her on the bed. His moist tongue came out to tickle the sensitive lobe of her ear before he pulled away long enough to undress himself. When Rob once again took her in his arms, he, too, was naked.

Reveling in the hardness of his body against hers, Kara pressed herself closer to him, molding herself to him. Rob's lips quickly reclaimed hers and his hands explored the body he'd been denied for five long years. Gently his hand roamed freely across her abdomen, along her side, and up her rib cage. He thrilled to touch her. Kara gasped with pleasure when his fingertips found the sensitive peak of her breast, and she bit her lip in order to restrain a cry of sheer pleasure when the desire grew to such a passionate strength that she wasn't sure she could stand it any longer. Flesh explored flesh with a mounting urgency as Rob moved to become part of her. She responded fully when they finally reached that ultimate moment of wondrous ecstasy. Once fulfilled, they fell back into the pillows, their energy spent, lanquid in the aftermath of their love.

Rob made no effort to leave and the reunited lovers

remained in each other's arms. Kara pressed her cheek against the strength of his warm, muscular chest and lay quietly, unmoving, listening contentedly to the steady pounding of his heart. Soon she was aware of his rhythmic heavy breathing and knew he was asleep. Wistfully, she hoped he would dream of her.

Even though Rob had effectively explained away her suspicions and had redeclared his love, Kara was almost afraid to believe it. It was too good to be true. If he really did feel about her the same as she did about him, she was sure they could make a marriage work this time. She grimaced as she thought of the five years they'd lost and what their life might be like had they not foolishly jumped to such wrong conclusions. She could've shared so much with him; there might have been children by now. Her stomach knotted at the thought that she could have gone the rest of her life miserably believing Rob had betrayed her and never knowing his love again. Kara had found joy again and rediscovered hope. Only briefly did she think of Maria and wonder anew about that relationship. It certainly had seemed as if they had more than friendship going for them, but Rob had assured her friendship was all. She decided to trust him and pushed it out of her mind.

Kara believed that this time their love would hold and a marriage would work. She planned to do everything in her power to see that it did. With only happy thoughts she drifted off into a peaceful sleep.

Chapter Nine

Without bothering to open her eyes, Kara reached out, expecting to find Rob in her bed, but all her fingers found were crumpled pillows and wrinkled sheets. Opening her eyes, she quickly searched the room. To her confusion she saw that she was alone.

Still groggy from sleep, she wondered if it might not have been another one of her overly imaginative dreams. Her mind must have been playing tricks on her. Blinking against the bright sunlight streaming in her window, Kara tried to clear her thoughts. There were no clothes where she remembered his to be, no real signs of Rob having been there at all. She was crestfallen. It had seemed so real.

Slamming her left fist into the pillow she had expected to find Rob's handsome cheek pressed against, she wanted to scream out with frustration. When she raised her hand to strike the pillow again, she noticed the ring. She froze with the hand in midair. Gingerly she ran a finger across the rough cut of the tiny diamond pressed into the smooth surface of the gold band. A warm, gentle smile spread across her face. Rob *had* been here. Last night *had* happened.

Throwing back the covers, Kara discovered the morning was cool and she was still naked. She quickly stepped over to her closet and pulled out her robe. Once snug in its terry warmth, she walked to the foot of the bed where she usually kept her houseshoes. There on the floor beside them were a pair of men's black shoes and a pair of black socks turned inside out. Had Rob left without his shoes?

Curiosity aroused, Kara hurried to the kitchen. She'd considered he might be trying to put something together for breakfast. She wondered if he'd be nearly as opposed to doughnuts for breakfast when he discovered that that's all there was. It was either doughnuts or starve. She could not even offer him her usual; she was ding-donged out. Grinning sheepishly, she walked into the kitchen ready to defend her junk-food diet.

The grin faded when her eyes scanned the room. Rob was not there as she had expected him to be. In fact it looked as if nothing had been tampered with at all. Out of habit she headed to the refrigerator and took out her usual diet cola. As she pulled on the tab to open it, she mulled over the possibilities. Maybe he had discovered her bare cupboard and had gone out to get something in the way of food. But without his shoes?

She shrugged. Rob had been known to do stranger things. Taking a big drink, Kara decided to see if her car was still in the driveway, having remembered that her car had his blocked in. When she was about halfway to the door, the phone rang.

Trying to think of a reason why Rob would be calling, Kara leaned against the kitchen counter and picked up the receiver.

"Hello?"

There was a pause as she waited for the reply.

"Oh, hi, Pat," she responded, recognizing the voice that had just greeted her in such a cheerful tone.

"I'm just calling to reconfirm our plans for this evening. Clint has decided we're going to eat at Ted-D's Supper Club. He wants to see the group that is scheduled to entertain tonight. They are supposed to perform the popular music and dances of the fifties. I'm not sure why he's so hooked on the fifties. It can't be nostalgia because Clint was only a toddler when everyone was hoppin' and boppin'," Pat chuckled. "Anyway, if that is all right with you, we'll just take in the supper club tonight."

"I don't know," Kara spoke hesitantly. "I don't think I can go out with Andy after all."

"Kara, don't you dare back out on me this late," Pat warned. "Give me one good reason why you would even want to."

Glancing down at the shiny gold ring on her finger, Kara replied, still a little mystified, "Well, I think I got engaged last night."

"What do you mean you *think* you got engaged?" Rob's voice boomed from only inches behind her.

Startled by his voice, not having heard him enter the room, Kara let out a yelp and sent the phone flying across the counter. Clutching her chest about where she supposed her pounding heart to be, Kara gasped for air. It was just an honest reaction that she had reached out and popped him on his head as she had. When she finally could, she shouted, "Rob Phillips, you scared the living breath out of me!"

Rob's face remained expressionless as he slowly repeated his question, "What do you mean you *think* you are engaged?" Narrowing his eyes to two icy slits, he also wanted to know just who this Andy guy was.

Still unnerved by Rob's sudden appearance, Kara breathed heavily. Taking the cord in her grasp, she slowly pulled, hand over hand, until she had retrieved the receiver. Watching Rob warily, she placed the receiver to her mouth and spoke quickly, "Pat, I'll have to call you back."

She could hear a tiny metallic voice continue to talk until she had placed the receiver securely in its cradle. She would apologize later.

"Where'd you come from?" she asked, finding it peculiar that he had been able to just appear out of nowhere. Looking down, she saw why she hadn't heard him come up behind her. Rob was still barefoot.

"I was in the bathroom," he said simply.

"You certainly were being quiet."

"I meant to be. I thought you were still asleep and didn't want to wake you. I had hoped to find a razor so I could shave, but all I could find was a strange-looking round thing that looked like it was designed by a clever Indian for the direct purpose of removing scalps," he explained. Then realizing he was getting off the subject he wanted to stay with, he added, "But when I heard the phone ring only once, I knew you had answered it and were awake, so I came in here hoping to find out if you had a more conventional tool for shaving. That's when I overheard your conversation about this Andy character. Just who is Andy?"

"Andy is Pat's brother from Houston," Kara explained, trying not to sound nervous when she felt as if she were being placed in front of the firing squad for an act of treason.

"And how do you know him?" Rob prompted, eyes still narrowed suspiciously.

"I don't know him," Kara said defensively.

"Then what are you doing going out with the guy?" Rob ran his hand through his hair as he waited for her reply. It seemed strange to him that she had not even met the guy, yet she planned to go out with him. That wasn't like Kara, or at least the Kara he thought he knew.

"He just came to Longview this weekend, and Pat wanted to show him a good time, so she asked me..." Kara started to explain further but was interrupted.

"And what sort of good time is it Pat wants you to show him?" he asked, widening his eyes and raising his eyebrows.

"Rob," she snapped flatly, having read his evil mind.

"I just want to know," he shrugged.

"I am simply supposed to accompany him for the evening to sort of even things out. Pat was afraid he would be uncomfortable being a third party to one of their evenings. She decided to find him a date, and as a result, she asked me."

"Why you?"

"Because I am a close friend of hers that she can trust, and I was available."

"*Was* is right," he stated firmly, putting special emphasis on the past tense. Reaching for her left hand, he raised it and pointed to the ring. "You aren't exactly available for dates anymore."

"That's what I was trying to explain to Pat," she sighed, shaking her head in exasperation.

"You weren't trying very hard," he pointed out.

"Well, I hate to disappoint her. She so wants tonight to be a lot of fun for Andy since he doesn't get to visit very often. I hate to ruin that for her. I never would've accepted at all if it didn't mean so much to her."

Rubbing the rough unshaven stubble on his chin, he thought aloud, "Then what we need to do is find a replacement for you so her brother will have company and be assured a nice time out. But who? Whom do we know that is available and fun to be with?"

Kara shrugged. She could only think of Jan but refused to do that to a total stranger, especially one that had such close family ties with her friend. He might have more fun than he could handle with Jan.

"I know!" Rob said, snapping his fingers. "Maria!"

"Maria?"

"Sure, she's perfect." His enthusiasm was pouring out of him. "I've been trying to get her to date again. She hardly has a social life except for coming over to my house for an occasional meal or once in a while going out for dinner and a show."

"Occasional," Kara repeated doubtfully.

Despite what Rob had told her last night, she still fought her jealousy where Maria was concerned. She knew she needed to overcome such feelings but realized it would take her a while.

"A few times a week," he shrugged, then proceeded with his idea. "Maria needs to get out and have a good time, to meet new people."

His concern didn't sit very well with Kara, but rather than chance an argument, she decided to go along with the idea. "Do you think Maria will be willing to go out with Andy?"

"She might if we promise to go along to lend her a little moral support. It's at least worth a try," he said, still enthusiastic. Then in a foreboding voice he added, "After all, you certainly can't go as Andy's date. Not when you plan to be my wife."

"And I don't want to. I'd much rather be with you," Kara said sweetly, grinning as the childlike pout on Rob's handsome face turned into a broad smile. "I'd better call Pat back and explain all this to her. I guess I need to start with an apology for having more or less hung up on her."

"And this time don't you tell her you *think* you are

engaged. You tell her you are definitely engaged and plan to be married next weekend.''

"W-what?" Kara stammered, stunned that he would want to make it that soon. She placed both hands on the counter to steady herself, fearing she would go into shock at any moment.

"I'd make it tomorrow, but there are legalities. And we have to tell your dad and my mom. Mom will want to be here, but being so afraid to fly, she'll need a day or two to drive in from Colorado. So I guess we'll just have to be patient and make it next weekend. Friday night will be fine."

"And that'll give us the whole weekend for the honeymoon," Kara put in. She wasn't about to argue for more time to get ready. If Rob wanted to hurry this along, she would be more than happy to oblige him.

"Weekend?" Rob asked, seeming confused. "I was thinking more along the lines of two weeks traipsing about Europe."

"What?"

"Well, I know how you've always wanted to see England. While we were at it, I thought we might as well check out France, Switzerland, and Germany. We might even take in the sights of Rome if time permits. Who knows?"

Kara stared at him in amazement. She was overwhelmed. This certainly was going to be different from their first honeymoon at the Daingerfield, Texas State Park. If this honeymoon in such a glamorous, romantic setting turned out to be only half as much fun as their first, she was in for a real treat.

"It might be better to plan on three weeks," Rob added thoughtfully, unaware Kara was temporarily lost in her lovely memories of a honeymoon past, remembering the secluded little cabin in the woods and how they had taken three times the provisions needed for their four-day stay. "What do you think? Should we make it three weeks?"

Only vaguely having heard what he had said, Kara asked, "How are we going to get three weeks free just like that?"

Rob shook his head as if he could not believe she was asking such trivial questions. "Clint can hold down the restaurant while you are away. Offer him a bonus of some sort or hire temporary help. If the restaurant can't afford it, I'll pay the added expense."

"And what about you?" Kara asked, already planning to offer Clint both a bonus in pay as well as more time off for his own honeymoon.

"I certainly have no problems getting time off. Maria can manage while I'm away. With Paula's help and a way to reach me by phone, Maria can manage just fine. Besides, we've left business matters on each other's shoulders on several occasions. She handled it when I went to Colorado last November to see Mom and do a little hunting, and I didn't complain when she dumped the whole thing on me over the holidays last year while she went to Hot Springs to see her folks. That was for almost three weeks."

A smile worked its way across Kara's face when she realized he really had thought this through. It wasn't sounding so spur-of-the-moment anymore. Come next weekend she would again become Mrs. Rob Phillips.

"If you want, you can extend an invitation to the ceremony when you call your friend. She might like to be there."

Kara not only intended to invite Pat to the wedding, she realized she would like to have her as her maid-of-honor. When she asked Rob if they were going to have a simple ceremony since this was a repeat performance, he shrugged and said, "Whatever you want."

What she wanted was a quiet moment in the presence of a minister with only very close friends and their parents there. Rob was quick to agree. It was not the size of a wedding that counted, it was the sincerity of their vows. A small wedding would be just as binding as a big elaborate affair. He considered their first wedding. Edison Ewan had spared no expense for the all-day extravaganza, and in spite of the thousands of dollars poured into the affair, the marriage had not lasted much over two years.

While Kara called Pat and explained everything to her, Rob went back to the bedroom to put on his shoes. He was going to a nearby convenience store to purchase decent food for breakfast and a proper razor for shaving.

Kara was relieved to find Pat not only agreeable to the change in plans but excited about the upcoming marriage "to that gorgeous hunk." Kara was still answering her friend's barrage of questions when Rob returned from the store. Quietly he set the small sack of groceries on the table, dug through until he located the razor, and walked over to her with a devilish grin. Pulling her hair back, he began placing delicate kisses along the nape of her neck. She suppressed the delicious shivers his lips sent down her spine. When his kisses did not get any more of a response than Kara's pulling in of her neck, he started rubbing her with his stiff whiskers. She paused in her conversation just long enough to give him a little push and ordered him to go shave. They would have time for such later. In fact they had all day. Meekly he let go of her and left the room, pouting like a three-year-old.

When he returned minutes later clean-shaven, Kara was off the phone and unpacking the groceries.

"When are you going to call Maria?" she asked while she pulled out the usual breakfast stuff: eggs, sausages, biscuits, and jelly. She grinned when she came across a large box of chocolate Ding-dongs snack cakes.

"Better do that right away," he admitted and went directly to the phone. Zipping through Maria's number with no hesitation, he leaned against the counter and waited for an answer. Kara tried not to feel annoyed that he knew her number so well. He ought to. They were business partners. She tried to keep the fact that they were only business partners in mind as she listened to Rob's friendly greeting.

"Hi, sweetheart," he began, pausing long enough for her reply.

"No, I didn't go home last night at all. Why? What's wrong?"

Another long pause before Kara heard him ask, "How bad is it?"

Oh, no. Trouble, Kara thought, having an odd feeling the trouble was going to directly affect her in some horrible way.

"Of course, I understand. It's never a problem to do you a favor."

Kara pretended not to be interested in this conversation at all and began putting the eggs into the small holes in her refrigerator door.

"You can count on me. You just do what you have to do. Hey, don't forget, I send my love."

Kara almost dropped an egg.

"And tell her I said to get well soon," he said gently before ending the conversation with a soft "Goodbye."

"Problems?" she asked sweetly as she rearranged the eggs for absolutely no reason.

"Maria won't be able to go out with Andy tonight," he frowned. "Her mother had a heart attack last night. Maria wasn't too clear on the details, but she was in the process of packing when I called. She's leaving for Hot Springs as soon as she can."

"Is it serious?" Kara asked, truly concerned. She had lost two of her grandparents to heart problems.

"Maria really doesn't know. She said her father called about five this morning and was pretty shaken. She told me she'd been trying to call ever since then to let me know she was going to be gone for a couple of days," Rob explained. His brow was pulled together showing how deeply worried he was. "I hope it's not too bad. She's such a nice lady."

"Maybe you should go with Maria," Kara said quietly, not believing what she had just suggested could come from her own lips. It would mean days of loneliness while Rob was away—with Maria, no less. But Rob did look concerned, for he obviously cared for her mother a great deal. Kara realized the woman had once been Rob's mother-in-law. There was reason for them to be close.

"No, someone has to stay here and tend to business. Besides, there's nothing I could do. I'd just get in the way. I'll probably call her when I'm sure she's feeling up to it," he said, then briskly changed the subject. "We still have to find someone for this Andy guy."

Reminded once again to make the call to Pat, Kara reluctantly explained that Maria was unavailable after all. Taking a deep breath, she forced out the suggestion to call the only other single female she knew—Jan.

After pausing a moment to search her memory for someone more suitable, Pat finally agreed. At this point they were getting desperate. Before hanging up, Pat asked Kara if she was planning to join them that evening and bring her gorgeous husband-to-be-again so they could get to know him.

Turning to Rob, Kara relayed the question. She covered the mouthpiece with her hand while she waited for Rob's reply.

"If we get back in time," he assured her, carefully folding the sack the groceries had been in.

"Get back? From where?"

"Don't you plan to tell your father about your engagement?" he asked as if she should have reached such a decision on her own. "Don't you want to drive over to Dallas and tell him in person? You weren't planning to break this to him over the phone, were you?"

Kara really had not thought about it. Of course, she would have to tell her father because she would certainly want him to be at the wedding. She had to agree, this was something she should tell him in person, and if they were getting married next weekend, she knew she could not put off telling him.

Placing the phone back up to her ear, Kara told Pat that she could not promise her anything definite, explaining where she was going and why. She promised that if they got back to Longview in time they would join them at the club and suggested they save them a couple of chairs, if possible. She ended the conversation with a good-natured warning, "If I don't get there early enough to save Clint from himself, tell him I don't like to see my employees hung over on Monday mornings." Pat just laughed and asked her to try her best to make it, telling her that they would be watching for them.

While Kara took a shower and got dressed in a pretty white sundress, Rob quickly prepared breakfast. As soon as they were through eating, they stacked the dishes in the sink and went over to his house so he could change clothes. He wanted to look his best when he faced Kara's father again. He was not sure what kind of a reception he would receive. Neither was Kara for that matter. Her father could be contrary when he chose to be.

Since they were going to be gone all day and didn't want the dogs to be lonely, Rob thought to let Redwood pay Princess a little visit. While Kara released Redwood in the backyard, Rob rushed upstairs to put on a pair of pale blue slacks, a blue multi-striped pullover and a dark blue blazer.

When he came back downstairs and joined Kara outside, Rob was delighted to see the two gangling Irish setters frolicking happily around the pool. When Redwood was not in hot pursuit of his new companion, he was enjoying her playful chasing across the yard. Princess nipped at his ears whenever he would slow down long enough for her to catch him. Rob and Kara watched this game of switch tag for several minutes before Rob courageously suggested they leave.

Heading west on I-20, the Trans Am made good time, almost too good as far as Rob was concerned. His anticipation grew with each mile they put behind them. It was midafternoon when they pulled into the large driveway that circled in front of the huge Victorian house that had been home to Kara for so many years. But rather than park in front, they drove back to the garage area and parked between the garage, a separate little building, and the main house.

"I hope he's home," Kara commented when she stepped out of the car. "Maybe we should have called after all." The solid-wood garage doors were closed, so she could not tell whether or not his car was inside, but there was no sign of life anywhere.

Rob nodded in agreement but was not quite certain he was as sincere as she was. The closer they came to the back door, the more he found himself hoping her father was out for the day. He was not sure if he was perspiring from the heat of the summer afternoon or from the worry of what might happen next. How well he remembered their last encounter when Edison had come to get Kara's things the day after she had left him. It had not exactly been pleasant. A heated bit of conversation had been exchanged. Edison's very last words had been a bold directive to leave his daughter alone. He had demanded that Rob stay out of her life, claiming she was better off without him. Now here he was, not only back in her life, but about to become her husband again.

When they reached the back door closest to the garage, Kara rapped lightly on it twice, then immediately tried the knob. To Rob's dismay, it was unlocked and Kara walked right in.

"Dad," she called out at the top of her voice. "You home?"

Seeing that Rob was still standing outside, she reached out and grabbed his arm, pulling him inside by his coat sleeve. "He isn't going to bite you," she whispered, stifling the grin that wanted to spread across her face. His eyes were stretched wide and his jaw worked nervously as he came inside. He reminded her of a little boy having been called before the principal for putting a tack on the teacher's chair.

"Up here, Buttons," they heard Edison's distant call. It sounded like his voice had come from upstairs. Kara smiled at being called Buttons, his pet name for her. It had something to do with the little pug nose she had as a child. Her nose had grown since then, but he still liked to call her Buttons and she liked to hear it.

"After you," Kara said to Rob in a deep foreboding voice. With a wave of her hand, she directed him to the door leading from the game room they were in to a short hall that would take them to the front stairway. When he did not move, she repeated herself, "After you."

"Said the spider to the fly," he mumbled before heading for the door.

Once they reached the stairs, they ascended side by side. Kara was becoming a little more apprehensive herself. She knew once her father was convinced this was what she wanted, he would give his blessing. Still she was not certain what his initial reaction would be or how much convincing it would take.

About halfway up the stairway, they could hear Edison's footsteps coming toward them from somewhere down the long upstairs corridor. Not an extremely tall man, standing just six feet, Edison Ewan was what he liked to call stocky. He was a few pounds heavier than he needed to be and much of it had settled in certain areas, mainly his stomach, and was due to his keen interest in food. Kara overlooked the added weight; to her it meant there was just that much more of him to love, and love him she did. If it ever came down to having to choose between Rob and her father, she was not sure she could make the decision. She would hate to ever be put in that position. She hoped she would not be put in that position now.

"Buttons, you should have called and told…" Her father's singsong voice cut short when he came into view and saw who was standing beside her on the top step. Looking bewildered, he finished his statement with his words far apart and his voice faltering, "me…you…were coming."

"I—I wanted to surprise you," she smiled sheepishly, looking rather guilty as she rushed over to give him her usual big hug.

Rob raised his hand and wiggled his fingers in an awkward greeting, aware that Edison's gaze was still directed at him. His dimples felt misplaced when Edison did not return his smile. Her father only raised a curious silver eyebrow at him.

When Kara pulled away, she immediately began explaining, "I know you're wondering why Rob is with me."

Edison's blue-gray eyes darted from Rob to Kara, then back to Rob. "You're right there."

"Well, he thought he should be with me when I break the news to you," Kara went on to say, aware that the two men's eyes were locked in a steady gaze.

"News?" he asked, narrowing his eyes, but never so much as blinking. Putting the pipe that had grown cold in his hand back in his mouth, he began to feel the pockets of the dark-blue nautical-style coveralls he wore. Never letting his steely gaze drop, he located the lighter and slipped it out of a front pocket. Flicking twice, he put the small flame to the pipe and drew heavily, causing the yellow flame to disappear into a red glow of tobacco.

"Yes, we plan to get married again," she blurted out, then bit her lip and waited for his reaction.

Edison's pale eyes continued to regard Rob's deep blue as he took several long draws from his pipe. For an extremely long moment he just stared through heavily lowered lashes, contemplating what Kara had told him.

"This true, Rob?"

"Yes sir," he replied firmly, squaring his shoulders. He was not going to let Edison intimidate him. "I still love her, and when I asked her to make another go of it, she accepted."

Glancing over at Kara for only a moment, he looked again at Rob. He studied Rob's eyes for sincerity as he demanded to hear him declare his feelings again. "You still love her?"

"Yes, very much," Rob told him, taking his gaze from Edison's to look lovingly at Kara. A smile played at his lips when he saw her wide-eyed expression. She was just as nervous about this as he was. "I've been miserable these past five years without her."

Edison slowly took the pipe out of his mouth and held it. He took several short steps toward Rob, who had not progressed past the top step, and threw open his arms. "Then welcome back, son," he said, giving Rob a bear hug. His voice was shaking with emotion. He was fully accepting what Rob had just told him.

A smile of relief broke out across Rob's face as he returned the man's embrace, but the smile faded when Edison pulled away abruptly.

"But you'd better keep her happy," her father warned, wagging his finger in front of Rob's nose. Then just as abruptly, he hugged him again. "I'm glad you've come back. She needs a man to tell her what to do."

Kara slowly let go of the breath she had been holding. This was turning out better than she had hoped, although she was not certain she liked that crack about needing a man to tell her what to do. She ignored such remarks from her father; that was just the way he was. She loved him in spite of it.

"This calls for a toast," Edison said, draping one arm around Rob and holding the other out for Kara. "I wonder if I have any champagne."

"I'm sure you do," Kara sighed, going to him.

"When's the big event going to take place?" he asked while the three of them made their way down the stairs arm in arm.

"Next weekend," Kara beamed. "As far as we know, it should be next Friday night."

"Next Friday night?" Edison asked, obviously surprised at her reply. He stopped midstride, causing Rob to stumble onto the next step. Kara had anticipated the sudden reaction and stood by her father's side, explaining further. "We've already wasted five years being apart, so why waste any more time?"

"Next Friday?" Edison repeated in the same astonished tone, still not sure he had heard right.

"Yes, next Friday, if we can find a minister to marry us on such short notice. Want to come?"

"You mean five-days-from-now Friday?"

"That's the one," Kara shrugged.

"Certainly I want to come. You couldn't keep me away," he said in a boisterous reply. Evidently he had now accepted the fact that they were not only getting married but that it would happen in just a matter of days. Grinning broadly, his eyes sparkling with amusement, he wanted to know what he should wear.

One toast led to another and soon the bottle of champagne Edison had located was empty. He then decided the celebration would not end there. Grabbing his coat, he demanded to take them out to the fanciest restaurant open on Sunday, which eliminated any of his own. It was well after ten o'clock before they returned to the house, and in spite of Edison's staunch objections, they left for Longview shortly after that but too late to join Kara's friends at Ted-D's Supper Club.

It was just after one o'clock when they reached Longview. Remembering Redwood, they went straight to Rob's house. But before allowing Kara to go to the backyard and get the dog, Rob insisted on phoning his mother to tell her the good news. Kara tried to reason with him, reminding him of the late hour, but Rob refused to wait until morning. It was easy to see that she was not going to be able to convince him otherwise, so Kara agreed to stay while he placed the call.

Minutes later Rob had dialed his mother's number and had Kara pick up the extension in the kitchen. Kara was glad to find out that Kathy Phillips had not gone to sleep yet; she had stayed up reading a book she just could not put down. When they told her the news, she squealed with delight, promising to be packed and on the road by Tuesday. Being a free-lance artist, she did not have to worry about arranging for free time.

"Well, don't get your suitcase down just yet," Rob warned her, causing Kara and his mother both a moment of worry.

"Why not?" his mother wanted to know.

"Because we haven't okayed it with a preacher yet," he admitted timidly. Kara sighed with relief, so did his mother.

"Well, why not?" his mother wailed, causing both Rob and Kara to pull the receivers away from their ears.

"Haven't really had much of a chance. We just decided to get married again last night."

"Then you'd better see to that first thing in the morning, young man, because I'm going to be there by Friday night and I expect to see a wedding," she said firmly.

"Yes, ma'am," Rob laughed. "First thing in the morning."

"See you Friday," she warned again before she soundly hung up the phone.

Kara was smiling happily when she rejoined Rob in the living room where his hand still lay on the phone. She was delighted at Rob's mother's reception. Although they had become close during the years she had been married to Rob, she had not been too sure how his mother felt about her now. She had worried that the divorce might have changed his mother's feelings for the worse. The woman could have placed the blame on her, since most mothers can see no wrong in their own sons. She was pleased that no ill feelings were harbored.

Taking his future bride into his arms, Rob kissed her lightly. "A ring, both our parents' blessings, all we need now is a preacher who doesn't bowl on Friday nights."

Kara laughed openly. She could not imagine anyone being happier than she was right now. Locking her arms around his powerful neck, she tilted her head back so he could easily claim more kisses. *Five more days,* she thought with a smile. *Five more days and this handsome man will be my husband again.*

Even though she had no intention of denying Rob whatever he wanted, he did not demand more than a half-dozen kisses before pulling away,

"I'd better take you on home now," he said in a low, husky voice, swallowing with some difficulty.

"If that's what you really want to do," she said, smiling seductively and putting her arms back around his neck.

"Look," he pouted, "I'm trying to be noble here."

"Then noble you shall be," she laughed, letting go of his neck and taking his proffered arm with both of hers. Together they walked out onto the back patio and found Redwood and Princess both asleep in the same lounge chair, snuggled closely together in one big red heap. Since Redwood would be returning permanently on Friday anyway, they decided to just let him stay. With all the preparations for a wedding, even a simple one, Kara felt she would not have any time to spend with him. He would just get lonely. If he stayed here, he would have Princess for company.

"I think Redwood's going to like living here," Rob bent close to her ear and whispered.

Hugging him close, she sighed, "Redwood's not the only one."

Chapter Ten

Although it wasn't unusual for Kara to come in early on Monday morning, she surprised Clint by getting to work even before he did, and he was almost always the first one there. She was already at her desk buried in a sea of paperwork when he poked his head through the open doorway.

"Aren't you the early bird," Clint said as he strode into her office. She could tell by the puffiness around his eyes that he had not been awake long and was very impressed that she had. "What's the matter? You checking up on me to see what time I really get here?"

"No," Kara smiled. "And absolutely nothing's the matter. Actually everything is perfect, simply perfect."

"On Monday?" he expressed his doubts. "I don't believe my ears."

Kara put the tip of her pen in her mouth and thought about what Clint had said. It did seem strange she could feel such complete happiness on a Monday.

"Does all this elation I see bubbling out of you have to do with the fact that you and your ex are giving it another go?" he asked, settling down comfortably in one of the chairs across from her desk.

"I guess Pat's already filled you in."

"She called me yesterday morning as soon as she'd

finished talking with you. She thinks this is the greatest thing since paper plates," he chuckled, draping a leg over one arm of the chair and sitting at an angle.

"And what do you think?" she wanted to know. She placed her pen aside and waited for his reply. She valued Clint's opinion.

"I don't want to say," he admitted, bobbing his foot nervously. "I've never even met the guy. All I know is what you've told me and what little your father has had to say about him. You know for yourself that it all wasn't good. I'd like at least to meet the guy before I offer a firm opinion. I thought I'd get a chance to meet him last night."

"We didn't leave Dad's until around ten," Kara explained quickly, hoping there wouldn't be any ill feeling on the matter. "But if you'd really like to meet him, stay late. He's coming for supper around seven."

"And I suppose you wouldn't mind if I covered the front while you joined him," he said suspiciously.

"Well, of course, I wouldn't mind, but I wasn't hinting at that. I just thought it would be a good opportunity for you to meet him."

"Since I don't have anywhere else to go at seven, with Pat having to go over to Tyler for a meeting, I guess I might as well hang around and see if the guy is worthy enough." Clint slowly smiled one of his charming smiles. "I might even find it in my big, wonderful heart to seat customers long enough for you to have dinner with him."

"That's truly wonderful of you."

"I agree," he nodded, then commented, "You never did tell me why you came in so early."

"I just want to get all the bookwork I can out of the way before the wedding Friday," Kara explained. "I don't want to leave you with more than you can handle."

"Leave me?" he asked, raising an eyebrow and leaning forward. She had his full attention.

"Didn't I mention that I'm going on a little honeymoon and want you to take care of things here?" she asked sweetly, batting her eyes to emphasize her innocence of having let it slip her mind. Actually it hadn't slipped her mind, she had just been waiting for the right time to tell him. She supposed now was as good a time as any. Grinning broadly, Kara continued, "I'm certainly glad you're sitting down for this."

"Why? Just how long is this little honeymoon going to last?" His eyes narrowed as he spoke, showing his distrust.

"Oh, only a couple of weeks, three at the most," she said, flinching with anticipation of his reaction. Clint was known to overreact at times.

"Three weeks?" His eyebrows shot up in surprise. At first he pretended to be very upset, waving his arms and wanting to know what he got out of it. Once she had explained the bonus in his paycheck as well as an added week for his own honeymoon, he became very agreeable, almost docile. He wanted to know more about what extra duties he would be responsible for and just how she was used to handling them.

For the rest of the day, they worked together so he could learn how to handle her many duties. By midafternoon Clint was well briefed on these and most of the rest of Kara's duties, claiming it was going to be a cinch. By the time Rob arrived just before seven, all of her doubts concerning Clint's ability to handle the overload were gone. She had most of her work out of the way and no major catastrophes had occurred all day. It was like living through a miracle, having everything going so smoothly on a Monday. But the miracle came to an end when Rob delivered his bad news.

"Maria called this afternoon," he began, having waited until they were sitting at a table and had placed their orders. "I wasn't in at the time, but she left a message with Paula. Seems her mother is in the Cardiac Care Unit of Preston General near Dallas and still is in serious condition. Maria claimed she would not be back to work for at least two weeks, maybe longer. She left phone numbers where she can be reached both at the hospital and at a motel nearby. She is planning to stay until her mother is out of danger."

The smile that had ridden triumphantly on Kara's lips all day quickly sagged. Her whole face seemed to wither sadly as she realized what this could do to their plans. "Does this mean we will have to put off getting married?"

"It leaves us with two choices," Rob explained while reaching across the table to take her hands in his. He was not smiling either. "We can postpone the wedding for a few weeks and still have our beautiful, long honeymoon, or we can go ahead as planned on Friday night and postpone the trip to Europe until some other time. We'd only have the weekend for our honeymoon. It's not enough time to bother with England, but I want you to make the decision as to what we do."

"Were you able to find a minister for Friday night?" she asked, wanting to know more before making a choice.

"Yes, Reverend Lanagan agreed to marry us. He said he could conduct a small ceremony in his chambers."

"But I'd rather be married at your house. I had thought we might have an outdoor ceremony in your lovely backyard," she told him, her eyes sparkling at the idea. "We could light the area near the gardens against the east fence with candles and hold a twilight ceremony."

"What if it rains?"

"It wouldn't dare," she retorted, then conceded, "If it should rain, we could still have it on the patio because the group will be small."

"Whatever you want," he smiled tenderly, enjoying her enthusiasm. "I'm leaving it all up to you."

"Then I want to get married this Friday evening in your backyard, and I'd like to return to the Daingerfield Park for our honeymoon," she told him with a determined nod. "I would really love to share that very same cabin, if we can get it."

"Always the sentimentalist." He smiled, shaking his head. "I'll see what I can do to arrange it. In fact we have a lot of arrangements to make in a very short time."

"We can share in the responsibilities," she offered quickly. "I'll take care of everything for the wedding and you can be in charge of honeymoon arrangements."

"What about moving?" Rob wanted to know, letting go of her hands and leaning back so the waitress could set his salad in front of him. "We need to get all of your belongings repacked and moved over to my house."

Kara waited until her own salad had been placed in front of her before commenting. "I can pack my clothes and whatever is immediately necessary to me and take them over this week. We'll just have to see to the heavy stuff later."

"Will you have time to pack?" he asked, while gently tossing his salad. He knew that the wedding arrangements would take a lot of her time, even for a small ceremony.

"I think so. I'm pretty well caught up here," she told him, reaching for the salt. "You'd be amazed at how much I can get done when pressed for time."

"I am always amazed when it comes to you," he grinned, deepening his long, narrow crescent dimples. His blue eyes glimmered brightly as he gave her a flirtatious wink.

"Oh, you silver-tongued devil, you," she laughed, appreciating how handsome he was.

They continued to discuss their plans for the wedding throughout the meal, laughing whenever Kara had to discard one of Rob's more ridiculous ideas. It was not until they had been served dessert that Clint found the opportunity to join them.

"So you're the guy Kara's so crazy about," he said while pulling a chair over from another table.

"I hope so," Rob commented, laying his napkin aside and staring curiously at Clint. He knew this guy was an employee but did not understand why he should be this bold until Kara was able to formally introduce the two. Remembering the name Clint Rutledge and that he was engaged to her friend, Pat Ray, he decided the guy posed no personal threat. With a friendly smile, he put out his hand and said, "Pleased to meet you. Kara's told me a lot about you."

None of it any good, I'll bet," Clint retorted, glancing at Kara. "But most of it true."

"No doubt," Rob laughed. As the two men became engrossed in deep discussions of important topics of the day, such as the coming football season and the pros and cons of light beer, Rob decided he liked Kara's friend, and it was obvious Clint felt the same. They had discovered several things they had in common: They both were faithful Dallas Cowboys fans, they both liked professional drag racing and neither one cared for raw oysters, despite their touted attributes.

Although Kara was glad the two hit it off so well, she

was feeling a little left out when they began talking in some foreign language—something about gear ratios and competition cams. She was not certain, but she thought they were back to discussing drag racing, a sport she had never been fond of, although she had gone to a few races with Rob years ago.

When a couple of late diners walked in and stood patiently by the podium, it was Kara that had to get up and seat them. Rob and Clint were now discovering friends that they had in common.

Later that evening Pat returned from her meeting early and came by wondering where Clint was. She joined them for a round of coffee and the group stayed for hours after closing, talking and getting to know one another better. It was almost one o'clock before anyone suggested going home.

The next morning Kara's father phoned, wanting to know if she intended to continue managing Pinewood or if he should be looking for a replacement. Kara had already been seriously considering the matter and told him that she still wanted to manage Pinewood, although she would prefer to give up the evening hostess duties. Now that she would have a home life again, Kara wanted her work hours to be more conventional. She promised to continue hostessing until they found someone he considered suitable. Edison was so particular about the type of person greeting the patrons in his restaurants that Kara had not felt insulted when he asked to be there during the interviews that would start the following week.

She told Rob when they met for lunch of her plans to start working a more normal nine-to-five day as soon as it could be arranged. He was pleased with the idea, preferring to have her home with him in the evenings. Rob had wanted to suggest such a change but did not want her to think he was making demands on her. He had hoped she would make this decision on her own.

Rob then told her about the phone call he had received from his mother early that morning. She was leaving Colorado as soon as she finished with a few errands and expected to reach Longview sometime Thursday.

"She wants to be here to help get things ready on Friday," he explained with a shrug. "She also plans to stay at my house over the weekend and oversee having your things moved in."

"We can't ask her to do that," Kara said quickly.

"I didn't ask her; she volunteered. You know what a work horse she is. She loves to be busy doing something for someone else. If it'll make her happy, let her do it. Besides, there shouldn't be too much for her to do. I've hired professional movers to do the heavy work. Mother's just going to supervise," he explained, then grinned. "And you know what a great supervisor Mother is."

"Yes, I remember," Kara laughed softly. Her mother-in-law had been quite opinionated in the way Rob's laundry should be done and how his meals should be prepared. That first visit of hers had been quite an experience.

"Then your mother will be staying at your house for a while?"

"Yes, but don't worry. She promised to be long gone by the time we return Sunday night."

"I wouldn't mind if she decided to stay for a visit," Kara said earnestly. "After all, that's quite a drive."

"You're truly understanding," he expressed with a wry smile. "But she insists. Besides she plans to come again for a visit in October. She'll be staying for two weeks then, taking in the Dallas State Fair, the Rhonesboro Museum, and the Gilmer Yamboree."

Kara decided that she'd better sharpen her cooking skills by then or be prepared for a few overly helpful suggestions; but then, she really didn't mind. Truth was she really liked Rob's mother. The lady always had a ready smile and never failed to be in a jovial mood. Even if his mother did something to irritate her now and then, she could never stay angry at such a person. No one could.

True to her word, Kathy Phillips arrived at Rob's house about midafternoon on Thursday. Kara had stopped by to leave off several elaborately engraved silver trays she intended to use Friday evening. She was just closing the door behind her when she noticed Rob's mother climbing out of her dark brown Mercury Marquis. The two rushed to each other with open arms and both were a little teary-eyed when they finally broke their welcoming embrace.

"Kara," is all his mother could say before throwing her arms around her again.

As soon as they were through with the emotional greeting, his mother began to ask question after question. They talked constantly while Kara helped her unload her suitcases. Kathy directed her to the guest bedroom she always used whenever she visited. Kara placed the two suitcases she was carrying on an old restored trunk and went to open the curtains to let a little light into the room.

"Now what can I do to help?" Kathy asked as soon as she'd placed the packages she'd carried on the bed.

"There's not much to be done today," Kara assured her. "I'm taking tomorrow off and have planned to get most of the work done then. I'd tell you that you don't need to bother at all, but I know you're going to have your hands in this one way or another."

Kathy laughed good-naturedly at Kara's remark. "There's nothing to be done today?" She frowned at the thought, her dark expressive eyes showing the disappointment.

"You have three hours to unpack and rest from the trip before Rob comes home. Then the two of you are supposed to dine at Pinewood," Kara told her. "Since I'll be working this evening, it'll give you a chance to be alone with your son. It might be the last chance you'll have for a while."

"Three hours is a long time to waste resting," Kathy stated, shaking her head and causing her short silver curls to seem animated with protest. "Are you sure there isn't something I can do today? How about the food preparations?"

Kara shrugged hopelessly, "There isn't that much to do. There are only going to be eight guests."

"Only eight?" she asked, surprised at such a small number. When remembering the hundreds that had been invited to the first wedding, it seemed odd.

"Just you, my father, and a few very close friends. We don't want a huge extravagant affair, just a simple, yet lovely, little ceremony here."

"Here? Well, then what about cleaning and decorating?" she asked, her dark blue eyes reflecting a sudden hope. Rob was right, she was a work horse.

"The place is spotless. Rob has a cleaning service come in once a week. There won't be any need in putting out the decorations and setting up the refreshments until tomorrow. Besides, many of the decorations are rented and won't arrive until tomorrow morning."

Finally giving up, Kathy Phillips agreed to unpack but chose a swim in the pool over lying around resting.

Kara mentioned seeing her later that evening at Pinewood before she left.

Kara awoke the following morning to find a bright, blue, cloudless sky. Sunshine was streaming through her window as she hurried to get dressed. Pulling on a pair of jeans and a sleeveless cotton top, she found herself actually singing with delight. Today was her wedding day. Running a quick brush through her hair and taking enough time to put on her makeup, Kara was soon on her way to Rob's. It was not even eight o'clock yet, and she was dressed and out of the house, quite an accomplishment for her.

Knowing Rob would be up, but not so sure about his mother, Kara knocked lightly on the kitchen door. Rob planned to work half a day, so she expected him to be dressed already and downstairs. Just when she was about to try the doorknob, the door swung open wide.

"Kara, you're just in time for breakfast," Kathy Phillips greeted her with her usual cheerful smile.

When she stepped inside, she was overcome by the delicious smells. Already on the table were sausage, bacon, biscuits, hash browns, pancakes, coffee, and a wide assortment of jellies, jams, and syrup. There was enough food for a dozen people, and Kathy had returned to the stove to oversee something still in the oven.

Rob entered moments later but did not seem too surprised to see such a feast laid out on the table. He looked impressed but not in the least surprised.

"Good morning," he greeted them both with a smile. His mother walked by him on her way to the table with a fluffy Spanish omelet and extended her cheek for a kiss before announcing everything was ready.

Before they all sat down, Rob went to Kara and

placed a warm kiss on her lips, sending tiny shivers of delight down her spine. "Today's the day," he whispered close to her ear. "You'll finally be mine again."

She kept that tingling feeling of his breath against her cheek with her for the rest of the day while she and Kathy worked to get everything ready. She set out the elaborate candelabra as soon as they arrived. Kathy helped her place the tables out on the patio and covered them with lovely cloths of silk and white lace.

Because Redwood and Princess refused to behave and constantly kept getting in the way, Kara finally had to take them over to her house and leave them in the backyard with plenty to eat in order to get them out of her way. Kathy promised to see to the dogs' needs while they were gone on their honeymoon.

By the time Rob came home at one, the backyard was almost finished. The large arrangements of assorted yellow flowers on tall golden stands had been delivered from the florist and had been placed on either side of the two main candelabra to be part of the backdrop for the ceremony. The smaller arrangements of varied yellow flowers and white sprays of forget-me-nots had been centered on each of the tables.

After a quick lunch Rob set to work rigging a small floodlight in a nearby tree to shine down on the area where they would speak their vows. Kara and his mother began preparing the large trays of food. By four o'clock everything had been done except for picking up the cake. Rob and Kara went together to get it. When they returned, they found his mother waiting with fresh coffee for Rob and a diet cola over ice for Kara. The three sat down for a brief moment of quiet before Kara had to rush home to get ready.

As promised, Pat arrived promptly at five to help

Kara get dressed. Although Kara knew she could manage by herself, she felt she needed her friend nearby. Kara was as nervous as she had been that first time. For a moment, she was drawn back in time. Her emotions had been a mess that day. She'd been anxious and scared at the same time. One minute she was laughing about something one of her girlfriends had said and the next moment she was crying over something that was mentioned. She also remembered how her father could never be found whenever he was needed and the fact that he was already late arriving today made Kara even more nervous.

By seven forty-five Kara and Pat were ready and anxiously glancing at the clock. Now not only was Kara's father late, Clint was, too. They were seriously considering going on without their escorts when the doorbell finally rang. Rushing to open it, Kara wondered if she would find Clint or her father on the other side. To her relief, she found them both.

"I had a little car trouble. The car died just blocks the other side of the restaurant and would not start again," her father began explaining immediately. "Rather than trouble you on such an important day, I walked to the restaurant to phone a garage for help. Clint was just leaving when I walked up and luckily he volunteered his assistance. It took him awhile to diagnose the trouble. Seems my electronic module bit the dust. But because it was getting so late, we decided to wait until tomorrow to replace it."

"Won't take five minutes to replace it once we find one," Clint put in reassuringly. "The old one pulls out easily and a new one plugs right in."

"Anyway, I'm having it towed over here," Edison went on to say. "Since Clint still had to change and time was already running out, I went ahead and dressed over there. Just show me where to dump my suitcase and we're ready to go."

Since the four of them decided to travel together, they wisely chose Clint's Olds 98 over Pat's MG and Kara's Vette. During the drive across town, Clint seemed to hit only red lights, and no matter which lane he moved into, it was the slowest. They were due to arrive at eight but were a good ten minutes late when they finally pulled to a stop in front of Rob's house.

Kathy Phillips rushed out of the house to greet them, having been beside herself with worry. Rob was out on the patio talking with his secretary Paula and her escort Darran. Rob was handsomely dressed in a camel-colored suit with a dark brown vest. He seemed calm and very self-assured as he led in the conversation. He smiled and politely excused himself when he spotted his beautiful bride-to-be coming through the patio door. He stood staring down at her a moment, drinking in the beauty he saw before him.

Kara wore an off-white, floor-length gown with a simple row of lace edging the low neckline. The silky fabric gathered just below her breasts to accent her slim figure, then flared in soft lines to the floor. Her hair was especially full with sprigs of forget-me-nots woven carefully into the curls surrounding her face. Rob was not really sure how, but he felt she looked far lovelier and more radiant than she had for that first wedding over seven years ago.

"Thought you had changed your mind," he finally said with a wink, not in the least angry, then turned to greet the other three. Leading them all over to where Paula and Darran were still standing, Rob made formal introductions all around.

The next to arrive was Jane Haught and her always-reluctant husband. Jane had been in Kara's photography class and had been the first one Kara had thought of when they had decided to have a photographer present. Kara liked Jane's work. In fact, she had been almost jealous of her unusual creativity when it came to photography. Jane breezed in wearing a loose creation of chiffon and around her neck she wore a 35MM camera. "It's what all the in-crowd wears," she had said laughingly when Kara had made a comment about her neckwear.

At 8:20 the Reverend Lanagan arrived and everything looked as if it would go on as scheduled. Rob's mother had discreetly managed to light all the candles without much notice, and as the sun settled behind the thick trees surrounding them, Rob and Kara were married again in the sight of God, their parents, and their closest friends.

Chapter Eleven

After the simple exchanging of vows, Rob and Kara's wedding guests were invited to help themselves to the many platters of food. Champagne was opened and flowed freely as many toasts were made. Clint and Pat were quieter than usual, exchanging tender glances. Their thoughts were on a similar event to happen soon. It was Rob's mother and Kara's father that kept the party lively. Edison was forever telling jokes and Kathy never failed to see the humor in them. Even Paula and Darran had finally relaxed among all these strangers and were joining in the merriment.

Kara and Rob did all the traditional things brides and grooms were supposed to do. They cut the cake and exchanged first bites; they graciously smiled through wave after wave of ridiculous toasts; and Kara turned and flipped the bridal bouquet over her shoulder. To Paula's delight and Darran's consternation, the bouquet flew right to the pretty blonde secretary. All the while Jane was continuously snapping her camera and advancing her film.

Just before midnight Rob and Kara eagerly made their departure amid a shower of rice and good wishes. An hour later the Blazer—with "Just Married" and "Just Remarried" written across every window in bold white letters—was headed along the winding, narrow park road that made its way down a wooded hillside. The headlights gave them only a glimpse of the thick majestic woodlands that closely surrounded them. In the midst of all this bountiful parkland, Cabin Three lay nestled on a tiny hill among many tall stately pines and sweet gums. Once the rangers had learned of the situation, they had made certain that Cabin Three was available.

Beautiful memories greeted them when they pulled up to the rustic little cabin made of dark, rough, wood planking. Quickly they unloaded only the suitcases and boxes they knew they would need that night and stacked them into a pile to be taken inside. They realized it would take several trips and decided not to try foolishly to take everything in at once. Although electricity was now available, they had chosen against using the lights and entered the small cabin by the dim glow of the lantern Kara carried. Putting down the first of the boxes from the Blazer, Rob swept Kara up in his arms and carried her across the threshold, causing her to squeal out in delightful surprise and almost making her drop the lantern.

After a bit of complaining and a lot of demanding, Kara was able to convince him to set her down so she could help make this place more comfortable. While Rob reluctantly brought in all the boxes and suitcases remaining outside, Kara set to work unrolling one of the mattresses and tucking sheets around it.

The lantern had been centered on a small wooden table, giving off a cozy, warm glow as they worked to get the cabin ready, stopping now and then for a little flirtatious petting that served only to drive them both to distraction. Soon the bed was made with fresh linen, some of the food was stored away in a small cabinet, while some of it was left in boxes to be put away later. Rob had laid open their suitcases for easier access to their clothes. Many of the contents of the huge ice chest had been quickly transferred to the small refrigerator. The ice chest containing only a few soft drinks now sat against the far wall. Towels had been hurriedly pitched into the little bathroom that stood in the middle of the far wall, dividing the large room into two alcoves with a bed in each alcove for semi-privacy should there ever be two couples sharing it.

After having rushed through all of that work, Kara and Rob noticed that the room began to feel stuffy and much warmer inside than it was outside. Rob raised the many windows in the cabin. The windows were small but placed on opposite walls so that a fresh breeze could easily pass through. Knowing that closing the curtains would only reduce the gentle breeze flowing through the windows, Rob decided to leave them open, but to assure their privacy, he walked over and extinguished the lamp on the table. Any further unpacking to be done could wait; Rob had tortured himself long enough.

Just enough moonlight filtered through the windows to allow Rob to easily find his way to his wife. He was reminded of a moonlit night seven years ago when he'd been just as eager and twice as nervous. He moved quietly toward her. Two silhouettes against a soft silvery backdrop became one when he took her into his arms.

"Kara, I love you," he breathed against her cheek while he trailed tender kisses there. "I love you so much and I swear you'll never have reason to want to leave me again."

"And I love you."

"My wife," he growled wickedly. "My beautiful, sexy wife, I love you almost more than I can bear."

Her response to his words came in the form of a delighted sigh. Gently bending her head back, she exposed her neck to his tantalizing kisses. A sweet burning sensation rippled through her when his lips touched the sensitive areas along the nape of her neck, his mouth sliding to the delicate hollow of her throat.

She felt herself eagerly yielding to his feathery touch. Her eyes grew heavy with passion as his head bent down and his scorching kisses searched for more intimate areas. Her hands went to caress his neck, then slipped upward to become entangled in the waves of his thick, blond hair. She was only vaguely aware that his fingers had moved to her zipper but was very much aware when the soft fabric fell away from her shoulders and drifted to the floor in a crumpled heap.

He released her bra with a practiced hand and his mouth sought one sensitive peak, then the other. Kara felt her need for her husband growing to unbearable heights when he eased her other lacy undergarments to the floor. Lifting her up out of the pile of discarded clothes, he carried her the few steps to their bed. Kara desperately wanted to feel the splendor of his body next to hers. Having already removed his jacket when they had first entered, all she needed to do was unbutton the shirt, unbuckle his belt, release the fastener of his pants, and ease down the zipper. In a very few moments he was just as naked as she was and just as eager.

Delighting in the feel of his hard body when he eased down on top of her, she let out a soft moan of pleasure. But the moan soon became more impatient and more demanding as he continued to work his magic on her. He bent his head and began making a slow circumnavigation of her breasts. Kara arched forward when his moist tongue finally moved in to flick and caress each hardened nipple. She breathed deeply his scent of cologne and excitement. Rob moaned as she pressed his face to her breast, encouraging him more. Kara quivered, thinking she could not bear any more of this sweet torture. She grew impatient to feel her husband inside her and began to pull him up, meeting his mouth with hers once again. They united and both were consumed with the wonder of their love for one another until finally they reached the ultimate height of their passions, until it eventually gave way to extreme satisfaction.

Pulling the sheet up over the both of them, they lay peacefully in each other's arms, marveling at the contentment and fulfillment they now felt. Those five years had not hindered their lovemaking in any way. It was still as wonderful and exciting as ever, maybe even more so.

Kara was the first to fall asleep in the warm comfort of Rob's arms. When he realized she was no longer awake, he tilted his head at an awkward angle in order to gaze down at her a moment. The moonlight created a wondrous aura around her, making him more aware of her special beauty. Her dark curls fanned out across the small pillow and her long dark lashes twitched slightly as she slept. By the gentle half-smile he was made aware of how sweet those dreams must be. With a loving smile of his own, he bent over just enough to be able to lightly touch his lips to her forehead without waking her. Gently, he lay back down, placing his head next to hers on the pillow.

"I love you," he sighed one last time before falling asleep.

Kara was first to wake up the next morning. Wanting to surprise her husband with an acceptable breakfast, she slowly eased out of bed, slipping out from under the arm he had draped over her waist. Quietly

she put on a pair of cutoffs, a tank top, and her tennis
shoes before going outside in search of the charcoal.
There was a stove inside the cabin, but she was afraid
she might wake him if she used it and spoil her
chances of surprising him. She decided to cook over
the open grill outside, but she needed to find the charcoal. Gathering firewood inside the park was not per-
mitted.

She finally found a large sack of self-starting bri-
quettes in the back of the truck under several other
things. With some difficulty she managed to unload the
sack by herself.

After filling the small rock-and-mortar fire grill with
an ample amount of charcoal, she began searching for
matches. They were not in the back of the truck, and
there were not any in the glove compartment. She
would have to go back inside and search the boxes and
chance waking Rob.

Carefully she tiptoed back into the cabin and gently
began to unpack the boxes, item by item, until she
found a large box of kitchen matches in the second
box. Gathering up the coffee pot and coffee and stopping by the ice chest for a diet cola, she snuck back
outside, got water from the nearby hydrant, and soon
had fresh coffee perking over the open fire.

She slipped back inside and got a pan, a spatula, and
enough bacon and eggs for their breakfast. Noticing a
loaf of bread, she picked it up, too, trying not to rattle
the plastic wrapper when she did. Kara felt very proud
of herself as she cooked the bacon over the grill. Not
only had she managed to go in and out of the cabin
several times without waking Rob but she was cooking
over an open fire for the first time and it was turning
out just fine. Rob had done the cooking during the first
honeymoon because Kara did not have the slightest

idea where to begin. Now her bacon was turning a light, crispy brown just the way Rob liked it.

Slipping the spatula under several pieces and lifting them, she suddenly realized she had not thought to get anything to put the cooked food on. Turning to hurry inside the house for a paper plate, she was startled to find Rob only a few feet away, leaning against the cabin doorframe, watching her.

Feeling a little embarrassed at having found him watching her, she demanded to know how long he had been standing there.

"Long enough to see what a domestic you've become, cooking breakfast no less," he grinned, his dimples deepening.

Realizing her bacon was still browning and soon would start to burn along the edges, she ordered him inside for paper plates. To her relief Rob did not poke fun at her for having overlooked getting something to put the cooked food on. Instead he worked with her to get their breakfast ready. He watched the eggs while she ran back inside to get margarine for toast. As soon as the eggs were ready, Rob poured off the bacon grease and they made toast by slowly frying it in the pan over the fire.

After a hearty breakfast they decided to take a long nature hike through the beautiful park woodlands. They walked along at a slow, leisurely pace, stopping to admire the abundance of wildflowers that grew wherever the trees allowed them enough room. Kara wished she could pick a colorful assortment of black-eyed Susans, coral paintbrush, honeysuckle, asters, and wild lilies, but dared not, knowing it was against park rules. Occasionally she bent over to see if a particular flower had an inviting scent or not and was rarely disappointed.

They took all the time they needed to explore the natural surroundings. They took time to breathe and to appreciate the moist coolness provided by the dense mixture of pines, oaks, sweet gums, dogwoods, hickories, chinquapins, and cottonwoods. Where the trees were the thickest, they walked on a deep carpet of dried pine needles and crushed leaves. They stopped to watch a reluctant bullfrog hop across a shallow area in a small, slow-moving creek.

Walking at such a slow pace gave them a chance to talk about nothing in particular and everything that happened to cross their minds. At that particular moment they hadn't a care in the world because they once again had each other.

After having explored several hills and wooded ravines, they emerged from the woods and headed for the small recreational lake that was the focal point of the park. Realizing it was well after noon, but not wanting to have to return to the cabin just yet, they lunched on potato chips and soft drinks at the snack bar.

The day was rapidly growing hotter and from the bench on which they had chosen to rest while they ate, they could see several people enjoying themselves in the water. There was a small platform built in the middle of the small lake where sun worshippers could tan or where the more energetic could climb to different levels and dive into the deep water. After their long hike the cool blue water reflecting the dense growth of trees along the far shoreline certainly looked inviting. Suddenly the walk back to the cabin did not seem so bad and they both hurried to get into their swimsuits. Slipping a terry top over her bikini and grabbing a couple of large fluffy towels, Kara was the first to leave the cabin but waited for Rob before heading back to the swimming area. All Rob had bothered to put on was a pair of faded cutoffs and jogging shoes. As they descended the grassy knoll leading to the lake, he kicked off the shoes and broke into a run. Once the water was up to his thighs, he plunged in head first.

Kara had stopped long enough to remove the top and lay their towels down on a large flat rock near the narrow sandy shore. Searching the water, she finally spotted Rob, shoulder-deep, waiting for her. Running into the water, she gasped aloud. The water was colder than she had expected, having become accustomed to Rob's warm pool. By the time the water was up to her thighs, she had slowed to a walk and when she was waist-deep, she was barely moving at all.

"Come on, it's not that cold," Rob laughed.

"It's cold enough," she complained, standing on tiptoe and stretching to keep as much of her as she could out of the water.

"You'll get used to it," he assured her. "Just dive in and get the initial shock of it over with." When she looked skeptical, he dove in and came back up smiling. "See, I'm used to it already. It doesn't bother me anymore."

"Yeah, lady, it's only cold for a second or two," a young boy, about twelve years old, put in as he pushed his long wet hair away from his eyes. He twisted up his face in disgust and shook his head, remarking, "Girls are such sissies." Then the boy dove into the water and disappeared from sight.

Kara was unable to resist sticking her tongue out at the ripple of water where the boy had just stood.

"Yeah, lady, girls are such sissies," Rob said in a high voice, mimicking the little boy. Then heading in her direction, he narrowed his devilish eyes. "I guess I'm going to have to help you through this situation and see that you get wet."

"Don't you dare, Rob Phillips," she squealed, backing away from him. "Stay away from me."

Rob continued to come at her like a menacing creature from the sea. His gleaming wet shoulders grew out of the water as he came ever closer.

"Rob, don't," she stammered, still trying to back away. She tried her best to hurry back to shore, but the water would not let her, causing her to lose her balance. With very little grace she fell backward into the cold water she had so hoped to avoid and disappeared from sight. When her head broke the surface, all she could hear over her own sharp intake of air was Rob's deep throaty laughter.

"I guess you didn't need my help after all. You managed to get yourself wet just fine."

Her initial reaction had been to try to wipe that silly grin off his handsome face, but she could easily see the humor in it and broke out laughing, too.

Rob had been right. Within minutes, Kara was used to the cold. After that, she was able to go in and out of the water with no problem. Only after she had collapsed from near exhaustion on the platform to relax and sunbathe awhile did the cold water once again pose a threat.

She and Rob swam for hours, sometimes playing, sometimes exploring the underwater world of the small lake, and many times relaxing on the platform or along the grassy shoreline. Rob was first to wonder if it was almost suppertime. Trying to judge the hour by the low position of the sun, he guessed that it was around six, earlier than he usually ate, but he was especially hungry. Kara frowned at his suggestion to return to the cabin to eat. She had just spotted a couple at the bend in the lake riding around in a small paddleboat and now wanted to go around the lake in the paddleboats. She She was not the least bit interested in eating yet.

Promising they would do that first thing in the morning, Rob convinced her he would soon grow weak from hunger if they did not do something about it right away. Reluctantly Kara gathered their things and they trudged back to the cabin. By the time they had changed into dry clothes and Rob had put two large steaks on the grill, she realized she was more than just a little hungry herself.

Once the sun had eased down behind the trees, the ninety-degree midday heat gave way to a cool breeze and settled into the comfortable seventies. Rob tied a hammock between two sturdy trees and they lay comfortably in each other's arms and listened to the melody of the approaching evening. Crickets had begun to chirp, frogs to croak. Some birds sang happy tunes while others called to their mates. Whispering along in soft accompaniment to nature's symphony was the evening breeze gently rustling through the thick leaves and pine needles overhead. There was a peaceful harmony in the nocturnal sounds of nature.

Kara could not imagine anyone being any happier than she was at that very moment, snuggled safely in the arms of the man she loved, her husband. She wished the moment would last forever. Neither one of them said a word to express the happiness they felt. Neither had to.

The next morning, Rob kept his promise. The first thing they did after breakfast was head for the pier at the far end of the lake. It was still early and not many people were around so they had their choice of paddleboats. Pushing down hard on the pedals, Kara and Rob got the little paddlewheel on the back of the boat to move. As they left the pier, a trio of fat white geese swam over to see if there were any prospects of a few tasty handouts. When all they received was Kara's poor apology, they turned and swam away, complaining to each other as they went. She shouted out behind them that she would make it up to them later, already having decided to have a picnic near the lake for lunch.

All too soon the day came to an end and it was time for them to leave the cabin and the wooded park. They packed with less enthusiasm than they had unpacked Friday night. It was almost dark by the time they stopped by the ranger's station and let her know they were leaving. For some reason that Kara could not explain, she felt an impending doom as they pulled out of the park and onto the highway. She couldn't explain it; it was an eerie feeling.

But no dreaded disasters occurred. They arrived home safely and found Rob's house, their home, still standing when they got there. Yet Kara still felt uneasy.

When they entered the house through the door going from the garage to the kitchen, they were surprised to see the table in the small kitchen alcove set for two. The table was graced with Rob's finest china and crystal on a white silk tablecloth. Two long, tapered candles sat in tall silver candlesticks with a cigarette lighter waiting beside them. One of the floral arrangements from the wedding sat between the candles. On the table were several notes: three in Rob's mother's neat handwriting and one in her father's burly scrawl.

Picking up the notes, Kara read them aloud. "'Dear Mr. and Mrs. Phillips,'"Kara began, then smiled. This was the one in her father's not-so-legible handwriting. She had always told him he should have become a doctor since he certainly wrote like one. "'You will find your dinner already prepared and waiting in the refrigerator. Just follow the directions taped to each dish to warm it. We wanted your first night home to be special.'"

"We?" Rob interrupted.

Shrugging, Kara continued. "'Light the candles and

enjoy yourselves. Since Kathy had such a long drive ahead of her and hates to drive it alone, and since I could use a little time off, I've decided to make the trip with her. We will leave my car in Dallas and travel together from there. I'll catch a plane home, probably by next weekend. I'll call from Colorado. Enjoy the meal. Love to both of you, Dad.'"

Kara raised her eyes from the paper to meet Rob's. They stared in astonishment at each other for a moment then at the paper again.

"You don't suppose," Rob began, doubtfully. "You don't actually suppose that your father and my mom ... no, not those two."

"You never know," Kara shrugged. "Stranger things have happened."

Rob blinked a few times, then shook his head as if dismissing the idea and repeated, "No, not those two."

Handing him the note to read for himself, Kara began to read the next message. "This one's from your mom. It says that some of my furniture is in the garage, but most of it has been put to use. She hopes we like the changes they've made."

"They?" he questioned curiously.

"I guess Dad stayed to help her."

Glancing down at the next note, Kara was able to announce that his mother and her father had brought the dogs back and had put them in the backyard with enough food to last them until Monday morning.

"The way Redwood devours food, I'd better check on them before I go to bed," Rob chuckled, then wanted to know, "What does that last note say?"

When Kara looked down to read the brief message, she had the same uneasy feeling she'd had earlier. "Rob, Maria called. Wants you to call her as soon as possible."

"Hope her mother's not any worse," Rob commented as he headed for the door. "Why don't you see about the food while I make the call. I'll unload the truck in a minute."

"Where are you going?" she asked, wondering why he could not use the kitchen phone.

"The numbers she left me are upstairs," he explained over his shoulder just before he disappeared.

Kara's shoulders sagged as she walked over toward the refrigerator. She wished he would make the call from the kitchen so she would be able to hear at least his end of the conversation. There was still a nagging doubt where Maria was concerned. When she passed the phone, she realized how easy it would be to gently lift the receiver and listen to both sides of the conversation. If it was just a call concerning her mother, it would certainly ease Kara's mind to know it. And by the tone of Maria's voice she would be able to satisfy herself that the relationship between the two was strictly the platonic friendship Rob had claimed it to be. It would be nice to be certain.

Watching the door Rob had disappeared through, Kara waited by the phone until he'd had enough time to walk upstairs, get the numbers, and place the call. Slowly placing her hand on the phone, she began wondering if she had the right to listen in. Her conscience began to warn her not to lift up the receiver. She should not doubt Rob because she really had no reason to. Not this time.

Kara removed her hand with the thought that she must trust her husband. If she did not believe in him, she never should have remarried him. Nodding firmly, she decided she did trust him and turned away from the phone to start getting the food ready, but she only took two steps before she froze. She trusted Rob, but did she trust Maria? Remembering the defiant smirk the woman had flashed at the restaurant, she knew she did not trust her. Should she reconsider listening in? Shouldn't she know if the woman was up to something? While she was still fighting her conscience on this one, Rob returned.

"Well, what goodies did they leave us?" he wanted to know, looking around for a clue.

"Huh?" He'd caught her so deeply in thought that she had heard his voice, but not what he had said to her.

"Where's the food?"

"Still in the refrigerator." When he looked slightly perplexed at her, she explained, "I guess I got lost in a daydream. I'm sorry; I'll get it out now."

"I guess new brides are entitled to a few daydreams," he smiled, stepping over to take her into his arms. "Even if it is the second time around, you are a new bride. My new bride."

Kara felt a little guilty when he held her close and rocked her lovingly in his arms. She had to stop being so jealous of the woman before it caused trouble in their marriage. She hoped she could get over the uneasy feelings and worry she had about Rob's beautiful blond partner—and soon.

"While you get that food ready, I think I'll go ahead and unload the truck," he said, finally breaking away.

He walked out while Kara went to examine the contents of the refrigerator. On the shelf she found four covered dishes with little notes taped to the lids. The notes just explained how long each needed to reheat in the microwave oven. As she raised the lids, she discovered sirloin tips in a dark sauce, green peas with tiny onions, corn in a cheese and pepper sauce, and a small fresh-peach cobbler.

Minutes later she had warmed the meat and peas and was waiting for the corn to finish when Rob came through carrying their suitcases. She wondered if he had made the call to Maria or not. He hadn't mentioned it. By the time he had taken the suitcases upstairs and returned, Kara was putting everything on the table and had decided to simply ask him. But when she opened her mouth to ask, he was already talking.

"Since you're taking the week off, do you mind waiting until tomorrow and unpacking all our stuff?"

"No, I'll be glad to," she replied, letting the question wait. "Shouldn't take too long."

"Well, I wasn't too sure. I know how you hate to unpack," he grinned. "You'd just as soon have your teeth pulled."

Kara looked at him with a raised brow, wondering if he'd just insulted her or not. But she knew it was the truth.

"And if you don't like where Mom has put things, or if you want to redecorate in any way, feel free to make any changes your heart desires," he said once they had sat down to eat. "This is your home now and I want you to be happy with it. And if you don't like some of the furniture, you can replace it with your own or go out and buy brand new pieces. Whatever you want. And since Clint has insisted you go ahead and take a week off, you might as well spend it getting this place exactly as you want it."

Kara's eyes lit up at the prospect of having the freedom to put a little of herself into their home. She delighted at the idea. "There are a few changes I would like to make," Kara said.

"I can imagine you have lots of changes in mind," he commented with a smile. "Buy anything you think necessary, but just don't go for broke in doing so."

Kara's mind was already filling his empty counter-space with glass canisters, a wooden bread box, a matching spice rack, and maybe a utensil rack. She decided to start with the kitchen and go from there. She could hardly wait to get started.

"Just promise to leave my study alone. I like it just the way it is," he stated adamantly.

Kara promised, knowing he kept the door to it shut anyway.

"Good. Everyone's always wanting to change it. Mom wants to get all my broken trophies out of there, and Maria hates my old scarred-up desk, but that was my father's desk and it stays."

"Maria?" Kara asked, not especially fond of the idea that the woman had seen his study, the room he was so particular about.

"Yes, Maria likes ultra-modern and detests my study. She hates even to go in there."

"Then why does she?" Kara asked, thinking the solution should be simple. Keep Maria out of there.

"Occasionally I bring work home to the study and then forget to take it back. Sometimes Maria has to come over and get the things I neglected to return to the office," Rob explained. "And then there are times when we have to put in a little extra time on a project. We usually do it over here unless we need access to the computer. No interruptions that way. You'll find out that Maria is a workaholic. That's why I wish she would get interested in someone and learn to relax. Life can't be all work. She's been that way ever since Juanita's death. Those two were very close. Now the only time she takes off is either to visit her family or because of an emergency, usually having to do with her family. Like now. But I guarantee that since her mother's better, she will be back at work very soon."

"How do you know her mother's better?"

"I called, remember?" Rob looked at her curiously.

"I didn't think you were gone long enough to have talked with her. The conversation must have been very short."

"It was. I caught her father at her motel room. She was in the shower, so I spoke to him instead. He told me how much better Ruby was doing. In fact they were getting ready to go out to eat. They've been living on hospital food until now, and since her mother is doing so much better, they were going to get a decent meal."

"What did he think about our having gotten married again?" she asked casually.

"I didn't mention it."

"What? Why not?"

"I didn't think about it," he shrugged.

Kara couldn't help but wonder if Rob was delaying telling Maria on purpose. It was hard to imagine that he just did not think about it. "But don't you think Maria would want to know?"

"I really think she has enough on her mind right now. Besides, she'll know soon enough," he reasoned. "And she will probably be more than a little upset when she does. She will hate it that she missed the wedding, and be a little angry about it, no doubt. Just don't let it worry you. I'll explain why we did not call her and tell her, as soon as she gets back home. She'll get over it."

"Oh, I won't let it worry me," Kara promised, knowing she was not going to lose any sleep over Maria's disappointment. It made her feel better that Rob did not seem very concerned either. Besides, she had too many important things to think about to dwell on anything so trivial. If Maria decided to be insulted because they did not change their wedding plans to in-

clude her, let her. Kara had a beautiful house to redecorate, plus endless crates and boxes to unpack again. She
would be blissfully busy for quite a while. In fact she
wondered where she was going to put everything. She
had a horrible feeling she was going to have to give up
her pack-rat ways and actually get rid of some of the
things she'd held onto for so many years.

To her surprise, when she went looking for all those
crates and boxes the next morning, she found only the
few boxes they had brought back from their honeymoon. Upon further investigation she found out Rob's
mother and her father must have unpacked everything
themselves. Her dishes were in the cabinets along with
Rob's, and her pans had been placed beside his. Inside
the walk-in pantry she discovered her appliances and
miscellaneous items sitting neatly on shelves.

Later when she examined linen closets and bathroom cabinets, she found all of her things mixed with
his. With only a fraction of the work she had thought
she would have, it only took a little over an hour to
unpack. Soon she had their honeymoon things put
away. By midmorning she was ready to start redecorating. The kitchen was too bare, so she made lists of what
she wanted to add. The living room was too crowded
now that much of her own furniture had been squeezed
in, and she made notes of what she wanted removed.
Taking the rooms one by one, she wrote down the
changes she had in mind for each.

She planned no major changes for their bedroom.
Rob's surprise had been that he'd had their old brass
bed moved into his room and the huge king-size bed
was now in the guest room. He had even kept the cro-
cheted bedspread they had used so many years ago.
The dark pine furniture was different but its rustic
beauty suited her just fine and the deep gold drapes

blended nicely with the carpet and the braided rug that lay across the large brick hearth of the fireplace. She liked the colors and the antique look and had absolutely no desire to change it.

When Rob came home at one for a quick bite to eat, he found her upstairs in the guest bathroom writing in her notepad. She stopped what she was doing long enough to prepare a light lunch for them both but was right back to making notations just as soon as he had left.

Tuesday she began eliminating everything she'd decided had to go. What she absolutely could not give up, she stored in the attic; the rest she put in the garage until they could decide what to do with it. She spent the day making endless trips to the garage. Some of the heavier pieces of furniture had to stay where they were until Rob came home, whether she liked it or not.

Wednesday Kara began shopping for some of the things on her lists and made arrangements for someone to come in the following week and wallpaper the bathroom. By lunchtime she had only marked through a third of the items on her lists and had made two trips home to unload the car. She and Rob met at a cafeteria near his office for lunch and she eagerly told him of all the wonderful treasures she'd bought. He found her enthusiasm delightful.

By the end of the day, Kara had only a few items left on her list and had begun to unpackage what she'd bought and put a few of the items where she wanted them.

Rob sent Walt and Wade, two teenage boys who worked in one of his auto parts stores, over on Thursday morning to help her with some of the heavy work. She'd had her doubts when she had opened the door to find a set of twins grinning at her. They weren't much bigger than she was, but they were willing to work and amazed her by the loads they managed to carry.

By Friday it was a matter of putting everything exactly where she wanted and cleaning each room as she finished. She was busy vacuuming the living room carpet when she thought she heard a door. Turning off the machine, she listened. Someone was in the house. It could not be Rob, who had gone out of town for the afternoon and was not due back until late. Wondering if she should pick up something to use as a weapon, she went to see who it was.

"Rob," she heard a very feminine voice call out. "Rob, darling, are you here?"

"No, he's not," Kara called back, imitating Maria's lofty singsong voice. She was irritated that this woman had barged into their home uninvited.

When they met in the living room doorway, Maria's emerald eyes sparked with anger. "What are you doing here?" she demanded sharply, placing her hands firmly on her shapely hips.

Kara was furious that she had dared use such a waspish tone with her. Her temper flared and she did little to hide it. "I live here. What are *you* doing here?"

Maria's eyes grew wide as she glanced around her. She noted the new furniture and wall decorations. Only a few of the pieces did she recognize as Rob's. "How dare you try to wheedle your way back into Rob's life!"

"I don't wheedle," Kara retorted triumphantly, knowing her next words were razor sharp. "It was Rob who did all the wheedling, if anyone did. He's the one who decided we should get married again." Kara watched as all the color seemed to drain from Maria's lovely face. Then sounding not too sincere, she added, "It's too bad you missed the ceremony. It was quite lovely. Rob really wanted you there to witness it since you are so much like a sister to him."

"You're already married?" Maria gasped, her hand going to her throat while her green eyes quickly sought the telltale wedding ring.

"Until death us do part."

"How can Rob be such a fool?" she spat, then turned on her heel and stalked back down the hall toward the kitchen. Kara hated how gracefully Maria moved even when angry.

"You never told me what you wanted," Kara shouted after her.

Maria stopped suddenly, turning to glare at Kara. Her narrow nostrils flared and her lips tightened when she gave her simple reply.

"Rob!" was all she said, then stormed out of the house.

Chapter Twelve

Still working in the living room, Kara was vigorously rubbing the coffee table with furniture polish, working off the frustration and anger Maria's visit had caused, when the phone rang.

Hoping it was Rob, Kara got up and hurried to answer it. She wanted to tell him just how his dear "friend" had treated her earlier.

"Hello?"

"Hi, Kara, it's me," Rob said in his usual cheerful voice.

"You're back early," she remarked curiously.

"Yes, I got back about thirty minutes ago. I'd be home by now, but I've been talking to Maria." Kara's stomach tightened as he continued, "I was right. She was pretty upset about the wedding."

"I know," Kara said in a flat tone. She wondered just what Maria had told him.

"Oh, you're the one that told her. What did she do, stop by the house for something?"

"Yes," Kara replied sharply, remembering just what that something was Maria wanted. "She was here earlier this afternoon."

"Then you know how upset she was to find out about the wedding."

"Yes, she made that very clear."

"I explained why we did not invite her or even tell her about it. We knew she would be too concerned over her mother's illness to worry about attending a wedding, but she still seemed pretty upset."

"I don't doubt it," Kara commented, knowing the woman had been in a furor the last time she'd seen her.

"But I told her I wanted to make it up to her and invited her to supper tomorrow night," he said sounding as if he had solved a major problem.

"You what?" she cried out over the phone.

"Invited her to supper tomorrow," he repeated, then asked, "That is all right, isn't it?"

"No! I'm not ready to entertain yet. The house isn't ready. Rob, please say you didn't."

"I did," he told her sheepishly. "I didn't think you'd mind. You seemed to have the house well in hand."

"Well, I don't. Most of the house is still a mess," she complained, wishing he would tell her this was all a joke.

"How about if I stop off and get something for supper so you don't have to take time off to cook and then help you get the rooms on the lower floor finished. You don't need to worry about upstairs. There's no reason for her to go up there anyway. Besides, didn't she already see the disorder this afternoon?"

Kara wanted to blurt out the truth. She wanted to tell him that she did not want Maria to come over because she did not like the woman and was terribly jealous of her and that Maria did not seem to care much for her either. She certainly did not want to play hostess to her and have to be hospitable to her. But all that sounded so childish, even to her. Finally, she relented and agreed to have Maria as their guest the next evening.

All the while Kara and Rob worked on the finishing

touches for the rooms on the lower floor, Kara's insides churned. She was apprehensive about how tomorrow's supper would turn out. It was extremely important to her that the food be especially delicious and the house look extra nice. And, of course, she wanted to look her best. She would try to be charming and witty, but above all else, she would show Maria just how happily married she and Rob were.

It was after midnight before she was satisfied enough with the house to stop working and go to bed. Because it was so late when they finally did go to sleep, Rob overslept the next morning and was late leaving for work. Promising only to be gone a few hours, he told Kara he would help her get supper ready when he returned. He wanted to take as much of the burden off her as possible, but she assured him she could handle it.

Kara left the house right after he did to go to the supermarket and buy everything she would need to make the oriental dishes she had planned. She was pulling out the wok and all the pans and utensils she would need when Rob came home that afternoon. He again volunteered his services in the kitchen, but she turned him down again. Kara had to do this herself. She suggested he go for a swim and relax awhile. He would help her best by getting out of her way.

Wanting to serve the food the minute it was done for peak flavor, Kara went ahead and got dressed in a wine-colored jumpsuit carefully fitted to her trim figure and worked with her hair and makeup until they were flawless. Slipping her robe over her outfit, she went back downstairs to start supper. So far everything was going smoothly.

While she cut up the vegetables she planned to stir-fry, she noticed the time. Maria was due to arrive in less than an hour and Rob was still out in the pool. Putting the vegetables aside and picking up a damp cloth to wipe her hands, she rushed outside to tell him it was time for him to get dressed. There was a sharp stab of pain in her stomach when she discovered Maria had already arrived and had joined Rob at the pool. The two of them were sitting in lounge chairs, subtly laughing about something they both found funny.

Rob was the first to notice Kara standing about halfway between the house and the pool. Waving to her, he shouted, "Guess who decided to come on over early."

"Hope you don't mind," Maria said sweetly. "I got ready too early and decided to come on over. Thought maybe I could help you with something." Maria's green eyes swept down briefly, then narrowed with amusement when she commented, "My, don't you look wifely in that robe."

Having forgotten she even had it on, Kara's face burned with embarrassment and anger. How she managed a smile, she was not quite sure. "I'm glad you were concerned enough to want to help, but I have everything under control." She wondered how long she was going to be able to keep her temper under control as well.

"Then I'll just sit out here and keep Rob company," she said, turning her back to Kara.

"It's time for Rob to be getting dressed," Kara put in, not about to be dismissed so easily.

"He looks all right to me," she remarked over her shoulder.

Looking down at his wet swimsuit, Rob offered, "I would like to put on some dry clothes before we eat. I'll be inside in a minute. I just want to make a few more laps in the pool first."

"Just don't take too long,' Kara warned. "Supper

will be ready in about thirty minutes." If she hurried, she might be able to have it on the table in twenty.

Once she was back in the kitchen she yanked off the robe and worked at breakneck speed. The table still had to be set and most of the food had not even been started yet, but she would have it ready when she had claimed she would or die trying. When Rob came through, she was frantically tossing the vegetables about in the wok and trying to keep an eye on the pepper steak and rice that were cooking on the stove.

"Need any help?" he asked, stopping near the stove.

"No," she said adamantly, then ordered him to go change. He was dripping water on the floor and she did not have time to mop.

"Be down in a minute," he smiled, then leaned over and kissed her cheek briefly before heading out of the room.

Kara smiled, concentrating on how warm his lips had felt against her cheek, as she raked the vegetables out of the wok and into a waiting serving bowl.

"Quite a little homebody, aren't you?" she heard a soft sarcastic voice say. Looking up, Kara saw Maria closing the patio door and heading in her direction. The flimsy fabric of her pants outfit flowed as she walked.

"Thank you," Kara replied politely, pretending not to have noticed the sarcasm in Maria's voice. "I try."

"Oh, I bet you do," Maria retorted, glaring at her a moment. Then briskly turning her back, she waltzed on through the kitchen and out the same door Rob had just used.

Although Kara did not really believe Maria would have the audacity to follow Rob up to his room, she hurried all the same to finish getting the meal on the table so she would have a reason to call her back to the kitchen. She preferred to keep this woman in sight.

Soon, Kara came through the door in search of their guest, the pepper steak and rice steaming from the serving platter she held. She found Maria and Rob coming toward her, arm in arm, laughing at a comment he had just made. It irked Kara that they always found something to laugh about.

Kara could not help but wonder if Maria had actually gone upstairs after him, but she did not have the nerve to ask either of them. Forcing a cordial smile, she announced that supper was ready.

Holding out his other arm, Rob hooked onto Kara's arm, turning her and escorting the two women to the small alcove off the kitchen where the steaming hot food waited. Pulling out a chair, he first seated their guest, then helped Kara with her chair. Before reaching for his own chair, he suggested they have wine and went to the refrigerator to get a liter.

"Rob knows how I enjoy wine with my meal," Maria commented, lifting her gaze to meet Kara's. Smiling a little too sweetly, she added, "Rob always keeps a bottle of my favorite."

Matching her mocking smile, Kara replied in a cordial tone, "Yes, Rob has always prided himself on being a good host. He even keeps Redwood's favorite doggie treats on hand."

Maria's smile faded momentarily. Kara could tell she was trying to think of something clever to retort and Kara was delighted the woman seemed to be coming up blank.

Setting three glasses on the table, Rob did not comment on the conflict growing between the two. Pouring the wine, he commented aloud, "Supper certainly smells good."

"Thank you, hon," Kara replied, sounding very affectionate. It took all the restraint she had not to go on to say that it was just a little something she threw together. She did not want to overplay her part as the model little homemaker.

Having filled the stemmed glasses, Rob put the bottle aside and sat down. Lifting the dish with the pepper steak, he held it for Maria to help herself. Kara noted the warm smile Maria produced for him. When Maria took only a couple of spoonfuls, he explained to Kara, "Don't take it personally. She barely ever eats enough to stay alive."

Laughingly Maria added, "That's because I don't want to get fat and ugly. I want to always be pleasing to look at."

"Well, you are that," he claimed with a smile, lifting the vegetables and offering them to her.

Maria looked at Kara to make certain she had caught what Rob had said, then returned her attention to Rob. "I must say, I am jealous of anyone who can eat as much as you and still look like a Greek god."

Kara had had enough of this honey-sweet conversation and decided it was time to butt in and change the subject. "You know Greece would be a nice place to visit. We might consider it for that next honeymoon of ours. What do you think, Rob?"

"Whatever you want," he stated, holding out the pepper steak for her.

"Another honeymoon?" Maria questioned in a cautious voice. Kara could tell the idea did not sit very well with her. She really had not expected it to.

"Originally we'd planned a three-week trip to Europe for our honeymoon," Rob explained as he heaped food onto his plate. "We decided to put it off when we found out your mother had become ill. I did not want to impose on you at such a time."

"I hope you don't expect to take this trip anytime

soon," Maria said worriedly. Placing her fork down and giving her full attention to Rob, she hurried on to say, "I'm too far behind in my work. Mother's illness really threw me off. I've got dozens of bills that need to be paid, new accounts to process, billings were supposed to go out Friday, we've got two gas pumps down, and there's a water drainage problem at that new site over on McCann Road. You just can't run off and leave me now, Rob. You just can't!"

Reaching out for and taking one of her hands in his, Rob patted it gently. "Calm down, Maria. You know I wouldn't leave you in a bind. It will probably be the end of summer before we can make the trip anyway. Kara has promised her father she will continue to be hostess at Pinewood until they can find a replacement, and she is supposed to be in a friend's wedding next month. We certainly won't be able to leave until after that. You have plenty of time to catch up, and you know I'm always willing to do whatever I can to help you."

"The end of summer?" she asked. Her frown lifted a little and her free hand, which had tightened into a fist, slowly relaxed. "I hope I can get all caught up by then. You know that summer is our busiest season and I am hopelessly behind."

"Just tell me what to do and I'll help you get caught up. With Kara still working evenings for a while, I'll be able to put in a few extra hours with no problem," he continued to reassure her.

Kara wanted to protest but could not think of a good reason that did not make her sound like a jealous wife or a selfish brat. After all Rob was right. She was not going to be home in the evenings for a while. It did seem reasonable that he could spend that time working if he was needed. The idea was a sound one.

"I really could use your help," Maria admitted in a

coy voice, looking up at him through lowered lashes. "You know how I hate to be behind in my duties."

"I know and if given half a chance, you would run yourself ragged trying to get it all done," Rob had gone on to say. Letting go of Maria's hand, he picked up his fork and resumed eating. Looking up between bites, he noticed Kara's look of concern. "You don't mind if I put in a few extra hours at work to help out Maria, do you?"

"No," Kara lied and attempted a pleasant smile. "Just don't overdo it."

"I'll watch him very closely and make sure he doesn't overwork himself," Maria promised, sounding most sincere.

"You just let me know what you want me to do," Rob told her just before helping himself to more pepper steak and abruptly changing the subject.

Maria took Rob at his word and was quick to take advantage of it. She called Sunday night to ask if he would go with her to City Hall the next morning and see if they could get something done about the drainage problem on McCann Road. Rob agreed to go as soon as he had made his morning phone calls.

Knowing a trip of that sort to City Hall could end up taking most of the day, Rob cancelled his plans with Kara. They were to have lunch at Pinewood since Kara always went in early on Mondays. Instead he planned to have Paula get him something to eat in his office when he got back. He then promised to come by Pinewood for supper after he was finished at work to make up for having to miss their lunch date.

Kara was not happy with the change in plans, but decided not to complain. It would only put a strain on him and that was not at all what she wanted to do. She would just have to make it through the day without seeing his smiling face. After having taken off a week herself, she had a lot of work to occupy her time until that evening. For Rob's sake and the sake of their new marriage, she would simply grin and bear it.

By midafternoon, Kara was looking forward to seeing Rob. The later in the day it became, the more she thought of her handome husband and the less interested she became in work. Since Monday evenings were usually rather slow, she felt she would be able to dine with Rob with very few interruptions. Just the thought of it kept her in good spirits all day. It gave her something to look forward to. When Clint opened the door just after five and leaned inside to tell her Rob was on the phone, she was so eager to hear his voice that her hand sprang for the phone on her desk.

"Hello, darling," she answered in a low, sultry voice.

"Who's this darling character?" Rob demanded loudly, although he really did not sound very concerned.

"Oh, Rob, it's you," she retorted, sounding as if she had expected it to be someone else. "What do you want?"

"I've got what I want," he said, lowering his voice seductively. "The sexiest, most beautiful wife a man could want."

"What you won't say to get a free meal around here," she laughed.

"Well, that is what I called about," he said in a hesitant voice. Suddenly his playful mood turned serious.

"You want to place your order already?" she asked, pretending she had not noticed the change in his voice.

"No, I won't be able to make our supper date after all," he began, then was quick to explain. "It was three thirty before we got back from City Hall and when we walked in, we found poor Paula chin-high in billings. They were really supposed to go out last week, and since our customers don't pay until we bill them, we really need to get them in the mail. I wouldn't feel right leaving Paula and Maria with it, so I'm going to stay and help stuff, stamp, and label envelopes. You understand, don't you?''

"Aren't you going to eat at all?" she asked, avoiding his question. At the moment she did not feel very understanding at all.

'We're going to have some pizza delivered here at the office," he explained. "Paula says it should only take us about four or five hours if we get right on it and don't have any interruptions. We should be through by nine or so. I'll stop by Pinewood on my way home."

Kara was so disappointed that she was afraid she was going to cry if she lingered on the phone long. "Okay, I guess I'll see you then," she said bravely, then added, "I love you."

"I love you, too," he said earnestly before telling her good-bye and hanging up.

Kara tried not to dwell on the fact that Maria was certainly taking advantage of Rob's offer to help. She tried to keep her thoughts on other things, but when Rob had not shown up by ten and did not answer the phone when she called home or the office, she was beginning to feel uneasy. Why hadn't he called? He could have at least been considerate enough to call.

By eleven, when he finally strode through the door, she was past being upset or irritated, she was just plain mad.

"Took longer than you expected, didn't it?" she asked abruptly when he walked over to where she was pouring herself a glass of water from a serving pitcher. She had two aspirin in her hand ready for her mouth.

"A guy called and said he had his gas card stolen and was afraid someone would charge up a lot of gasoline to his account. We had to stop stuffing envelopes and key his account out of the computer. Just when we got the data cleared, he called back and said he found his card on the floorboard of his truck. We had to process him all over again," Rob began to explain, frowning because Kara was questioning him in such a brusque manner.

"And it took two hours to do that?" she asked doubtfully. She did not know much about computers, but it seemed highly unlikely to her. Tossing the two white tablets to the back of her throat, she took several large swallows of water, twisting her face as she tried to get the aspirin to go down. They were as hard to swallow as his excuse.

"Well, it took us about thirty minutes," he replied defensively. "Then we had a guy get his card jammed in one of the pumps over on Oakley Street. He was determined to fit it in sideways. He had it in so tightly that I had to dismantle the thing to get it out." His voice rose as he continued, "Then after I got the card and handed it to the guy, he blamed the pump and cussed me out because he had better things to do with his time. Then on my way back to the office, I actually ran out of gas. I own my own gas stations and I ran out of gas. Luckily Maria and Paula had finished the billings and Maria passed by on her way to the post office. She drove me to get enough gas to get me here. After all that, I walk in here hoping for a few comforting words and you jump all over me for being late!"

Although they were not in the area with the diners, Kara was certain they had heard his tirade. Putting her finger to her lips, she apologized softly, "I'm sorry.

I've just had a very trying day myself. My head hurts and my shoulders ache. I shouldn't take it out on you. I'm sorry.''

Taking the glass out of her hand and setting it on the serving cart beside the pitchers of ice water, he slid his arms around her. "I'm sorry, too. Do you still love me?''

"Of course I do," she chuckled. Rob was putting on his little boy act for her and she loved it.

"I'm sorry I was bad," he continued. "I'll try to do better.''

"Promises, promises," Kara chanted with skepticism. Little did she know, her skepticism was warranted. The next day, just half an hour before he was to meet her for lunch at home, he called and explained that the head of Daniel's Trucking, Jeb Daniels himself, was in his office setting up multiple accounts with them, and it was going to take a couple of hours to process the data and set up the accounts. By then he would be due at a meeting with his main supplier for the auto parts stores. He claimed he would make it up to her somehow and promised to see her that evening at Pinewood. Under no circumstances would he miss having supper with her. He swore she could count on seeing him later. What Kara did not count on was Maria being at his side when he walked in.

Kara had kept a small table for two within sight of the podium vacant so that she could join him when she was not seating guests. The table was not large enough to properly accommodate the three of them, but she was not about to let them have it alone.

"Maria is going to join us for supper," he said casually when they approached the podium. "She was going to work late again, but I convinced her she deserved a break. Since she hasn't had a chance to go to the grocery store lately and her cupboard is bare, I suggested she eat with us."

"I wasn't in the mood to cook anyway," Maria put in. "I'd much rather come here and let someone else do the cooking and have someone wait on me."

For lack of something nice to say, Kara remained silent. She simply gathered a couple of menus and led them toward the small table. Just before she reached it, several guests got up from a larger table just a few feet beyond. Since that table would better accommodate the three of them, she went over and began clearing the table herself. Glancing back at Maria, she silently dared her to say anything about her having to clean tables; but Maria was too engrosed in something Rob was saying to even notice. After she had cleared the table, she had to move it a few feet in order to be able to watch the front where another couple was already waiting. With restrained politeness she interrupted their conversation and asked them to be seated. She placed the menus on the table before she told them, "Decide what you would like to eat. I have to greet those two. I'll be right back."

A steady stream of customers kept Kara busy for almost an hour. When she finally had a chance to return to the table, Rob and Maria were enjoying a liter of rosé wine and each other's company. They did not seem very concerned about the time Kara had spent away from them.

"Are you ready to order?" Kara asked as she sat down to rejoin them.

"We've just been waiting for you, hon," he shrugged, pouring the last of the wine into his glass. "We're ready when you are."

Motioning to Shellie, the waitress who took care of that area, they placed their orders. Kara did not even have time to go with them to the salad bar before she noticed a small group standing at the podium. Telling Rob and Maria not to wait for her, she went back to the podium.

Kara did not know whether to be delighted that Pinewood was so busy or to be irritated at the fact, but it was hours before there was another lull long enough for her to return to the table where Rob and Maria had long since finished eating. Rather than have them watch over her while she ate, she announced that she had been nibbling and was not really very hungry. She pushed the fish she had ordered hours ago out of her way and waited to be included in a conversation that had turned into another business discussion. Maria was now trying to convince Rob to put the auto parts stores on computer, but Rob was afraid their countermen would have trouble adapting. Kara did not get to listen long; more customers walked in.

It was almost closing time when Kara again got a moment to spend with them. She apologized for having neglected them when she eased back down.

"It's a good thing I came along," Maria cooed, her lips lifting into a sly grin. "Poor Rob would have had to wait for you all this time by his lonesome if I hadn't been here."

"I'd have probably put him to work," Kara commented, trying not to let Maria's smile unsettle her.

"Then it's a good thing you did come," Rob laughed, winking at Maria who quickly joined in with a soft chuckle of her own. Kara did not see the humor but lifted her face into a forced smile.

"I just hope you don't forget your promise to help me get the checks written tomorrow that I had planned to take care of tonight."

Kara's eyes narrowed. She was getting a little sick of

Maria constantly finding ways to monopolize Rob's time, and as the week progressed, Kara found it harder and harder not to let Maria's constant manipulations worry her. Even though Kara was not yet free to spend evenings with her husband, she resented his spending most of them with Maria. She had to keep reminding herself that Maria was his business partner and had a right to ask for his help, which she did with growing regularity. Rob was constantly calling Kara to explain why he would be out late but would always assure her that this would last only until Maria was caught up in her work, but Kara had her doubts.

On Saturday, even though it was the Fourth of July, Rob went in to work. Kara had no reason to ask him not to, since she, too, had to work. Pinewood always did well on holidays. About four o'clock Rob called to inform her that as soon as they posted the accounts receivable and processed two new accounts that they would finally be caught up. He would be home in time to cook what he termed a midnight special. Kara was so delighted that she hurried home after work with a small bottle of champagne to celebrate. She was even more delighted to discover that Maria had not found some way to invite herself to Rob's midnight special.

Kara found Rob lounging out by the pool. By the dim light of a candle burning in a yellow globe and the soft light of the pool, she could see the small feast on the table near him. There was a platter of fresh fruits cut into manageable pieces and a plate filled with cubed cheeses and different crackers. Rob, too, had thought of champagne. A small green bottle was already nestled in a bucket of ice, awaiting their pleasure.

The night was made for lovers. The black sky was spattered with glittering stars and a gentle breeze cooled the summer night. Rob heard her approach and quickly rose, rushing to greet her. The gleam in his eye matched that of the stars when he slipped his arms around her and welcomed her with a kiss.

"Hungry?"

"Mmmm," she nodded and they both knew she was not referring to food.

Desire flared in his eyes, lighting his face, as he reached out to run a hand over her yellow blouse. The hand came to rest over her breast and lovingly began to caress her through the soft fabric. Kara's hand stroked the hard muscle of his arm and she smiled seductively at her husband.

"You're so beautiful," he growled just before meeting her lips in a wild passionate kiss. Knowing the tall fence surrounding the yard gave them complete privacy, Rob began to unbutton her clothes, and she did likewise for him. Quickly, they freed themselves of their clothing and stood kissing and embracing, enjoying each other's nudity. Running his hands along her back, he finally slipped them down to the soft flesh of her rounded hips and pressed her to him. Instinctively, Kara began to move toward the lounge chair Rob had just abandoned and they made love not once, but twice, beneath the star-filled Texas skies.

The next morning they left early for a day of waterskiing at the Lake o' the Pines. Reflecting on the previous evening's activities, Kara felt as if a great weight had been lifted from her. She was reassured that Rob did love her, and Maria's name was not even mentioned once in the course of the day. And with interviews for a new hostess scheduled to begin Monday afternoon, she soon would be able to spend all her evenings with her husband. She would have started interviewing women earlier, but her father had stayed in

Colorado until late Thursday and she had promised not to start without him.

When Edison walked into Kara's office Monday morning, there was something decidedly different about him. He looked happier and more rested than he had in years. Kara knew then that her suspicions were true. So many years after her mother's death, her father had finally fallen in love again. She could see it in his sparkling eyes, in the way he walked, and especially in the lively lilt of his voice. Her mother-in-law someday could very well become her stepmother. *Now couldn't that be confusing?* she thought with a lift of her brow.

She found she did not have to question her father on the matter, since he was overflowing with tales of his visit with Kathy Phillips. Kara wondered how Rob was going to react to this new development. She figured she would find out at lunch when he was supposed to join them for a while, but a forgotten dentist appointment made months ago kept Rob from being able to make it. Although disappointed, Kara was glad it had not been something concerning Maria.

That afternoon Kara and her father interviewed fourteen prospects for Pinewood's hostess. Edison asked most of the questions, while Kara glanced over their references and took notes on each one. At the end of the day, they both agreed that there was no reason to interview any more women. They had both been impressed with Gina Tillery, a pretty young applicant who had shown poise, displayed a pleasant sense of humor, and had worked as a hostess once before for a rival restaurant in Dallas. Best of all, she could report to work immediately.

Picking up the phone, Kara called the number on the application and asked Gina to come in the next day.

Although the woman offered to start that same evening, Kara assured her the next day would be soon enough.

Having gotten that out of the way, she and her father went to inspect the kitchen to make certain everything was under control. When Clint came to tell her Rob was on the phone, Kara felt her mood go from happy to worried. Her stomach tightened into one twisted knot. Her first thought was that Maria had found another reason to keep him at the office.

Kara's father looked concerned when she walked over to the kitchen extension and leaned heavily against the counter for support before reaching for the receiver. He noticed that she was a shade paler than before. She closed her eyes as she put the phone to her ear.

"Hello," she said weakly, dreading what she was about to hear.

"Hi, hon, how'd it go? Did you find yourself a hostess?" he asked cheerfully.

"Yes, as a matter of fact, we did. She starts to work tomorrow."

"Good, glad to hear it. Hope she's half as good as your present hostess."

Kara's eyes eased open as he continued with a normal conversation concerning his day. It had been another trying Monday for him. They had three of the pumps at one location vandalized, and the man who usually repaired their equipment was in the hospital with a hernia, forcing Rob to do the work himself. He explained how he still had to go by the house to clean up before he could join them for supper but that he would be there eventually.

"You sound tired," Kara pointed out, sounding worried yet at the same time sighing with relief. He was not calling to tell her he would be working late with Maria again.

"I am a little," he admitted. "It was hot out there."

"Why don't you just stay home and rest? I'm sure you can find something to eat," she offered with apparent concern.

"Are you sure you won't mind?" he asked. "I know I've cancelled out on you quite a lot lately."

"No, I won't mind. Besides, Dad is still here to keep me company. You just take it easy and I'll see you in a little while."

When she returned to her father's side, she was frowning slightly. She felt a bit guilty at having assumed the worst and a little silly for having reacted the way she had when Clint had told her Rob was on the phone.

"What's wrong?" her father asked, having noted the moody expression on his daughter's face.

"Nothing really," she assured him, although not convincingly. "Rob called to tell me he would have to go by the house and change before coming over for supper, but he sounded so tired, I told him not to come. I ordered him to stay home and rest."

"Ah, newlyweds," he sighed, clutching at his heart in an exaggerated gesture. "Can't stand to be away from one another. Tell you what. I've got nothing better to do. Why don't you go home early? I can handle things here."

"I appreciate the offer, but I can't let you do that."

"Why not? You think I can't handle it?" He pretended to be offended.

"I don't doubt that you can handle it, but you have that long drive back to Dallas and you don't need to be driving that late at night."

"Traffic will be lighter then," he pointed out, wielding logic at her.

"That may be true, but I promised you my fine company for supper and I know how you hate to eat alone."

"Okay, you will leave right after supper," he stated as if it were a fact not to be argued. When she opened her mouth to offer another protest, he narrowed his blue-gray eyes and spoke with authority. "As owner of Pinewood, I have a right to tell my employees what to do."

Knowing how bullheaded her father could be at times, Kara finally gave in. Shortly after they had finished eating, she handed him her spare set of keys and reminded him not to leave the money in the cash register, but to lock it in her desk drawer. She was reluctant to leave, but once she was in her car, she was eager to hurry home and surprise Rob.

Kara parked near the street, not wanting to alert him to her presence just yet. She was so excited as she ran to the front door that she did not notice Maria's car parked in the shadows at the side of the house near the garage.

Quietly she slipped her key in the lock and turned it as gently as she could. She could not keep the silly grin off her face as she eased the door open and stepped inside. Noting that all of the lights on the lower floor were off, even with it being a little after nine and already dark outside, she assumed Rob was upstairs, probably already in bed. Carefully closing the door without making a sound, she headed for the stairs.

With the agility of a thief, Kara climbed the stairs and crept down the hall to their room, but when she peeked inside, she saw that he was not there. Looking across to the bathroom, she noticed that it was dark. Rob was not there either, but his clothes were piled in a chair. He had come home.

As she headed back down the hall, Kara realized that

he was probably out by the pool. Undaunted she hurried down the stairs, still anxious to surprise him. She eased open the patio door and stepped outside, but she was the one in for an unexpected surprise. In spite of the darkness, she could clearly make out the shapes of Rob and Maria out by the pool. They were standing in each other's arms in what could not be denied as a loving embrace.

Chapter Thirteen

Kara's first impulse had been to run away. She rushed back inside the house with every intention of leaving, but something stopped her. She stood in the dark for a moment, not sure why she had decided not to run. Not this time. Swallowing hard to loosen the tightness in her throat, she called out Rob's name as if she was still looking for him. She called his name again when she stepped back onto the patio, trying to sound casual and unconcerned.

"Out here," he called to her.

When she crossed the patio the second time, she discovered the two had separated. They still were standing close and facing each other, but both of them now had their arms crossed in front of them. Kara felt that they looked terribly guilty, but then they had a reason to.

"What are you doing home?" Rob asked as she joined them. Raising his arm, he eased it around her and pulled her to his side. He kissed her temple lightly while he expressed how surprised he was. Kara felt it was repulsive the way he could appear so affectionate toward her right in front of the very woman he had just embraced in his arms. She could not help but pull away from him.

"I expected you to be surprised," Kara commented in

a shallow voice, looking at Maria and noticing how upset this little interruption had made her. The woman's delicate fingers pressed deeply into her bared arms and her lower lip twitched ever so slightly. "Dad thought I needed an evening off, so he stayed to take over my job. He's busy seating the guests."

"That certainly is generous of him," Rob pointed out. She was aware that his eyes never quite met hers but kept cutting a glance to Maria.

Turning to stare at Maria, Kara said in a silky voice, "Why, hello, Maria. I certainly didn't expect to see you here. How nice of you to drop by. We just don't get to see enough of you."

Maria's eyes narrowed and her nose flared in anger, but she remained silent. It was Rob who finally offered an excuse as to why Maria was there. "Maria has a few problems she wanted to discuss with me."

"Business problems?" Kara probed, pretending to have accepted what Rob had just said.

"Some of them," he replied quickly, then was quick to change the subject. "I sure could use a cool drink on a warm night like tonight. What about you two? How about a glass of chilled wine?" Before anyone could answer, Rob was walking toward the house to get the wine.

No sooner was he in the house than Maria finally found her voice. "You are such a fool for marrying him again."

"Am I?" Kara asked in amazement.

"You should have learned something with that first marriage. Only fools make the same mistake twice."

"I guess that means Rob is a fool, too," Kara said doubtfully. Although she did have a few names in mind for him, fool was not one of them.

"He is," she nodded. Stepping closer, Maria glared

at Kara, looking almost demonic in the upward glow of light from the pool. She added intently, "He is just as much of a fool as you are. This marriage is a marriage of fools. You will never be able to make him happy. You didn't the first time. Why do you bother?"

"That is an interesting question," Kara replied calmly while fighting back her frustrations.

Maria opened her mouth to say more but caught sight of Rob. He was headed back in their direction with three glasses of wine.

Rob suggested they make themselves comfortable, motioning to several webbed chairs around an enameled table near the pool. As they sipped their wine, Rob tried to keep a conversation going but could not get any interaction from either Maria or Kara. He acted very relieved when Redwood trotted up and demanded his attention.

While she watched Rob roughly stroking Redwood's thick red coat, Maria's words haunted Kara's thoughts. Slowly she sipped her wine and contemplated what she had said. As hard as it was to admit, the woman was right. She was a fool to have married Rob again, and she would be a bigger fool if she stayed any longer. Drinking down the last of her wine, she placed the empty glass on the table and politely excused herself, explaining how tired she was before calmly walking away. She was proud of the way she was handling herself in front of the two when she really wanted to scream at the top of her lungs and throw things.

Once inside, Kara broke into a run. She hurried up the stairs, two steps at a time, and into their room. Taking the largest suitcase from the top of her closet, she flung it open across the cedar chest at the foot of the bed and began to fill it with clothes. She did not know exactly where she was going at this point. She had returned the keys to the other house so she could not go back there. She did not feel like facing her father with this just yet, and until after closing hours when everyone had gone, she could not go to her office. Deciding to either stay at a motel or drive around until she could slip into the restaurant and stay the night on the couch in her office, Kara continued to toss things into the suitcase. She would prefer anywhere to here. She was angry and hurt, but mostly she was confused. How could he? The marriage was barely two weeks old and he was already cheating on her. It dawned on her that he had lied to her in order to get her to marry him again. He probably had been having an affair with Juanita that first time. But what really confused her was why he had even bothered to lie. Why had he been that intent on remarrying her? If it was love he felt for her, why did he always end up cheating on her?

Something was wrong with the guy. She decided that there must be a tiny flaw in his character, preventing him from being true to her and forcing him to seek out other women. It was now obvious one woman would never possess his heart. Why did she remarry him? Why couldn't she have spotted his lies?

Tears stung her eyes but she fought them back. Upset as she was, she refused to let herself get too emotional as she gathered up her makeup, hair brushes, and blow dryer in the bathroom. While she was tucking in the last of the things she planned to take with her, she heard heavy footsteps. When she looked toward the door, Rob walked in.

"What do you think you are doing?" he demanded angrily when he had realized she was packing.

"Leaving," she replied coolly, still trying not to become overly emotional in spite of her straining heart and churning stomach. She was amazed at how steady her hands were when she closed the suitcase and snapped the locks shut.

His blue eyes glowed with anger as he stared at her. "You are not going anywhere."

"Oh, yes, I am," she replied, yanking up the heavy case. Taking several steps toward the door, she came face to face with him. "Would you please get out of my way?"

"Kara, you are *not* going anywhere," he shouted angrily and grabbed the suitcase out of her hands. "You are my wife and you are staying right here."

"Give me that suitcase," she demanded, reaching for it. "I'm leaving."

Rob was so overcome with rage that his voice trembled when he spoke. "You are not leaving me. Do you hear me?"

When she made another attempt to grab the handle of the suitcase, he reared back and heaved it through the window, shattering glass everywhere. Before Kara could protest, he had grabbed her by the shoulders and pushed her backward toward the bed. When she fell across it, he came down on top of her and pinned her shoulders to the mattress. His angry blue eyes bore into hers.

"Suppose you tell me why you are leaving this time," he demanded bitterly. His face was so near hers, she felt his warm, moist breath on her cheek.

"Rob, you somehow convinced me that you and Juanita did not have anything going during our first marriage," she began, her eyes lowering to narrow slits of anger.

"And we didn't."

"Oh, and now I suppose you are going to tell me you and Maria don't have a little something going," she came back, her voice thick with sarcasm.

"We don't."

"Come off it, Rob. I saw you two tonight out by the pool."

"When I was holding her?" he asked, his expression going from anger to concern when he realized what had happened.

"Bingo!" she said bitterly. "I saw the little clench you two were in."

"And, no doubt, you assumed the worst."

"I know what I saw," she spoke defiantly. "And I'm leaving you for good! I hate you!"

Without warning, Rob's mouth came down on hers with such a force that it actually hurt her lips. Kara struggled to pull away from his savage kisses, but found her efforts were useless. He had her trapped beneath him. She tried to wrench her shoulders free but could not manage. When she finally gave up her futile struggle, the pressure of his mouth lessened and his kisses became more gentle, more probing. The familiar taste and feel of his lips brought her an exquisite pain. Damn it all. She may hate him, but she still desired the man.

When he felt her relax, his hands eased their grip on her shoulders and began to glide down the length of her body. Kara tried to ignore the ache growing inside her; she did not want to feel anything for this man, especially desire. While his lips continued to pursue hers with growing passion, he slid a hand beneath her blouse and skillfully teased the sensitive peaks of her breasts.

Kara could not believe that her body was actually responding to his lovemaking after what he had done, but she was quickly becoming aroused. By the time he had unbuttoned her blouse and had trailed sizzling kisses to first one hardened peak, then the other, she knew she had passed the point of no return. She silently cursed him all the while her body's needs were mounting.

Waves of sensuous desire were spreading through her. Although her mind said no, her body wanted him with more passion than she'd ever felt before. Damn him. When he guided a hand beneath her skirt and up along her inner thigh, she moaned with pleasure despite herself. It was as if he had cast a demon's spell over her; she could not deny him what he was after. She *was* a fool.

Rob was deliberate as he continued to kiss and caress her body until he was certain she would submit. Taking a deep breath, he pulled away from her and in a low, decisive voice, he commented, "I thought you hated me."

Infuriated, Kara struck quickly, landing her opened hand across his face. His eyes blazed with rage as he felt his reddening cheek.

"You don't have to leave, Kara," he snarled, glowering down at her, "because I'm going."

Standing abruptly, he stalked out of the room, leaving Kara trembling and confused. It had all happened so quickly, she could scarcely believe any of it. She had struck him. Angry as she was, she had never wanted to do that. She was no longer in control of herself. Bewildered by her own actions, Kara reached her emotional limit and broke into loud rasping sobs. Turning over, she buried her face in the covers and cried helplessly.

As her thoughts rambled, reviewing all that had just happened, it occurred to her that it was her own lovemaking that caused Rob to seek out other women. The flaw must be inside her. He could have had her, for she had been more than willing to yield to him, to succumb to his every need, yet he chose to ignore it, to go elsewhere for it. Kara had no doubt that he was headed for Maria's and the thought of it tormented her very heart and soul.

Kara eventually cried herself numb, although she never managed to actually fall asleep. She wrestled with thoughts of how she had hoped it would be this time and tried to analyze exactly what had gone wrong. She could not decide if the blame was entirely Rob's or if she might be partly responsible.

She was not aware of the time, only that the sun had been up for hours, when there came a knock at the door. Thinking Rob had come back, she hurriedly straightened her clothes, buttoned her blouse, and ran her fingers through her hair. She was anxious to talk about it. She had to know if any of the fault had been hers, and if so, how much. If it had been her fault, could it be rectified or was their relationship unsalvageable. Her hands shook violently when she turned the knob and opened the door. Her face twisted with disappointment when a man she had never seen before greeted her.

"Howdy, ma'am," the chubby young man wearing coveralls said with a smile. "Is this the Robert Phillips address?"

"Yes," she answered curiously.

"Good. I'm here to repair that broken window upstairs," he explained in a friendly manner. "Shouldn't take long."

After presenting her with a carbon of the work order, he asked her to show him to the window. Once she had led him to their bedroom, she went back downstairs. Not wanting to give this guy too much to think about, she hurried outside to retrieve the suitcase. She was amazed at how far from the house she found it and was glad it had not sprung open and scattered its contents.

When she carried the suitcase back inside, she set it by the door in the kitchen leading to the garage. She was not yet sure if she was going to go ahead and leave or wait for an opportunity to talk to Rob. One thing she was certain of and that was that she did not feel up to going to work. Seeing that it was barely nine, she called Clint at his apartment and gave him the partial truth. She told him how terrible she felt and asked if he could manage without her. She apologized for not being able to make it for Gina Tillery's first day but admitted Clint could train her just as well as she could, maybe better. Clint was quick to agree and told her to take care of herself.

Having gotten her responsibilities out of the way, she poured herself a diet drink out of habit and sat down at the kitchen table trying to decide what to do. Kara knew they were headed for a second divorce. Her pride wanted her to get her things together and clear out, but something else nagging at her caused her to want to stay, face Rob, and find out why this had happened. Just the fact that it had happened was not enough this time. She desperately wanted to know why and knew she would have a better chance of finding out if she stayed right here in his house. With that thought in mind, Kara waited until the repairman had left, then carried her suitcase back upstairs. She was staying.

For days she waited for word from Rob. She continued to call in sick for fear Rob might call or come by while she was out, but he never did. Although she knew she could easily call his office and leave a message for him, she refused to, being determined to wait until he was ready to contact her. Kara intended to be there when he did.

She had assumed he would eventually contact her in

person. It never occurred to her that he would send Maria over to do his dirty work, but late Friday afternoon there was a knock at the front door and it was Maria in all of her glory. She was decked out in one of her designer pants outfits of flowing satin. She wore an overly contented smile and held her nose at a haughty angle. She had come to get a few of Rob's things, and before Kara could say anything, Maria had pushed past her and was headed for the stairway.

Kara was right behind her uninvited visitor when the woman breezed into their bedroom and immediately went to his closet and pulled out a brown leather suitcase. Silently Maria went about collecting Rob's things, knowing right where everything was. She ignored Kara's presence until she had neatly filled the suitcase with his clothes and various personal articles. Then as she slammed the suitcase shut, she finally spoke.

"You don't actually intend to live here after the divorce, do you?" she asked in an icy voice, as if the thought of it was totally outrageous.

"I haven't really thought about it," Kara admitted. She had not really thought that far ahead. She was worried enough with what was going on now.

"Well, you'd better think about it, lady. This is my sister's house, not yours. You have no right to it."

"Your sister's house?" Kara's brow drew into a frown. What did she mean that this is her sister's house? Her sister was dead.

"My sister helped him plan this house. She helped pick out the design and selected the tile and carpets. This is *her* house and I can't stand the thought of your being in it!"

"I never really planned to stay here long."

"Good." Jerking up the heavy suitcase with both hands, she stalked out.

Kara's mind was busy reviewing what had just happened. She suddenly realized that Maria probably did not want Rob for herself at all, that her reasons for wanting to break them up were far different. Maria was being loyal to her sister's memory and felt as if Rob had betrayed Juanita somehow by having remarried her.

It all seemed rather clear now. Kara felt sorry for Maria, but she overcame the urge to call out to her or to run after her and explain it all to her. How could she tell her that Rob had never truly loved Juanita but had married her out of loneliness and gratitude? Besides, she didn't expect Maria to believe her anyway. Maria would suspect anything she had to say.

The front door slammed with a loud bang and Maria's car pulled away with a screech. Kara sank down on the bed and sat thinking everything through. She now believed Rob had indeed told her the truth about everything. She winced as she remembered having as much as called him a liar and exclaimed how she hated him. Remembering the way she had slapped him, she doubted he would ever forgive her. Kara wasn't sure she deserved to be forgiven. But she had been so sure that Maria was out to get him for herself. It had never entered her mind that she resented their remarriage because of her sister. Always the wrong conclusion.

Just then the phone rang. Kara's heart leapt into action. She wondered if it might be Rob. She so wanted the opportunity to apologize, even if she might chance an angry rejection. She was somewhat disappointed when she answered the phone and heard her father's concerned voice on the other end. He had called Pinewood to see how the new hostess was working out and was informed Kara was sick and had not been in since she had left early Monday evening.

"What's wrong, Buttons?" he wanted to know. "You looked just fine Monday. Why didn't you call me or have Rob call me? You know I would want to know when you're sick."

Kara decided to be honest with him; besides, he had an uncanny knack of knowing when she was lying, especially about something important. "I'm not really sick, not physically anyway."

"Explain," he prompted her briefly.

Taking a deep breath, Kara admitted she should not have left Clint to do all the work but explained that she would not have been much help anyway. Her mind would never have been on what she was doing. Then she went on to tell him most of what had happened, even the part where she had lost control and had slapped Rob across the face. By the time she had finished, she was sniffing back tears. "Daddy, I've lost him for good this time."

There was a long pause as Edison took in what she had just told him. Finally he commented, "Don't cry, Buttons. You're coming home." He did not give her time to protest before going on to say, "I'm going to be down there first thing in the morning with one of the trucks to help you move. You're coming back to Dallas."

"What about Pinewood?"

"Clint knows enough now to take over the manager's position. After all, he's done it twice now. I'll send someone from one of my Dallas restaurants to help him until he can hire an assistant and get him or her oriented to the job. Start packing; I'll be there early." He was very serious about what he had just said. He wanted her home where he could take care of her and see her through the initial pain.

Part of Kara was reluctant to give up Pinewood, but she knew she needed somewhere to go, to think things through. She couldn't stay here. She'd already promised to leave. Besides, she knew she could always talk her father into letting her have Pinewood back, if she decided that's what she wanted. Finally Kara agreed to go home for a while, and as soon as she had hung up, she drove to the nearest supermarket and got as many large boxes as they would let her have, which was more than she could fit in her car in one trip, so she had to make three trips.

Taking one room at a time, Kara started packing her things into the boxes. What she could not fit on the truck the next morning, she would store in the garage until she could send for them. She was glad now that they had not gotten rid of the extra furniture.

While packing, whenever Kara came to anything she had selected in the course of redecorating or something the two of them had collected on their honeymoon, she left it. She was not sure if she could consider these things really hers or not and knew that they would only serve to remind her of the horrible mistake she'd made and the way she'd managed to ruin her life in one fell swoop. She grew incredibly remorseful as she continued to put her things into boxes. She could not help but think about how desperately she still loved Rob and how stupid she'd been to have doubted him again. Why was she so quick to jump to conclusions?

Although growing tired, Kara continued with the packing. Maria was right, she had no right to be in this house. The sooner she was out, the sooner she could start to sort through all that had happened; and if she had truly lost Rob, the sooner she could put some of the heartache and misery behind her. She knew from experience that the pain could eventually mellow into a hollow emptiness that was almost bearable, but it would take time.

Just after midnight Kara's shoulder and neck muscles were beginning to ache. She was just too tired to continue. Her recent lack of sleep had drained her of her strength. She decided to take a hot bath to soothe her muscles and catch a few hours sleep before resuming her task.

While she was soaking in a tub filled just inches from the top with tepid water, Kara was temporarily able to ignore her troubles. Leaning back against the porcelain edge, she began to drift off to sleep. The wonderfully peaceful moment was disrupted by the faint sound of the doorbell. Not really certain she had heard the familiar chimes, she sat up and listened. Seconds later it rang again. Quickly she got out of the tub and dried off. Slipping into her robe, Kara rushed downstairs to see just who was at the door. Surely her father had not decided to come straight to Longview to help her pack. Glancing at the clock in the entryway, she realized he'd had more than enough time to arrange for a truck and make the trip. It was almost one.

Just before Kara reached the door, she heard the metallic sound of a key being fitted into the lock. Suddenly she was aware it was Rob. A cold wave of anticipation ran through her while she stood watching the doorknob quietly turn, then the door slowly swing open. The muscular shape of the silhouette in the doorway confirmed that it was indeed Rob. When he stepped from the darkened area into the dimly lit entryway, she could finally see his face. Kara was stunned to see how tired and haggard he looked. He had four day's growth of beard on his face and there were dark semicircles beneath his dismal red-rimmed eyes. He looked dreadful.

"Kara, please, we have to talk," Rob said, almost pleading with her.

"I know," she replied softly, going to the door and gently closing it. "Come on in and sit down."

Glancing around at the boxes still lying on the floor as he made his way to the couch, he shook his head sadly. "Maria was right. You are moving out for good. Where are you going?"

"Dad wants me to come stay with him a while," she explained quietly.

"So you are going back to Dallas?"

Kara shrugged. She was afraid to try to talk. The tears were already straining to overtake her eyes.

"Look, it wasn't fair of you to pass judgment on me just like that. You didn't even bother hearing my side."

"I know. I'm not a fair or truly rational person when I'm in one of my rages. I've had time to calm down though."

"Then can we talk? I want to have a chance to tell my side."

"I don't think you have to."

"But I want to. I want you to know that had you come out by the pool Monday when you found Maria in my arms, you would have seen she was crying. She had come over here to convince me to reconsider our marriage. She actually believes that I am dishonoring Juanita's memory in some way by being remarried to you. Maria's very confused right now. Her grief has the best of her. She wanted me to see that our remarriage had been a mistake and claimed it would break Juanita's heart to know I had let you trick me into remarrying you. For a minute she even acted as if she believed Juanita was still alive."

Rob rubbed his tired eyes and continued, "Knowing she was overworked and near exhaustion, I figured she was just out of her head. When I tried to explain that I loved you and always had, she broke down and started to cry. I was only trying to console her by taking her into my arms like I did. Kara, please believe me. I never cheated on you and I've never lied to you.''

"I'd already figured that out, but I lied to you," Kara admitted bravely.

Rob's eyes grew wide with concern, imploring her to say more.

"Rob, I lied when I said I hated you. I don't. I didn't then.''

Rob let out the breath he had been holding. He hadn't known what to expect. "Are you sure? You were pretty convincing, you know.'' He grinned, rubbing his cheek.

"I want to apologize for that. You have every right to hate me.''

"I should apologize too. I should have told you what was happening but I was just so afraid I'd lose you.''

"Do you hate me?'' Her voice was so weak she barely heard herself.

"No.''

"Are you still mad at me?''

"No.''

"Do you still love me?''

Kara's stomach tightened when he did not answer right away. He looked down at her, thoughtful.

"Well, do you?'' her voice quivered.

"Yes.'' A grin moved slowly across his face, deepening his crescent dimples as it spread. Holding out his arms, Kara went to him, burying her face in his strong chest, hiding her tears of relief.

"Any more questions?'' he asked, leaning his cheek against the top of her head and placing a kiss in her soft hair.

"Just one,'' she replied, her voice muffled by his shirt. Then she looked up and peered over his shoulder.

"What's that?" Rob asked, lifting his head and staring down at her.

Glancing up, her eyes were large brown circles of concern.

"Well?" he prompted her, taking a deep breath and holding it. He didn't like the troubled look he saw.

"Will you please help me unpack all my things?"

"Tomorrow," he promised, kissing first one damp cheek then the other. "I've got better things to do right now."

Epilogue

"Hey, sleepyhead, I asked you a question," Rob said as he sat down on the redwood lounge chair beside his wife.

"You did?" Kara asked, blinking with confusion. She hadn't meant to fall asleep, but it was something she did a lot of lately.

"I explained that the steaks are almost done and asked if everything else was ready."

"Ready and waiting," she told him, referring to the potato salad and baked beans she had made earlier.

Just then their attention was drawn to Redwood, who was patiently nudging a stray puppy back toward its mother. Princess was lying on the cool brick of the patio only a few feet away while five of her puppies suckled hungrily. The sixth puppy had struck out on its own in search of better things.

"Tell me, Redwood. Is fatherhood all it's cracked up to be?" Rob wanted to know, watching the determined puppy struggle against Redwood's efforts to return it to the fold. Reaching over to gently pat Kara's rounded belly, he remarked proudly, "I guess I'll find out soon enough."

"Oh, you still have a month yet," Kara reminded him, watching as his dimples disappeared. Rob was tired of waiting. "Maybe he'll be born on our anniversary."

"Just have it before Pat and Clint have theirs."

"Pat's still got two months to go," she reminded him. "This fella better be out by then."

"Still positive it's a boy, are you?"

"The way he kicks, he could be twins," she chuckled. Rob's eyes grew wide at the thought, so Kara quickly added, "But the doctor assures me it's not."

"You know, it wouldn't be so bad to have twins. One of each."

"I like the idea of two children, too, but one at a time," she laughed, shifting to make herself more comfortable. Sniffing the delicious hickory aroma drifting through the warm spring air, she commented, "I thought you said those steaks were about ready. We're hungry." Gently she stroked her protruding stomach to emphasize the word "we".

"They are. You just sit there and take it easy. I'll bring your plate to you."

Kara sighed. She'd never been able to get Rob to believe that just because she was expecting their first child didn't mean that she was helpless and unable to do for herself. Ever since Rob had found out she was pregnant, he had ordered her to take it easy and had refused to let her lift a single box when they had moved into their new home. Although Maria had finally come to accept their marriage and claimed she no longer resented Kara's being in the house Juanita had helped plan, Rob had insisted they build a new home. This one was smaller than the first, but that was what Kara had wanted. She wanted a house she could manage by herself. It had as many rooms as the other house had but was not quite as pretentiously large, and it was every inch Kara. She'd had a hand in every aspect of it, from designing the layout to picking out the mailbox. And when Rob was not looking, she actually helped plant much of the shrubbery and flowers.

So much had happened in a year: first Pat and Clint's wedding, then the construction of their new home, and most recently her father's announcement that Rob's mother had consented to be his wife. But the best was still to come, for within the next few weeks they were to have a child, their first. This year had indeed been a good year. And as Kara shifted once again in her chair, she thought of all the wonderful years to come.

Harlequin Photo
~ Calendar ~

Turn Your Favorite Photo into a Calendar.

Uniquely yours, this 10x17½" calendar features your favorite photograph, with any name you wish in attractive lettering at the bottom. A delightfully personal and practical idea!

Send us your favorite color print, black-and-white print, negative, or slide, any size (we'll return it), along with **3 proofs of purchase** (coupon below) from a June or July release of Harlequin Romance, Harlequin Presents, Harlequin Superromance, Harlequin American Romance or Harlequin Temptation, plus $5.75 (includes shipping and handling).